W9-DAV-814

ARIZONA GUNS

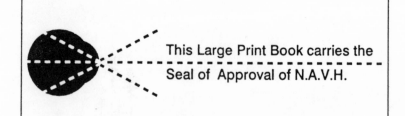

was more to the boy's taste, but he enjoyed the flavor of the camouflage he was employing. It fitted into his new role of Bud Proctor, Scout of the Pecos.

The fugitives slipped down the back stairway of the Proctor House and into the garden. In another moment they were astride and moving out to the sparsely settled suburbs of town.

"Did you notice the brand on the horse you're ridin', Jim?" asked Prince with a grin.

"Same brand's on your bay, Billie — the Lazy S M. Did you tell that kid to steal us two horses?"

"No, but you've said it. I'm on the bronc Sanders rides, and you an' I are horse-thieves now as well as killers. This certainly gets us in bad."

"I've a notion to turn back yet," said Jim, with the irritability of a sick man. "How in Mexico did he happen to light on Snaith-McRobert stock? Looks like he might have found somethin' else for us."

"Bud has too much imagination," admitted Prince ruefully. "I'd bet a stack of blues he picked these hawsses on purpose — probably thought it would be a great joke on Sanders an' his crew."

"Well, I don't like it. They've got us where they want us now."

Billie did not like it either. To kill a man on the frontier then in fair fight was a misdemeanor. To steal a horse was a capital offense. Many a bronco thief ended his life at the end of a rope in the hands of respectable citizens who had in the way of business snuffed out the lives of other respectable citizens. Both of the Flying V Y riders knew that if they were caught with the stock, it would be of no avail with Sanders to plead that they had no intention of stealing. Possession would be *prima facie* evidence of guilt.

"It's too late to go back now," Prince decided. "We'll travel night an' day till we reach the old man an' have him send the broncs back. I hate to do it, but we have no choice. Anyhow, we might as well be hanged for stealin' a horse as for anything else."

They topped a hill and came face to face with a rider traveling townward. His gaze took in the animals carrying the fugitives and jumped to the face of Billie. In the eyes of the man was an expression blended of suspicion and surprise. He passed with a nod and a surly " 'Evenin'."

"Fine luck we're havin', Billie," commented his friend with a little laugh. "I give Sanders twenty minutes to be on our trail."

Chapter XI

The Fugitives

Through the gathering darkness Prince watched the figure of his companion droop. The slim, lithe body sagged and the shoulders were heavy with exhaustion. Both small hands clung to the pommel of the saddle. It took no prophet to see that in his present condition the wounded man would never travel the gun-barrel road as far as the dust of the Flying V Y herd. Even by easy stages he could not do it, and with pursuit thundering at their heels the ride would be a cruel, grilling one.

"How about pullin' a little strategy on Sanders, Jim? Instead of hittin' the long trail, let's circle back around the town, strike the river, make camp, an' lie low in the chaparral. Does that listen good to you?"

Young Clanton looked at his friend suspiciously. The younger man was fagged out and in a good deal of pain. The jolting of the pony's movements jarred the bandages on the wound. Already his fever was high and he had moments of light-headedness. He knew that his partner was proposing to jeopardize his own chances of escape in order to take care of him.

"No, sir. We'll keep goin' right ahead," he said irritably. "Think I'm a quitter? Think I'm goin' to lie down on you?"

"Would I be likely to think that?" asked Billie gently. "What I'm thinkin' is that both of us would be better for a good night's rest. Why not throw off an' camp in the darkness? While we're sleepin' Sanders an' his posse will be ridin' the hearts out of their horses. It looks like good business to me to let 'em go to it."

"No," said Jim obstinately. "No. We'll keep ridin'."

Prince knew that the other understood what he was trying to do, and that his pride — and perhaps something better than pride — would not accept such a sacrifice. Billie said no more, but his mind still wrestled with the problem before him. It was impossible, while his comrade was so badly hurt, to hold a pace that would keep them ahead of the Lazy S M riders. Already Sanders must be gaining on them, and to make matters worse Clanton drew down to a walk. His high-pitched voice and disjointed expressions told the older man that he was at the beginning of delirium.

"What do you mean, standin' there and

grinnin' at me like a wolf, Dave Roush? I killed you once. You're dead an' buried. How come you alive again? Then shoot, both of you! Come out from cover, Hugh Roush." He stopped, and took the matter up from another angle. "You're a liar, you coyote. I'm not runnin' away. Two to one . . . two to one . . . I'll ride back an' gun you both. I'm a-comin' now."

He pulled up and turned his horse. Faintly there came to Billie the thudding of horses' hoofs. In five minutes it would be too late to save either the sick man or himself. It never occurred to him for a moment to desert Clanton. Somehow he must get him into the chaparral, and without an instant's delay. His mind seized on the delirious fancy of the young fellow.

"You're sure right, Jim," he said quietly. "I'd go an' gun them too. I'll ride with you an' see fair play. They're out here in the brush. Come on."

"No. They're back in town. Leave 'em to me. Don't you draw, Billie."

"All right. But they're over here to our right. I saw 'em there. Come. We'll sneak up on 'em so that they can't run when they hear you."

Billie turned. He swung his horse into the mesquite. His heart was heavy with anxiety.

Would the wounded man accept his lead? Or would his obstinacy prevail?

"Here they are. Right ahead here," continued Prince.

Followed a moment of suspense, then came the crashing of brush as Clanton moved after him.

"S-sh! Ride softly, Jim. We don't want 'em to hear us an' get away."

"Tha's right. Tha's sure right. You said somethin' then, Billie. But they'll not get away. Haven't I slept on their trail four years? They're mine at last."

Prince was drawing him farther from the road. But the danger was not yet over. As the posse passed, some member of it might hear them, or young Clanton might hear it and gallop out to the road under the impression he was going to meet Dave Roush. Billie twisted in and out of the brush, never for an instant letting his friend pull up. On a moving horse one cannot hear so distinctly as on one standing still.

At last Billie began to breathe more easily. The pursuers must have passed before this. He could give his attention to the sick man.

Jim was clutching desperately to the saddlehorn. The fever was gaining on him and the delirium worse. He talked incessantly, sometimes incoherently. From one subject to another he went, but always he came back to Dave Roush and his brother. He dared them to stand up and fight. He called on them to stop running, to wait for him. Then he trailed off into a string of epithets usually ending in sobs of rage.

The sickness of the young man tore the heart of his companion. Every instinct of kindness urged him to stop, make up a bed for the wounded boy, and let him rest from the agony of travel. But he dared not stop yet. He had to keep going till they reached a place of temporary safety.

With artful promises of immediate vengeance upon his enemies, by means of taunts at him as a quitter, through urgent proddings that reached momentarily the diseased mind, Prince kept him moving through the brush. The sweat stood out on the white face of the young fellow shining ghastly in the moonlight.

After what seemed an interminable time they could see from a mesa the lights of Los Portales. Billie left the town well to his right, skirted the pastures on the outskirts, and struck the river four miles farther down.

While they were still a long way from it the boy collapsed completely and slid from the saddle to which he had so long clung. His friend uncinched and freed the sorrel, lifted the slack body to his own horse, and walked beside the animal to steady the lurching figure.

At the bank of the river he stopped and lifted the body to the ground. It lay limp and slack where the cowpuncher set it down. Through the white shoulder dressings a stain of red had soaked. For a moment Billie was shaken by the fear that the Arizonian might be dead, but he rejected it as not at all likely. Yet when he held his hand against the heart of the wounded man he was not sure that he could detect a beating.

From the river he brought water in his hat and splashed it into the white face. He undid the shoulder bandages, soaked them in cold water, and rebound the wound. Between the clenched teeth he forced a few drops of whiskey from his flask.

The eyelids fluttered and slowly opened.

"Where are we, Billie?" the sick man asked; then added: "How did we get away from 'em?"

"Went into the brush an' doubled back to the river. I'm goin' to hunt a place where we can lie hid for a few days."

"Oh, I'll be all right by mornin'. Did I fall off my hawss?"

"Yes. I had to turn your sorrel loose. Soon as I've picked a permanent camp I'll have to

let mine go too. Some one would be sure to stumble on it an' go to guessin'."

After a moment the sick man spoke quietly. "You're a good pal, Billie. I haven't known many men would take a long chance like this for a fellow they hadn't met a month ago."

"I'm not forgettin' how you rode up Escondido when I asked you to go."

"You got a lot of sabe, too. You don't go bullin' into a fight when there's a good reason for stayin' out. At Tolleson's if you had drawn yore gun when the shootin' was on, the whole Lazy S M would have pitched in an' riddled us both. They kept out because you did. That gave me a chance to come through alive."

The Texan registered embarrassment with a grin. "Yes, I'm the boy wonder of the Brazos," he admitted.

A faint, unexpected gleam of humor lay for a moment in the eyes of the sick man. "I got you where the wool's short, Billie. I can throw bouquets at you an' you got to stand hitched because I'm sick. Doc says to humor me. If I holler for the moon you climb up an' get it."

"I'll rope it for you," assented the cow-puncher. "How's the game shoulder?"

"Hurts like Heligoland. Say, ain't I due for one of them sleep powders Doc fixed up so careful?"

His companion gave him one, after which

he folded his coat and put it under the head of Clanton. Over him he threw a saddle blanket.

"Back soon," he promised.

The sick man nodded weakly.

Billie swung to the saddle and turned down the river. Unfortunately the country here was an open one. Along the sandy shore of the stream the mesquite was thin. There was no soapweed and very little cactus. The terrain of the hill country farther back was rougher, more full of pockets, and covered with heavier brush. But it was necessary for the fugitives to remain close to water.

What Prince hoped to find was some sort of cave or overhanging ledge of shale under which they could lie hidden until Jim's strength returned sufficiently to permit of travel. The problem would be at best a difficult one. They had little food, scarce dared light a fire, and Clanton was in no condition to stand exposure in case the weather grew bad. Even if the boy weathered the sickness, it would not be possible for him to walk hundreds of miles in his weakened condition. But this was a matter which did not press for an answer. Billie intended to cross no bridges until he came to them. Just now he must focus his mind on keeping the wounded man alive and out of the hands of his enemies.

Beyond a bend he came upon a jutting bank

that for lack of better might serve his purpose. He could scoop out a cave in which his partner might lie protected from the hot midday sun. If he filled the mouth with tumble weeds during the day they might escape observation for a time.

When the Texan returned to his friend, he found him in restless slumber. He tossed to and fro, muttering snatches of incoherent talk. The wound seemed to pain him even in his sleep, for he moved impatiently as though trying to throw off some weight lying heavy upon it.

But when he awoke his mind was apparently clear. He met Billie's anxious look with a faint, white-lipped smile. To his friend the young fellow had the signs of a very sick man. It was a debatable question whether to risk moving him now or take the almost hopeless chance of escaping detection where they were.

Prince put the decision on Jim himself. The answer came feebly, but promptly.

"Sure, move me. What's one little — bullet in the shoulder, Billie? Gimme some sleep — an' I'll be up an' kickin'."

Yet the older man noticed that his white lips could scarcely find strength to make the indomitable boast.

Very gently Billie lifted the wounded man and put him on the back of the cowpony. He held him there and guided the animal through the sand to the bend. Clanton hung on with clenched teeth, calling on the last ounce of power in his exhausted body with his strong will.

"Just a hundred yards more," urged the walking man as they rounded the bend. "We're 'most there now."

He lifted the slack body down and put it in the sand. The hands of the boy were ice cold. The sap of life was low in him. Prince covered him with the blankets and his coat. He gave him a sip or two of whiskey, then gathered buffalo chips and made a fire in which he heated some large rocks. These he tucked in beneath the blankets beside the shivering body. Slowly the heat warmed the invalid. After a time he fell once more into troubled sleep.

Billie drove his horse away and pelted it with stones to a trot. He could not keep it with him without risking discovery, but he was almost as much afraid that its arrival in Los Portales might start a search for the hidden fugitives. There was always a chance, of course, that the bay would stop to graze on the plains and not be found for a day or two.

The rest of the night the Texan put in digging a cave with a piece of slaty shale. The clay of the bank was soft and he made fair progress. The dirt he scooped out was thrown by him into the river.

Chapter XII

The Good Samaritan

A girl astride a buckskin pony rode down to the river to water her mount. She carried across the pommel of her saddle a small rifle. Hanging from the cantle strings was a wild turkey she had shot.

It was getting along toward evening and she was on her way back to Los Portales. The girl was a lover of the outdoors and she had been hunting alone. In the clear, amber light of afternoon the smoke of the town rose high into the sky, though the trading post itself could not be seen until she rounded the bend.

As her horse drank, a strange thing happened. At a point directly opposite her a bunch of tumble weeds had gathered against the bank of the shrunken stream. Something agitated them, and from among the brush the head and shoulders of a man projected.

Without an instant of delay the girl slipped from the pony and led it behind a clump of mesquite. Through this she peered intently, watching every move of the man, who had by this time come out into the open. He went down to the river, filled his hat with water, and disappeared among the tumble weeds, gathering them closely to conceal the entrance of his cave.

The young woman remounted, rode downstream an eighth of a mile, splashed through to the other side, and tied her pony to a stunted live-oak. Rifle in hand she crept cautiously along the bank and came to a halt behind a cottonwood thirty yards from the cave. Here she waited, patiently, silently, as many a time she had done while stalking the game she was used to hunting.

The minutes passed, ran into an hour. The westering sun slid down close to the horizon's edge. Still the girl held her vigil. At last the brush moved once more and the man re-appeared. His glance swept the landscape, the river-bank, the opposite shore. Apparently satisfied, he came out from his hiding-place, and began to gather brush for a fire.

He was stooped, his back toward her, when the voice of the girl startled him to rigidity.

"Hands in the air!"

He did not at once obey. His head turned to

see who this Amazon might be.

"Can't you hear? Reach for the sky!" she ordered sharply.

She had risen and stepped from behind the tree. He could see that she was dark, of a full, fine figure, and that her steady black eyes watched him without the least fear. The rifle in her hands covered him very steadily.

His hands went up, but he could not keep a little, sardonic smile from his face. The young woman lowered the rifle from her shoulder and moved warily forward.

"Lie down on the sand, face to the ground, hands outstretched!" came her next command.

Billie did as he was told. A little tug at his side gave notice to him that she had deftly removed his revolver.

"Sit up!"

The cowpuncher sat up and took notice. Stars of excitement snapped in the eyes of this very competent young woman. The color beat warmly through her dark skin. She was very well worth looking at.

"What's your name?" she demanded.

"My road brand is Billie Prince," he answered

"Thought so. Where's the other man?"

He nodded toward the cave.

"Call him out," she said curtly.

"I hate to wake him. He's been wounded.

129

All day he's been in a high fever and he's asleep at last."

For the first time her confidence seemed a little shaken. She hesitated. "Is he badly hurt?"

"He'd get well if he could have proper attention, but a wounded man can't stand to be jolted around the way he's been since he was shot."

"Do you mean that you think he's going to die?"

"I don't know." After a moment he added: "He's mighty sick."

"He ought never to have left town."

"Oughtn't he?" said Prince dryly. "If you'll inquire you'll find we have a good reason for leavin'."

"Well, you're going to have another good reason for going back," she told him crisply. "I'll send a buckboard for him."

"Aren't you takin' a heap of trouble on our account?" he inquired ironically.

"That's my business."

"And mine. Are you the sheriff of Washington County, ma'am?"

A pulse of anger beat in her throat. Her long-lashed eyes flashed imperiously at him. "It doesn't matter who I am. You'll march to town in front of my horse."

"Maybe so."

The voice of the sick man began to babble querulously. Both of those outside listened.

"He's awake," the girl said. "Bring him out here and let me see him."

Billie had an instinct that sometimes served him well. He rose promptly.

"Para sirvir usted" ("At your service"), he murmured.

"Don't try to start anything. I'll have you covered every second."

"I believe you. It won't be necessary to demonstrate, ma'am."

The cowpuncher carried his friend out from the cave and put him down gently in the sand.

"Why, he's only a boy!" she cried in surprise.

"He was man enough to go up against half a dozen 'Paches alone to save Pauline Roubideau," Billie said simply.

She looked up with quick interest. "I've heard that story. Is it true?"

"It's true. And he was man enough to fight it out to a finish against two bad men yesterday."

"But he can't be more than eighteen." She watched for a moment the flush of fever in his soft cheeks. "Did he really kill Dave and Hugh Roush? Or was it you?"

"He did it."

"I hate a killer!" she blazed unexpectedly.

"Does he look like a killer?" asked Prince gently.

"No, he doesn't. That makes it worse."

"Did you know that Dave Roush ruined his sister's life in a fiendish way?"

"I expect there's another side to that story," she retorted.

"This boy was fourteen at the time. His father swore him to vengeance an' Jim followed his enemies for years. He never had a doubt but that he was doin' right."

She put her rifle down impulsively. "Why don't you keep his face sponged? Bring me water."

The Texan put his hat into requisition again for a bucket. With her handkerchief the girl sponged the face and the hands. The cold water stopped for a moment the delirious muttering of the young man. But the big eyes that stared into hers did not associate his nurse with the present.

"I done remembered you, 'Lindy, like I promised. I'm a-followin' them scalawags yet," he murmured.

"His sister's name was Melindy," explained Prince.

The girl nodded. She was rubbing gently the boy's wrist with her wet handkerchief.

"It's getting dark," she told Billie in her

sharp, decisive way. "Get your fire lit — a big one. I've got some cooking to do."

Further orders were waiting for him as soon as he had the camp-fire going. "You'll find my horse tied to a live-oak down the river a bit. Bring it up."

Billie smiled as he moved away into the darkness. This imperious girl belonged, of course, in the camp of the enemy. She had held him up with the intention of driving them back to town before her in triumph. But she was, after all, a very tender-hearted foe to a man stricken with sickness. It occurred to the Texan that through her might lie a way of salvation for them both.

Until he saw the turkey the cowpuncher wondered what cooking she could have in mind, but while he cantered back through the sand he guessed what she meant to do.

"Draw the turkey. Don't pick it," she gave instructions. Her own hands were busy trying to make her patient comfortable.

After he had drawn the bird, which was a young, plump one, he made under direction of the young woman a cement of mud. This he daubed in a three-inch coating over the turkey, then prepared the fire to make of it an oven. He covered the bird with ashes, raked live coals over these, and piled upon the red-hot coals piñon knots and juniper boughs.

"Keep your fire going till about two or three o'clock, then let it die out. In the morning the turkey will be baked," the young Diana gave assurance.

The cowpuncher omitted to tell her that he had baked a dozen more or less and knew all about it.

She rose and drew on her gauntlets in a business-like manner.

"I'm going home now. After the fever passes keep him warm and let him sleep if he will."

"Yes, ma'am," promised Billie with suspicious meekness.

The girl looked at him sharply, as if she distrusted his humility. Was he laughing at her? Did he dare to find amusement in her?

"I haven't changed my mind about you. Folks that come to town and start killing deserve all they get. But I'd look after a yellow dog if it was sick," she said contemptuously, little devils of defiance in her eyes.

"I'm not questionin' your motives, ma'am, so long as your actions are friendly."

"I haven't any use for any of Homer Webb's outfit. He's got no business here. If he runs into trouble he has only himself to blame."

"I'll mention to him that you said so."

Picking up the rifle, she turned and walked

to the horse. There was a little devil-may-care touch to her walk, just as in her manner, that suggested a girl spoiled by over-much indulgence. She was imperious, high-spirited, full of courage and insolence, because her environment had moulded her to independence. It was impossible for the young cowpuncher to help admiring the girl.

"I'll be back," she called over her shoulder.

The pony jumped to a canter at the touch of her heel. She disappeared in a gallop around the bend.

Already the fever of the boy was beginning to pass. He shivered with the chill of night. Billie wrapped around him his own coat, a linsey-woolen one lined with yellow flannel. He packed him up in the two blankets and heated stones for his feet and hands. Presently the boy fell into sound sleep for the first time since he was wounded. He had slept before, but always uneasily and restlessly. Now he did not mutter between clenched teeth nor toss to and fro.

His friend accepted it as a good omen. Since he had not slept a wink himself for forty hours, he lay down before the fire and made himself comfortable. His eyes closed almost immediately.

Chapter XIII

A Friendly Enemy

"Law sakes, Miss Bertie Lee, yo' suppah done been ready an hour. Hit sure am discommodin' the way you go gallumphin' around. Don't you-all nevah git tired?"

Aunt Becky was large and black and bulgy. To say that she was fat fails entirely of doing her justice. She overflowed from her clothes in waves at all possible points. When she moved she waddled.

Just now she was trying to be cross, but the smile of welcome on the broad face would have its way.

"Set down an' rest yo' weary bones, honey. I'll have yo' suppah dished up in no time a-tall. Yore paw was axin' where is you awhile ago."

"Where's dad?" asked Miss Bertie Lee Snaith carelessly as she flung her gloves on a chair.

"He done gone down to the store to see if anything been heerd o' them vilyainous killers of Mr. Roush."

When Bertie Lee returned from washing her hands and face and giving a touch or two to her hair, she sat down and did justice to the fried chicken and biscuits of Aunt Becky. She had had a long day of it and she ate with the keen appetite of youth.

Her father returned while she was still at the table. He was a big sandy man dressed in a corduroy suit. He was broad of shoulder and his legs were bowed.

"Any news, dad?" she asked.

"Not a thing, Lee. I reckon they've made their get-away. They must have slipped off the road somewhere. The wounded one never could have traveled all night. Maybe we'll git 'em yet."

"What will you do with them, if you do?"

"Hang 'em to a sour apple tree," answered Wallace Snaith promptly.

His daughter made no comment. She knew that her father's resentment was based on no abstract love of law and order. It had back of it no feeling that crime had been committed or justice outraged. The frontier was in its roistering youth, full of such effervescing spirits that life was the cheapest thing it knew. Every few days some unfortunate was buried on Boot Hill, a victim of his own inexpertness with the six-shooter. The longhorned cattle of Texas were wearing broad trails to the north and the northwest and such towns as Los Portales were on the boom. Chap-clad punchers galloped through the streets at all hours of the day and night letting out their joyous "Eee-yip-eee." The keys of Tolleson's and half a dozen other gambling places had long since been lost, for the doors were never closed to patrons. At games of chance the roof was the limit, in the expressive phrase of the country. Guns cracked at the slightest difference of opinion. It was bad form to use the word "murder." The correct way to speak of the result of a disagreement was to refer to it as "a killing."

Law lay for every man in a holster on his own hip. Snaith recognized this and accepted it. He was ready to "bend a gun" himself if occasion called for it. What he objected to in this particular killing was the personal affront to him. One of Webb's men had deliberately and defiantly killed two of his riders when the town was full of his employees. The man had walked into Tolleson's — a place which he, Snaith, practically owned himself — and flung down the gauntlet to the whole Lazy S M outfit. It was a flagrant insult and Wallace Snaith proposed to see that it was avenged.

"I'm going duck-hunting to-morrow, dad," Lee told him. "I'll likely be up before daylight, but I'll try not to disturb you. If you hear me rummaging around in the pantry, you'll know what for."

He grunted assent, full of the grievance that was rankling in his mind. Lee came and went as she pleased. She was her own mistress and he made no attempt to chaperon her activities.

The light had not yet begun to sift into the sky next morning when Lee dressed and tiptoed to the kitchen. She carried saddlebags with her and into the capacious pockets went tea, coffee, flour, corn meal, a flask of brandy, a plate of cookies, and a slab of bacon. An old frying-pan and a small stew kettle joined the supplies; also a little package of "yerb" medicine prepared by Aunt Becky as a specific for fevers.

Lee walked through the silent, pre-dawn darkness to the stable and saddled her pony, blanketing and cinching as deftly as her father could have done it. With her she carried an extra blanket for the wounded man.

The gray light of dawn was beginning to sift into the sky when she reached the camp of the fugitives. Prince came forward to meet her. She saw that the fire was now only a bed of coals from which no smoke would rise to betray them.

The girl swung from the saddle and gave a

little jerk of her head toward Clanton.

"How is he?"

"Slept like a log all night. Feels a heap better this mo'nin'. Wants to know if he can't have somethin' to eat."

"I killed a couple of prairie plover on the way. We'll make some soup for him."

The girl walked straight to her patient and looked down at him with direct and searching eyes. She found no glaze of fever in the ones that gazed back into hers.

"Hungry, are you?"

"I could eat a mail sack, ma'am."

She stripped the gauntlets from her hands and set about making breakfast. Jim watched her with alert interest. He was still weak, but life this morning began to renew itself in him. The pain and the fever had gone and left him at peace with a world just emerging from darkness into a rosily flushed dawn. Not the least attractive feature of it was this stunning, dark-eyed girl who was proving such a friendly enemy.

Her manner to Billie was crisp and curt. She ordered him to fetch and carry. Something in his slow drawl — some hint of hidden amusement in his manner — struck a spark of resentment from her quick eye. But toward Jim she was all kindness. No trouble was too much to take for his comfort. If he had a whim it must be gratified. Prince was merely a servant to wait upon him.

The education of Jim Clanton was progressing. As he ate his plover broth he could not keep his eyes from her. She was so full of vital life. The color beat through her dark skin warm and rich. The abundant blue-black hair, the flashing eyes, the fine poise of the head, the little jaunty swagger of her, so wholly a matter of unconscious faith in her place in the sun: all of these charmed and delighted him. He had never dreamed of a girl of such spirit and fire.

It was inevitable that both he and Billie should recall by contrast another girl who had given them generously of her service not long since. There were in the country then very few women of any kind. Certainly within a radius of two hundred miles there was no other girl so popular and so attractive as these two. Many a puncher would have been willing to break an arm for the sake of such kindness as had been lavished upon these boys.

By sunup the three of them had finished breakfast. Billie put out the fire and scattered the ashes in the river. He went into a committee of ways and means with Lee Snaith just before she returned to town.

"You can't stay here long. Some one is sure to stumble on you just as I did. What plan have you to get away?"

"If I could get our horses in three or four days mebbe Jim could make out to ride a little at a time."

"He couldn't — and you can't get your horses," she vetoed.

"Then I'll have to leave him, steal another horse, and ride through to Webb for help."

"No. You mustn't leave him. I'll see if I can get a man to take a message to your friends."

A smile came out on his lean, strong face. "You're a good friend."

"I'm no friend of yours," she flashed back. "But I won't have my father spoiling the view by hanging you where I might see you when I ride."

"You're Wallace Snaith's daughter, I reckon."

"Yes. And no man that rides for Homer Webb can be a friend of mine."

"Sorry. Anyhow, you can't keep me from being mighty grateful to my littlest enemy."

He did not intend to smile, but just a hint of it leaped to his eyes. She flushed angrily, suspecting that he was mocking her, and swung her pony toward town.

On the way she shot a brace of ducks for the sake of appearances. The country was a paradise for the hunter. On the river could be found great numbers of ducks, geese, swans, and pelicans. Of quail and prairie chicken there was no limit. Thousands of turkeys roosted in the timber that bordered the streams. There were times when the noise of pigeons returning to their night haunt was like thunder and the sight of them almost hid the sky. Bands of antelope could be seen silhouetted against the skyline. As for buffalo, numbers of them still ranged the plains, though the day of their extinction was close at hand. No country in the world's history ever offered such a field for the sportsman as the Southwest did in the days of the first great cattle drives.

Miss Bertie Lee dismounted at a store which bore the sign

SNAITH & McROBERT
General Merchandise

Though a large building, it was not one of the most recent in town. It was what is known as a "dugout" in the West, a big cellar roofed over, with side walls rising above the level of the ground. In a country where timber was scarce and the railroad was not within two hundred miles, a sod structure of this sort was the most practicable possible.

The girl sauntered in and glanced carelessly

about her. Two or three chap-clad cowboys were lounging against the counter watching another buy a suit of clothes. The wide-brimmed hats of all of them came off instantly at sight of her. The frontier was rampantly lawless, but nowhere in the world did a good woman meet with more unquestioning respect.

"What's this hyer garment?" asked the brick-red customer of the clerk, holding up the waistcoat that went with the suit.

"That's a vest," explained the salesman. "You wear it under the coat."

"You don't say!" The vaquero examined the article curiously and disdainfully. "I've heard tell of these didoes, but I never did see one before. Well, I'll take this suit. Wrop it up. You keep the vest proposition and give it to a tenderfoot."

No cowpuncher ever wore a waistcoat. The local dealers of the Southwest had been utterly unable to impress this fact upon the mind of the Eastern manufacturer. The result was that every suit came in three parts, one of which always remained upon the shelf of the store. Some of the supply merchants had several thousand of these articles deluxe in their stock. In later years they gave them away to Indians and Mexicans.

"Do you know where Jack Goodheart is?"

asked Lee of the nearest youth.

"No, ma'am, but I'll go hunt him for you," answered the puncher promptly.

"Thank you."

Ten minutes later a bronzed rider swung down in front of the Snaith home. Miss Bertie Lee was on the porch.

"You sent for me," he said simply.

"Do you want to do something for me?"

"Try me."

"Will you ride after Webb's outfit and tell him that two of his men are in hiding on the river just below town. One of them is wounded and can't sit a horse. So he'd better send a buckboard for him. Let Homer Webb know that if dad or Sanders finds these men, the cottonwoods will be bearing a new kind of fruit. Tell him to burn the wind getting here. The men are in a cave on the left-hand side of the river going down. It is just below the bend."

Jack Goodheart did not ask her how she knew this or what difference it made to her whether Webb rescued his riders or not. He said, "I'll be on the road inside of twenty minutes."

Goodheart was a splendid specimen of the frontiersman. He was the best roper in the country, of proved gameness, popular, keen as an Italian stiletto, and absolutely trustworthy. Since the first day he had seen her Jack had been devoted to the service of Bertie Lee Snaith. No dog could have been humbler or less critical of her shortcomings. The girl despised his wooing, but she was forced to respect the man. As a lover she had no use for Goodheart; as a friend she was always calling upon him.

"I knew you'd go, Jack," she told him.

"Yes, I'd lie down and make of myself a doormat for you to tromple on," he retorted with a touch of self-contempt. "Would you like me to do it now?"

Lee looked at him in surprise. This was the first evidence he had ever given that he resented the position in which he stood to her.

"If you don't want to go I'll ask some one else," she replied.

"Oh, I'll go."

He turned and strode to his horse. For years he had been her faithful cavalier and he knew he was no closer to his heart's desire than when he began to serve. The first faint stirrings of rebellion were moving in him. It was not that he blamed her in the least. She was scarcely nineteen, the magnet for the eyes of all the unattached men in the district. Was it reasonable to suppose that she would give her love to a penniless puncher of twenty-eight, lank as a shad, with no recommendation but honesty? None the less, Jack began to doubt whether eternal patience was a virtue.

Chapter XIV

The Gun-Barrel Road

Jack Goodheart followed the gun-barrel road into a desert green and beautiful with vegetation. Now he passed a blooming azalea or a yucca with clustering bellflowers. The prickly pear and the catclaw clutched at his chaps. The arrowweed and the soapweed were everywhere, as was also the stunted creosote. The details were not lovely, but in the sunset light of late afternoon the silvery sheen of the mesquite had its own charm for the rider.

Back of the saddle he carried a "hot roll" of blankets and supplies, for he would have to camp out three or four nights. Flour, coffee, and a can of tomatoes made the substance of his provisions. His rifle would bring him all the meat he needed. The one he used was a seventy-three because the bullets fired from it fitted the cylinder of his forty-four revolver.

Solitude engulfed him. Once a mule deer stared at him in surprise from an escarpment back of the mesa. A rattlesnake buzzed its ominous warning.

He left the road to follow the broad trail made by the Flying V Y herd. A horizon of deep purple marked the afterglow of sunset and preceded a desert night of stars. Well into the evening he rode, then hobbled his horse before he built a camp-fire.

Darkness was still thick over the plains when he left the buffalo wallow in which he had camped. All day he held a steady course northward till the stars were out again. Late the next afternoon he struck the dust of the drag in the ground swells of a more broken country.

The drag-driver directed Goodheart to the left point. He found there two men. One of them — Dad Wrayburn — he knew. The other was a man of sandy complexion, hard-faced, and fishy of eye.

"Whad you want?" the second demanded.

"I want to see Webb."

"Can't see him. He ain't here."

"Where is he?"

"He's ridden on to the Fort to make arrangements for receiving the herd," answered the man sulkily.

"Who's the big auger left?"

148

"I'm the foreman if that's what you mean?"

"Well, I've come to tell you that two of yore men are hidin' in the chaparral below Los Portales. There was trouble at Tolleson's. Two of the Lazy S M men were gunned an' one of yours was wounded."

"Which one was wounded?"

"I heard his name was Clanton."

"Suits me fine," grinned the foreman, showing two rows of broken, stained teeth. "Hope the Lazy S M boys gunned him proper."

Dad Wrayburn broke in softly. "Chieto, compadre!" ("Hush, partner!") He turned to Goodheart. "The other man with Clanton must be Billie Prince."

"Yes."

"I reckon the Lazy S M boys are lookin' for 'em."

"You guessed right first crack out of the box."

"Where are our boys holed up?"

"In a cave the other side of town. They're just beyond the big bend of the river. I'll take you there."

"You've seen 'em."

"No." Goodheart hesitated just a moment before he went on. "I was sent by the person who has seen 'em."

"Listens to me like a plant," jeered Yankie.

149

"Meanin' that I'm a liar?" asked Goodheart coldly.

"I wasn't born yesterday. Come clean. Who is yore friend that saw the boys?"

"I can't tell you that."

"Then yore story doesn't interest me a whole lot."

"Different here," dissented Wrayburn. "Do you know how badly Clanton is hurt, Jack?"

"No. He was able to ride out of town, but my friend told me to say he wasn't able to ride now. You'll have to send a wagon for him."

Wrayburn turned to the foreman. "Joe, we've got to go back an' help the boys."

"Not on yore topknot, Dad. I'm here to move these beeves along to the Fort. Prince an' that Clanton may have gone on a tear an' got into trouble or they may not. I don't care a plugged nickel which way it is. I'm not keepin' herd on them, an' what's more I don't intend to."

"We can't leave 'em that away. Dad gum it, we got to stand by the boys, Joe. That's what Webb would tell us if he was here."

"But he ain't here, Dad. An' while he's gone I'm major-domo of this outfit. We're headed north, not south."

"You may be. I'm not. An' I reckon you'll find several of the boys got the same notion I have. I taken a fancy to both those young fellows, an' if I hadn't I'd go help 'em just the same."

"You ain't expectin' to ride our stock on this fool chase, are you?"

"I'll ride the first good bronc I get my knees clamped to, Joe."

"As regards that, you'll get my answer like shot off'n a shovel. None of the Flyin' V Y remuda is goin'."

Wrayburn cantered around the point of the herd to the swing, from the swing back to the drag, and then forward to the left point. In the circuit he had stopped to sound out each rider.

"We-all have decided that ten of us will go back, Joe," he announced serenely. "That leaves enough to loose-herd the beeves whilst we're away."

Yankie grew purple with rage. "If you go you'll walk. I'll show you who's foreman here."

"No use raisin' a rookus, Joe," replied the old Confederate mildly. "We're goin'. Yore authority doesn't stretch far enough to hold us here."

"I'll show you!" stormed the foreman. "Some of you will go to sleep in smoke if you try to take any of my remuda."

"Now don't you-all be onreasonable, Joe.

We got to go. Cayn't you get it through yore cocoanut that we've got to stand by our pardners?"

"That killer Clanton is no pardner of mine. I meant to burn powder with him one of these days myself. If Wally Snaith beats me to it I'm not goin' to wear black," retorted Yankie.

"Sho! The kid's got good stuff in him. An' nobody could ask for a squarer pal than Billie Prince. You know that yore own self."

"You heard what I said, Dad. The Flyin' V Y horses don't take the back trail to-day," insisted the foreman stubbornly.

The wrinkled eyes of Wrayburn narrowed a little. He looked straight at Yankie.

"Don't get biggety Joe I'm not askin' you or any other man whether I can ride to rescue a friend when he's in trouble. You don't own these broncs, an' if you did we'd take 'em just the same."

The voice of Wrayburn was still gentle, but it no longer pleaded for understanding. The words were clean-cut and crisp.

"I'll show you!" flung back the foreman with an oath.

When the little group of cavalry was gathered for the start, Yankie, rifle in hand, barred the way. His face was ugly with the fury of his anger.

Dad Wrayburn rode forward in front of his

152

party. "Don't git promiscuous with that cannon of yours, Joe. You've done yore level best to keep us here. But we're goin' just the same. We-all will tell the old man how tender you was of his remuda stock. That will let you out."

"Don't you come another step closeter, Dad Wrayburn!" the foreman shouted. "I'll let you know who is boss here."

Wrayburn did not raise his voice. The drawl in it was just as pronounced, but every man present read in it a warning.

"This old sawed-off shotgun of mine spatters like hell, Joe. It always did shoot all over the United States an' Texas."

There was an instant of dead silence. Each man watched the other intently, the one cool and determined, the other full of a volcanic fury. The curtain had been rung up for tragedy.

A man stepped between them, twirling carelessly a rawhide rope.

"Just a moment, gentlemen. I think I know a way to settle this without bloodshed." Jack Goodheart looked first at the ex-Confederate, then at the foreman. He was still whirling as if from absent-minded habit the loop of his reata.

"We're here to listen, Jack. That would suit me down to the ground," answered Wrayburn.

The loop of the lariat snaked forward, whistled through the air, dropped over the head of Yankie, and tightened around his neck. A shot went wildly into the air as the rifle was jerked out of the hands of its owner, who came to the earth with sprawling arms. Goodheart ran forward swiftly, made a dozen expert passes with his fingers, and rose without a word.

Yankie had been hog-tied by the champion roper of the Southwest.

Chapter XV

Lee Plays a Leading Rôle

A man on horseback clattered up the street and drew up at the Snaith house. He was a sandy-complexioned man with a furtive-eyed, apologetic manner. Miss Bertie Lee recognized him as one of the company riders named Dumont.

"Is yore paw home, Miss Lee?" he asked breathlessly.

"Some one to see you, dad," called the girl over her shoulder.

Wallace Snaith sauntered out to the

porch. " 'Lo, Dumont!"

"I claim that hundred dollars reward. I done found 'em, Mr. Snaith."

Lee, about to enter the house, stopped in her tracks.

"Where?" demanded the cattleman jubilantly.

"Down the river — hid in a dugout they done built. I'll take you-all there."

"I knew they couldn't be far away when that first hawss came in all blood-stained. Hustle up four or five of the boys, Dumont. Get 'em here on the jump." In the face of the big drover could be read a grim elation.

His daughter confronted him. "What are you going to do, dad?"

"None o' yore business, Lee. You ain't in this," he answered promptly.

"You're going out to kill those men," she charged, white to the lips.

"They'll git a trial if they surrender peaceable."

"What kind of a trial?" she asked scornfully. "They know better than to surrender. They'll fight."

"That'll suit me too."

"Don't, dad. Don't do it," the girl begged. "They're game men. They fought fair. I've made inquiries. You mustn't kill them like wolves."

"Mustn't I?" he said stubbornly. "I reckon that's just what I'm goin' to do. I'll learn Homer Webb to send his bad men to Los Portales lookin' for trouble. He can't kill my riders an' get away with it."

"You know he didn't do that. This boy — Clanton, if that's his name — had a feud with the Roush family. One of them betrayed his sister. Far as I can find out these Roush brothers were the scum of the earth." Her bosom rose and fell fast with excitement.

"Howcome you to know so much about it, girl? Not that it makes any difference. They may have been hell-hounds, but they were my riders. These gunmen went into my own place an' shot 'em down. They picked the fight. There's no manner o' doubt about that."

"They didn't do it on your account. I tell you there was an old feud."

"Webb thinks he's got the world by the tail for a downhill pull. I'll show him."

"Dad, you're starting war. Don't you see that? If you shoot these men he'll get back by killing some of yours. And so it will go on."

"I reckon. But I'm not startin' the war. He did that. It was the boldest piece of cheek I ever heard tell of — those two gunmen goin' into Tolleson's and shootin' up my riders. They got to pay the price."

Lee cried out in passionate protest. "It'll be just plain murder, dad. That's all."

"What's got into you, girl?" he demanded, seizing her by the arms. The chill of anger and suspicion filmed his light-blue eyes. "I won't stand for this kind of talk. You go right into the house an' 'tend to yore own knittin'. I've heard about enough from you."

He swung her round by the shoulders and gave a push.

Lee did not go to her room and fling herself upon the bed in an impotent storm of tears. She stood thinking, her little fists clenched and her eyes flashing. Civilization has trained women to feebleness of purpose, but this girl stood outside of conventional viewpoints. It was her habit to move directly to the thing she wanted. Her decision was swift, the action following upon it immediate.

She lifted her rifle down from the deer-horn rack where it rested and buckled the ammunition belt around her waist. Swiftly she ran to the corral, roped her bronco, saddled it, and cinched. As she galloped away she saw her father striding toward the stable. His shout reached her, but she did not wait to hear what he wanted.

The hoofs of her pony drummed down the street. She flew across the desert and struck the river just below town. The quirt attached to her wrist rose and fell. She made no allowance for prairie-dog holes, but went at racing speed through the rabbit weed and over the slippery salt-grass bumps.

In front of the cave she jerked the horse to a halt.

"Hello, in there!"

The tumble weeds moved and the head of Prince appeared. He pushed the brush aside and came out.

"Buenos tardes, señorita. Didn't know you were comin' back again to-day."

"You've been seen," she told him hurriedly as she dismounted. "Dad's gathering his men. He means to make you trouble."

Billie looked away in the direction of the town. A mile or more away he saw a cloud of dust. It was moving toward them.

"I see he does," he answered quietly.

"Quick! Get your friend out. Take my horse."

He shook his head slowly. "No use. They would see us an' run us down. We'll make a stand here."

"But you can't do that. They'll surround you. They'll send for more men if they need 'em."

"Likely. But Jim couldn't stand such a ride even if there was a chance — and there isn't, not with yore horse carryin' double. We'll hold the fort, Miss Lee, while you make yore get-away into the hills. An' thank you for comin'. We'll never forget all you've done for us these days."

"I'm not going."

"Not goin'?"

"I'm going to stay right here. They won't dare to shoot at you if I'm here."

"I never did see such a girl as you," admitted Prince, smiling at her. "You take the cake. But we can't let you do that for us. We can't skulk behind a young lady's skirts to save our hides. It's not etiquette on the Pecos."

The red color burned through her dusky skin. "I'm not doing it for you," she said stiffly. "It's dad I'm thinking about. I don't want him mixed up in such a business. I won't have it either."

"You'd better go to him and talk it over, then."

"No. I'll stay here. He wouldn't listen to me a minute."

Billie was still patient with her. "I don't think you'd better stay, Miss Lee. I know just how you feel. But there are a lot of folks won't understand how come you to take up with yore father's enemies. They'll talk a lot of foolishness likely."

The cowpuncher blushed at his own awkward phrasing of the situation, yet the thing had to be said and he knew no other way to say it.

She flashed a resentful glance at him. Her cheeks, too, flamed.

"I don't care what they say since it won't be true," she answered proudly. "You needn't argue. I've staked out a claim here."

"I wish you'd go. There's still time."

The girl turned on him angrily with swift, animal grace. "I tell you it's none of your business whether I go or stay. I'll do just as I please."

Prince gave up his attempt to change her mind. If she would stay, she would. He set about arranging the defense.

Young Clanton crept out to the mouth of the cave and lay down with his rifle beside him. His friend piled up the tumble weeds in front of him.

"We're right enough in front — easy enough to stand 'em off there," reflected Billie, aloud. "But I'd like to know what's to prevent us from being attacked in the rear. They can crawl up through the brush till they're right on top of the bank. They can post sharpshooters in the mesquite across the river so that if we come out to check those snakin' forward, the snipers can get us."

"I'll sit on the bank above the cave and

160

watch 'em," announced Lee.

"An' what if they mistook you for one of us?" asked Prince dryly.

"They can't, with me wearing a red coat."

"You're bound to be in this, aren't you?" His smile was more friendly than the words. It admitted reluctant admiration of her.

The party on the other side of the river was in plain sight now. Jim counted four — five — six of them as they deployed. Presently Prince threw a bullet into the dust at the feet of one of the horses as they moved forward. It was meant as a warning not to come closer and accepted as one.

After a minute of consultation a single horseman rode to the bank of the stream.

"You over there," he shouted.

"It's dad," said Lee.

"You'd better surrender peaceable. We've come to git you alive or dead," shouted Snaith.

"What do you want us for?" asked Prince.

"You know well enough what for. You killed one of my punchers."

Clanton groaned. "Only one?"

"An' another may die any day. Come out with yore hands up."

"We'd rather stay here, thank you," Billie called back.

Snaith leaned forward in the saddle. "Is

161

that you over there, Lee?"

"Yes, dad."

"Gone back on yore father and taken up with Webb's scalawags, have you?"

"No, I haven't," she called back. "But I'm going to see they get fair play."

"You git out of there, girl, and on this side of the river!" Snaith roared angrily. "Pronto! Do you hear?"

"There's no use shouting yourself hoarse, dad. I can hear you easily, and I'm not coming."

"Not comin'! D' ye mean you've taken up with a pair of killers, of outlaws we're goin' to put out of business? You talk like a — like a — "

"Go slow, Snaith!" cut in Prince sharply. "Can't you see she's tryin' to save you from murder?"

"We're goin' to take those boys back to Los Portales with us — or their bodies. I don't care a whole lot which. You light a shuck out of there, Lee."

"No," she answered stubbornly. "If you're so bent on shooting at some one you can shoot at me."

The cattleman stormed and threatened, but in the end he had to give up the point. His daughter was as obstinate as he was. He retired in volcanic humor.

"I never could get dad to give up swearing," his daughter told her new friends by way of humorous apology. "Wonder what he'll do now."

"Wait till night an' drive us out of our hole, I expect," replied Prince.

"Will he wait? I'm not so sure of that," said Jim. "See. His men are scattering. They're up to somethin'."

"They're going down to cross the river to get behind us just as you said they would," predicted Lee.

She was right. Half an hour later, from her position on the bank above the cave, she caught a glimpse of a man slipping forward through the brush. She called to Prince, who crept out from behind the tumble weeds to join her. A bullet dug into the soft clay not ten inches from his head. He scrambled up and lay down behind a patch of soapweed a few yards from the girl. Another bullet from across the river whistled past the cowpuncher.

Lee rose and walked across to the bushes where he lay crouched. Very deliberately she stood there, shading her eyes from the sun as she looked toward the sharpshooters. Twice they had taken a chance, because of the distance between her and Prince. She intended they should know how close she was to him now.

Billie could not conceal his anxiety for her. "Why don't you get back where you were? I got as far as I could from you on purpose. What's the sense of you comin' right up to me when you see they're shootin' at me?"

"That's why I came up closer. They'll have to stop it as long as I'm here."

"You can't stay there the rest of yore natural life, can you?" he asked with manifest annoyance. Even if he got out of his present danger alive — and Billie had to admit to himself that the chances did not look good — he knew it would be cast up to him some day that he had used Lee Snaith's presence as a shield against his enemies. "Why don't you act reasonable an' ride back to town, like a girl ought to do? You've been a good friend to us. There's nothin' more you can do. It's up to us to fight our way out."

He took careful aim and fired. A man in the bushes two hundred yards back of them scuttled to his feet and ran limping off. Billie covered the dodging man with his rifle carefully, then lowered his gun without firing.

"Let him go," said Prince aloud. "Mr. Dumont won't bother us a whole lot. He's gun-shy anyhow."

From across the river came a scatter of bullets.

"They've got to hit closeter to that before

164

they worry me," Jim called to the two above.

"I don't think they shot to hit. They're tryin' to scare Miss Lee away," called down Billie.

"As if I didn't know dad wouldn't let 'em take any chances with me here," the girl said confidently. "If we can hold out till night I can stay here and keep shooting while you two slip away and hide. Before morning your friends ought to arrive."

"If they got yore message."

"Oh, they got it. Jack Goodheart carried it."

The riflemen across the river were silent for a time. When they began sniping again, it was from such an angle that they could aim at the cave without endangering those above. Both Clanton and Prince returned the fire.

Presently Lee touched on the shoulder the man beside her.

"Look!"

She pointed to a cloud of smoke behind them. From it tongues of fire leaped up into the air. Farther to the right a second puff of smoke could be seen, and beyond it another and still a fourth jet.

After a moment of dead silence Prince spoke. "They've fired the prairie. The wind is blowin' toward us. They mean to smoke us out."

"Yes."

"We'll be driven down into the open bed of the river where they can pick us off."

The girl nodded.

"Now, will you leave us?" Billie turned on her triumphantly. He could at least choose the conditions of the last stand they must make. "They've called our bluff. It's a showdown."

"Now I'll go less than ever," she said quietly.

Chapter XVI

Three Modern Musketeers

The fierce crackling of the flames rolled toward them. The wind served at least the one purpose of lifting the smoke so that it did not stifle those on the river-bank. Clanton crept up from the cave and joined them.

"Looks like we're goin' out with fireworks, Billie," he grinned.

"That's nonsense," said Lee sharply. "There's a way of escape, if only we can find it."

"Blamed if I see it," the young fellow answered. As he looked at her the eyes in his pale face glowed. "But I see one thing. You're the best little pilgrim that ever I met up with."

The heat of the flames came to them in waves.

"You walk out, climb on yore horse, an' ride down the river, Miss Lee. Then we'll make a break for cover. You can't do anything more for us," insisted Prince.

"That's right," agreed the younger man. "We'll play this out alone. You cut yore stick an' drift. If we git through I'll sure come back an' thank you proper some day."

Recently Lee had read "The Three Musketeers." From it there flashed to her a memory of the picture on the cover.

"I know what we'll do," she said, coughing from a swallow of smoke. She stepped between them and tucked an arm under the elbow of each. "All for one, and one for all. Forward march!"

They moved down the embankment side by side to the sand-bed close to the stream, each of the three carrying a rifle tucked close to the side. From the chaparral keen eyes watched them, covering every step they took with ready weapons. Miss Lee's party turned to the right and followed the river-bed in the direction of Los Portales. For the wind was driving the fire down instead of up. Those in the mesquite held a parallel course to cut off any chance of escape.

Some change of wind currents swept the smoke toward them in great billows. It enveloped the fugitives in a dense cloud.

"Get yore head down to the water," Billie called into the ear of the girl.

They lay on the rocks in the shallow water and let the black smoke waves pour over them. Lee felt herself strangling and tried to rise, but a heavy hand on her shoulder held her face down. She sputtered and coughed, fighting desperately for breath. A silk handkerchief was slipped over her face and knotted behind. She felt sick and dizzy. The knowledge flashed across her mind that she could not stand this long. In its wake came another dreadful thought. Was she going to die?

The hand on her shoulder relaxed. Lee felt herself lifted to her feet. She caught at Billie's arm to steady herself, for she was still queer in the head. For a few moments she stood there coughing the smoke out of her lungs. His arm slipped around her shoulder.

"Take yore time," he advised.

A second shift of the breeze had swept the smoke away. This had saved their lives, but it had also given Snaith's men another chance at them. A bullet whistled past the head of Clanton, who was for the time a few yards from his friends. Instantly he whipped the rifle up and fired.

"No luck," he grumbled. "My eyes are sore from the smoke. I can't half see."

Lee was not yet quite herself. The experience through which she had just passed had shaken her nerves.

"Let's get out of here quick!" she cried.

"Take yore time. There's no hurry," Prince iterated. "They won't shoot again, now Jim's close to us."

The younger man grinned, as he had a habit of doing when the cards fell against him. "Where'd we go? Look, they've headed us off. We can't travel forward. We can't go back. I expect we'll have to file on the quarter-section where we are," he drawled.

A rider had galloped forward and was dismounting close to the river. He took shelter behind a boulder.

Billie swept with a glance the plain to their right. A group of horsemen was approaching. "More good citizens comin' to be in at the finish of this man hunt. They ought to build a grandstand an' invite the whole town," he said sardonically.

A water-gutted arroyo broke the line of river-bank. Jim, who was limping heavily, stopped and examined it.

"Let's stay here, Billie, an' fight it out.

No use foolin' ourselves. We're trapped. Might as well call for a showdown here as any-where."

Prince nodded. "Suits me. We'll make our stand right at the head of the arroyo." He turned abruptly to the girl. "It's got to be good-bye here, Miss Lee."

"That's whatever, littlest pilgrim," agreed Clanton promptly. "If you get a chance send word to Webb an' tell him how it was with us."

Her lip trembled. She knew that in the shadow of the immediate future red tragedy lurked. She had done her best to avert it and had failed. The very men she was trying to save had dismissed her.

"Must I go?" she begged.

"You must, Miss Lee. We're both grateful to you. Don't you ever doubt that!" Billie said, his earnest gaze full in hers.

The girl turned away and went up through the sand, her eyes filmed with tears so that she could not see where she was going. The two men entered the arroyo. Before they reached the head of it she could hear the crack of ex-ploding rifles. One of the men across the river was firing at them and they were throwing bullets back at him. She wondered, shivering, whether it was her father.

It must have been a few seconds later

that she heard the joyous "Eee-yip-eee!" of Prince. Almost at the same time a rider came splashing through the shallow water of the river toward her.

The man was her father. He swung down from the saddle and snatched her into his arms. His haggard face showed her how anxious he had been. She began to sob, overcome, perhaps, as much by his emotion as her own.

"I'll blacksnake the condemned fool that set fire to the prairie!" he swore, gulping down a lump in his throat. "Tell me you-all aren't hurt, Bertie Lee. . . . God! I thought you was swallowed up in that fire."

"Daddie, daddie, I couldn't help it. I had to do it," she wept. "And — I thought I would choke to death, but Mr. Prince saved me. He kept my face close to the water and made me breathe through a handkerchief."

"Did he?" The man's face set grimly again. "Well, that won't save him. As for you, miss — you're goin' to yore room to live on bread an' water for a week. I wish you were a boy for about five minutes so's I could wear you to a frazzle with a cowhide."

Snaith's intentions toward Clanton and Prince had to be postponed for the present, the cattleman discovered a few minutes later.

171

When he and Lee emerged from the river-bed to the bank above, the first thing he saw was a group of cowpunchers shaking hands gayly with the two fugitives. His jaw dropped.

"Where in Mexico did they come from?" he asked himself aloud.

"I expect they're Webb's riders," his daughter answered with a little sob of joy. "I thought they'd never come."

"You thought . . . How did you know they were comin'?"

"Oh, I sent for them." The girl's dark eyes met his fearlessly. A flicker of a smile crept into them. "I've had the best of you all round, dad. You'd better make that two weeks on bread and water."

Wallace Snaith gathered his forces and retreated from the field of battle. A man on a spent horse met him at his own gate as he dismounted. He handed the cattleman a note.

On the sheet of dirty paper was written:

> The birds you want are nesting in a dugout on the river four miles below town. You got to hurry or they'll be flown.
>
> J. Y.

Snaith read the note, tore it in half, and

tossed the pieces away. He turned to the messenger.

"Tell Joe he's just a few hours late. His news isn't news any more."

Chapter XVII

"Peg-Leg" Warren

Webb drove his cattle up the river, the Staked Plains on his right. The herd was a little gaunt from the long journey and he took the last part of the trek in easy stages. Since he had been awarded the contract for beeves at the Fort, by Department orders the old receiving agent had been transferred. The new appointee was a brother-in-law of McRobert and the owner of the Flying V Y did not want to leave any loophole for rejection of the steers.

With the clean blood of sturdy youth in him Clanton recovered rapidly from the shoulder wound. In order to rest him as much as possible, Webb put him in charge of the calf wagon which followed the drag and picked up any wobbly-legged bawlers dropped on the trail. During the trip Jim discovered for himself the truth of what Billie had said, that the settlers with small ranches were lined up as allies of the Snaith-McRobert faction. These men, owners of small bunches of cows, claimed that Webb and the other big drovers rounded up their cattle in the drive, ran the road brand of the traveling outfit on these strays, and sold them as their own. The story of the drovers was different. They charged that these "nesters" were practically rustlers preying upon larger interests passing through the country to the Indian reservations. Year by year the feeling had grown more bitter. That Snaith and McRobert backed the river settlers was an open secret. A night herder had been shot from the mesquite not a month before. The blame had been laid upon a band of bronco Mescaleros, but the story was whispered that a "bad man" in the employ of the Lazy S M people, a man known as "Mysterious Pete Champa," boasted later while drunk that he had fired the shot.

Jim had heard a good deal about this Mysterious Pete. He was a killer of the most deadly kind because he never gave warning of his purpose. The man was said to be a crack shot, quick as chain lightning, without the slightest regard for human life. He moved furtively, spoke little when sober, and had no scruples against assassination from ambush. Nobody in the Southwest was more feared than he.

This man crossed the path of Clanton when the herd was about fifty miles from the Fort.

The beeves had been grazing forward slowly all afternoon and were loose-bedded early for the night. Cowpunchers are as full of larks as schoolboys on a holiday. Now they were deciding a bet as to whether Tim Mc-Grath, a red-headed Irish boy, could ride a vicious gelding that had slipped into the remuda. Billie Prince roped the front feet of the horse and threw him. The animal was blindfolded and saddled.

Doubtful of his own ability to stick to the seat, Tim maneuvered the buckskin over to the heavy sand before he mounted. The gelding went sunfishing into the air, then got his head between his legs and gave his energy to stiff-legged bucking. He whirled as he plunged forward, went round and round furiously, and unluckily for Tim reached the hard ground. The jolts jerked the rider forward and back like a jack-knife without a spring. He went flying over the head of the bronco to the ground.

The animal, red-eyed with hate, lunged for the helpless puncher. A second time Billie's rope snaked forward. The loop fell true over the head of the gelding, tightened, and swung the outlaw to one side so that his hoofs missed the Irishman. Tim scrambled to his feet and fled for safety.

The cowpunchers whooped joyously. In their lives near-tragedy was too frequent to carry even a warning. Dad Wrayburn bummed a stanza of "Windy Bill" for the benefit of McGrath:

"Bill Garrett was a cowboy, an' he could
    ride, you bet;
He said the bronc he couldn't bust was
    one he hadn't met.
He was the greatest talker that this coun-
    try ever saw
Until his good old rim-fire went a-driftin'
    down the draw."

Two men had ridden up unnoticed and were watching with no obvious merriment the contest. Now one of them spoke.

"Where can I find Homer Webb?"

Dad turned to the speaker, a lean man with a peg-leg, brown as a Mexican, hard of eye and mouth. The gray bristles on the unshaven face advertised him as well on into middle age. Wrayburn recognized the man as "Peg-Leg" Warren, one of the most troublesome nesters on the river.

"He's around here somewhere." Dad turned to Clanton. "Seen anything of the old man, Jim?"

"Here he comes now."

Webb rode up to the group. At sight of Warren and his companion the face of the drover set.

"I've come to demand an inspection of yore herd," broke out the nester harshly.

"Why demand it? Why not just ask for it?" cut back Webb curtly.

"I'm not splittin' words. What I'm sayin' is that if you've got any of my cattle here I want 'em."

"You're welcome to them." Webb turned to his segundo. "Joe, ride through the herd with this man. If there's any stock there with his brand, cut 'em out for him. Bring the bunch up to the chuck wagon an' let me see 'em before he drives 'em away."

The owner of the Flying V Y brand wasted no more words. He swung his cowpony around and rode back to the chuck wagon to superintend the jerking of the hind quarters of a buffalo.

He was still busy at this when the nester returned with half a dozen cattle cut out from the herd. In those days of the big drives many strays drifted by chance into every road outfit passing through the country. It was no reflection on the honesty of a man to ask for an inspection and to find one's cows among the beeves following the trail.

177

Webb walked over to the little bunch gathered by Warren and looked over each one of the steers.

"That big red with the white stockin's goes with the herd. The rest may be yours," the drover said.

"The roan's mine too. My brand's the Circle Diamond. See here where it's been blotted out."

"I bought that steer from the Circle Lazy H five hundred miles from here. You'll find a hundred like it in the herd," returned Webb calmly.

Warren turned to his companion. "Pete, you know this steer. Ain't it mine?"

"Sure." The man to whom Warren had turned for confirmation was a slight, trim, gray-eyed man. Sometimes the gray of the eyes turned almost black, but always they were hard as onyx. There was about the man something sinister, something of eternal wariness. His glance had a habit of sweeping swiftly from one person to another as if it questioned what purpose might lie below the unruffled surface.

Homer Webb called to Prince and to Wrayburn. "Billie — Dad, know anything about this big red steer?"

"Know it? We'd ought to," answered Wrayburn promptly. "It's the ladino beef that started the stampede on the Brazos — made us more trouble than any ten critters of the bunch."

"You bought it from the Circle Lazy H," supplemented Billie.

Peg-Leg Warren laughed harshly. "O' course they'll swear to it. You're givin' them their job, ain't you?"

The drover looked at him steadily. "Yes, I'm givin' the boys a job, but I haven't bought 'em body an' soul, Warren."

The eyes of the nester were a barometer of his temper. "That's my beef, Webb."

"It never was yours an' it never will be."

"Raw work, Webb. I'll not stand for it."

"Don't overplay yore hand," cautioned the owner of the trail herd.

Clanton had ridden up and was talking to the cook. A couple of other punchers had dropped up to the chuck wagon, casually as it were.

Warren glared at them savagely, but swallowed his rage. "It's yore say-so right now, but I'll collect what's comin' to me one of these days. You're liable to find this trail hotter 'n hell with the lid on."

"I'm not lookin' for trouble, but I'm not runnin' away from it," returned Webb evenly.

"You're sure goin' to find it — a heap more

of it than you can ride herd on. That right, Pete?"

The gray-eyed man nodded slightly. Mysterious Pete had the habit of taciturnity. His gaze slid in a searching, sidelong fashion from Webb to Prince, on to Wrayburn, across to Clanton, and back to the drover. No wolf in the encinal could have been warier.

"Cut out the roan," ordered Webb.

The ladino was separated from the bunch of Circle Diamond cattle. Warren and his satellite drove the rest from the camp.

"War, looks like," commented Dad Wrayburn.

"Yes," agreed the drover. "I wish it didn't have to be. But Peg-Leg called for a showdown. He came here to force my hand. As regards the beef, he might have had it an' welcome. But that wouldn't have satisfied him. He'd have taken it for a sign of weakness if I had given way."

"What will he do?" asked young McGrath.

"I don't know. We'll have to keep our eyes open every minute of the day an' night. Are you with me, boys?"

Tim threw his hat into the air and let out a yell. "Surest thing you know."

"Damfidon't sit in an' take a hand," said Wrayburn.

One after another agreed to back the boss.

"But don't think it will be a picnic," urged Webb. "We'll know we've been in a fight before we get through. With a crowd of gunmen like Mysterious Pete against us we'll have hard travelin'. I'd sidestep this if I could, but I can't."

Chapter XVIII

A Stampede

Clanton took his turn at night herding for the first time the day of Warren's visit to the camp. Under a star-strewn sky he circled the sleeping herd, humming softly a stanza of a cowboy song. Occasionally he met Billie Prince or Tim McGrath circling in the opposite direction. The scene was peaceful as old age and beautiful as a fairy tale. For under the silvery light of night the Southwest takes on a loveliness foreign to it in the glare of the sun. The harsh details of day are lost in a luminous glow of mystic charm.

Jim had just ridden past Billie when the silence was shattered by a sudden fury of sound. The popping of revolvers, the clanging of cow bells, the clash of tin boilers — all that medley of discord which lends volume to the horror known as a charivari — tore to shreds the harmony of the night.

"What's that?" called Billie.

The hideous dissonance came from the side of the herd farthest from the camp. Together the two riders galloped toward it.

"Peg-Leg Warren's work," guessed Clanton.

"Sure," agreed Billie. "Trying to stampede the herd."

Already the cattle were bawling in wild terror, surging toward the camp to escape this unknown danger. Both of the punchers drew their revolvers and fired rapidly into the air. It was impossible to check the rush, but they succeeded in deflecting it from the sleeping men. Before the weapons were empty, the ground shook with a thunder of hoofs as the herd fled into the darkness.

Billie found himself in the van of the stampede. He was caught in the rush and to save himself from being trampled down was forced to join the flight. He was the center of a moving sea of backs, so hemmed in that if his pony stumbled life would be trodden out of him in an instant. Except for occasional buffalo wallows the ground was level, but at any moment his mount might break a leg in a prairie-dog hole.

For the first mile or two the cattle were packed in a dense mass, shoulder to shoulder, all lumbering forward in wild-eyed panic. The noise of their hoofs was like the continuous roll of thunder and the cloud of dust so thick that the throat of Prince was swollen with it. It was only after the stampeded cattle had covered several miles that the formation of their aimless charge grew looser. The pace slackened as the steers became leg-weary. Now and again small bunches dropped from the drag or from one of the flanks. Gradually Billie was able to work toward the outskirts. His chance came when the herd poured into a swale and from it emerged into a more broken terrain. Directly in front of the leaders was a mesa with a sharp incline. Instead of taking the hill, the stampede split, part flowing to the right and part to the left. The cowpuncher urged his fagged horse straight up the hill.

He had escaped with his life, but the bronco was completely exhausted. Billie unsaddled and freed the cowpony. He knew it would not wander far now. Stretched out at full length on the buffalo grass, the cowboy drank into his lungs the clean, cold night air. His tongue was swollen, his lips cracked and bleeding. The alkali dust, sifting into his eyes, had left them red and sore. Every inch of his unshaven face, his hands, and his clothes was covered with a fine, white powder. For a long drink of mountain water he would gladly have given a month's pay.

Within the hour Billie resaddled and took the back trail. There was no time to lose. He must get back to camp, notify Webb where the stampede was moving, and join the other riders in an all-night and all-day round-up of the scattered herd. Since daybreak he had been in the saddle, and he knew that for at least twenty-four hours longer he would not leave it except to change from a worn-out horse to a fresh one.

When Prince reached camp shortly after midnight he found that the stampede of the cattle had for the moment fallen into second place in the minds of his companions. They were digging a grave for the body of Tim Mc-Grath. The young Irishman had been shot down just as the attack on the herd began. It was a reasonable guess to suppose that he had come face to face with the raiders, who had shot him on the theory that dead men tell no tales.

But the cowpuncher had lived till his friends reached him. He had told them with his dying breath that Mysterious Pete had shot him without a word of warning and that after he fell from his horse Peg-Leg Warren rode up and fired into his body.

Jim Clanton called his friend to one side. "I'm goin' to sneak out an' take a lick at them fellows, Billie. Want to go along?"

"What's yore notion? How're you goin' to manage it?"

"Me, I'm goin' to bushwhack Warren or some of his killers from the chaparral."

Prince had seen once before that cold glitter in the eyes of the hill man. It was the look that comes into the face of the gunman when he is intent on the kill.

"I wouldn't do that if I was you, Jim," Billie advised. "This ain't our personal fight. We're under orders. We'd better wait an' see what the old man wants us to do. An' I don't reckon I would shoot from ambush anyhow."

"Wouldn't you? I would." The jaw of the younger man snapped tight. "What chance did they give poor Tim, I'd like to know? He was one of the best-hearted pilgrims ever rode up the trail, an' they shot him down like a coyote. I'm goin' to even the score."

"Don't you, Jim; don't you." Billie laid a hand on the shoulder of his partner in adventure. "Because they don't fight in the open is no reason for us to bushwhack too. That's no way for a white man to attack his enemies."

But the inheritance from feudist ancestors was strong in young Clanton. He had seen a

185

comrade murdered in cold blood. All the training of his primitive and elemental nature called for vengeance.

"No use beefin', Billie. You don't have to go if you don't want to. But I'm goin'. I didn't christen myself Jimmie-Go-Get-'Em for nothin'."

"Put it up to Webb first. Let's hear what he has got to say about it," urged Prince. "We've all got to pull together. You can't play a lone hand in this."

"I'll put it up to Webb when I've done the job. He won't be responsible for it then. He can cut loose from me if he wants to. So long, Billie. I'll sleep on Peg-Leg Warren's trail till I git him."

"Give up that fool notion, Jim. I can't let you go. It wouldn't be fair to you or to Webb either. We're all in this together."

"What'll you do to prevent my goin'?"

"I'll tell the old man if I have to. Sho, kid! Let's not you an' me have trouble." Billie's gentle smile pleaded for their friendship. "We've been pals ever since we first met up. Don't go off on this crazy idea like a half-cocked hogleg."

"We're not goin' to quarrel, Billie. Nothin' to that. But I'm goin' through." The boy-ish jaw clamped tight again. The eyes that looked at his friend might have been of tempered steel for hardness.

"No."

"Yes."

Clanton was leaning against the rump of his horse. He turned, indolently, gathered his body suddenly, and vaulted to the saddle. Like a shot he was off into the night.

Billie, startled at the swiftness of his going, could only stare after him impotently. He knew that it would be impossible to find one lone rider in the darkness.

Slowly he walked back to the grave. The riders of the Flying V Y were gathered round in a quiet and silent group. They were burying the body of him who had been the gayest and lightest-hearted of their circle only a few hours before.

As soon as the last shovelful of earth had been pressed down upon the mound, Webb turned to business. The herd scattered over thirty miles of country must be gathered at once and he set about the round-up. He had had bad runs on the trail before and he knew the job before his men was no easy one.

They jogged out on a Spanish trot in the trail of the stampede. The chuck wagon was to meet them at Spring River next morning, where the first gather of beeves would be brought and held. All night they rode, tough as hickory, strong as whipcord. Into the desert sky sifted the gray light which preceded the coming of day. Banners of mauve and amethyst and topaz were flung across the horizon, to give place to glorious splashes of purple and pink and crimson. The sun, a flaming ball of fire, rose big as a washtub from the edge of the desert.

In that early morning light crept over the plain little bunches of cattle followed by brown, lithe riders. Like spokes of a wheel each group moved to a hub. Old Black Ned, the cook, was the focus of their travel. For at Spring River he had waiting for them hot coffee, flaky biscuits, steaks hot from the coals. Each rider seized a tin cup, a tin plate, a knife and fork, and was ready for the best Uncle Ned had to offer.

The remuda had been brought up by the wranglers. While the horses milled about in a cloud of dust, each puncher selected another mount. He moved forward, his loop trailing, eye fixed on the one pony, out of one hundred and fifty, that he wanted for the day's work. Suddenly a rope would snake forward past half a dozen broncos and drop about the neck of an animal near the heart of the herd. The twisting, dodging cowpony would surrender instantly and submit to being cut out from the band. Saddles were slapped on in a hurry and the riders were again on their way.

Through the mesquite they rode, slackening speed for neither gullies nor barrancas. Webb gave orders crisply, disposed of his men in such a way as to make of them a dragnet through which no cattle could escape, and began to tighten the loops for the drive back to camp.

By the middle of the afternoon the chuck wagon was in sight. The ponies were fagged, the men weary. For thirty-six hours these riders, whose muscles seemed tough as whalebone, had been almost steadily in the saddle. They slouched along now easily, always in a gray cloud of dust raised by the bellowing cattle.

The new gather of cattle was thrown in with those that had been rounded up during the night. The punchers unsaddled their worn mounts and drifted to the camp-fire one by one. Ravenously they ate, then rolled up in their blankets and fell asleep at once. To-night they had neither heart nor energy for the gay badinage that usually flew back and forth.

Night was still heavy over the land when Uncle Ned's gong wakened them. The moon was disappearing behind a scudding cloud, but stars could be seen by thousands. Across the open plain a chill wind blew.

All was bustle and confusion, but out of the

turmoil emerged order. The wranglers, already fed, moved into the darkness to bring up the remuda. Tin cups and plates rattled merrily. Tongues wagged. Bits of repartee, which are the salt of the cowpuncher's life, were flung across the fire from one to another. Already the death of Tim McGrath was falling into the background of their swift, turbulent lives. After all the cowboy dies young. Tim's soul had wandered out across the great divide only a few months before that of others among them.

Out of the mist emerged the desert, still gray and vague and without detail. The day's work was astir once more. With the nickering of horses, the bawling of cattle, and the shouts of men as an orchestral accompaniment, light filtered into the valley for the drama of the new sunrise. Once more the tireless riders swept into the mesquite through the clutching cholla to comb another segment of country in search of the beeves not yet reclaimed.

That day's drive brought practically the entire herd together again. A few had not been recovered, but Webb set these down to profit and loss. What he regretted most was that the cattle were not in as good condition as they had been before the stampede.

The drover spent the next day cutting out the animals that did not belong to him. Of these a good many had been collected in the round-up. It was close to evening before the job was finished and the outfit returned to camp.

Billie rode up to the wagon with the old man. Leaning against a saddle on the ground, a flank steak in one hand and a cup of coffee in the other, lounged Jim Clanton.

Webb, hard-eyed and stiff, looked at the young man. "Had a pleasant vacation, Clanton?"

"I don't know as I would call it a vacation, Mr. Webb. I been attending to some business," explained Jim.

"Yours or mine?"

"Yours an' mine."

"You've been gone forty-eight hours. The rest of us have worked our heads off gettin' together the herd. I reckon you can explain why you weren't with us."

Yellow with dust, unshaven, mud caked in his hair, hands torn by the cat-claw, Homer Webb was red-eyed from lack of sleep and from the irritation of the alkali powder. This young rider had broken the first law of the cowpuncher, to be on the job in time of trouble and to stay there as long as he could back a horse. The owner of the Flying V Y was angry clear through at his desertion and he intended to let the boy know it.

"I went out to look for Peg-Leg Warren," said Clanton apologetically.

Webb stopped in his stride. "You did? Who told you to do that?"

"I didn't need to be told. I've got horse sense myself." Jim spoke a little sulkily. He knew that he ought to have stayed with his employer.

"Well, what did you do when you found Peg-Leg — make him a visit for a couple of days?" demanded the drover with sarcasm.

"No, I don't know him well enough to visit — only well enough to shoot at."

"What's that?" asked Webb sharply.

"Think I was goin' to let 'em plug Tim McGrath an' get away with it?" snapped Jim.

"That's my business — not yours. What did you do? Come clean."

"Laid out in the chaparral till I got a chance to gun him," the young fellow answered sullenly.

"And then?"

"Plugged a hole through him an' made my get-away."

"You mean you've killed Peg-Leg Warren?"

"He'll never be any deader," said Clanton coolly.

The dark blood flushed into Webb's face. He wasted no pity on Warren. The man was a cold-hearted murderer and had reaped only what he had sowed. But this was no excuse for Clanton, who had deliberately dragged the Flying V Y into trouble without giving its owner a chance to determine what form retribution should take. The cowpuncher had gone back to primitive instincts and elected the blood feud as the necessary form of reprisal. He had plunged Webb and the other drovers into war without even a by-your-leave. His answer to murder had been murder. To encourage this sort of thing would be subversive of all authority and would lead to anarchy.

"Get yore time from Yankie, Clanton," said his employer harshly. "Sleep in camp to-night if you like, but hit the trail in the mornin'. I can't use men like you."

He turned away and left the two friends alone.

Prince was sick at heart. He had warned the young fellow and it had done no good. His regret was for Jim, not for Warren. He blamed himself for not having prevented the killing of Peg-Leg. Yet he knew he had done all that he could.

"I'm sorry, Jim," he said at last.

"Oh, well! What's done is done."

But Billie could not dismiss the matter casually. He saw clearly that Clanton had come to the parting of the ways and had unconsciously made his choice for life. From this time he would be known as a bad man. The brand of the killer would be on him and he would have to make good his reputation. He would have to live without friends, without love, in the dreadful isolation of one who is watched and feared by all. Prince felt a great wave of sympathy for him, of regret for so young a soul gone so totally astray. Surely the cards had been marked against Jim Clanton.

Chapter XIX

A Two-Gun Man

Webb delivered his beeves at the Fort and endured with what fortitude he could the heavy cut which the inspector chose to inflict on him. He paid off his men and let them shift for themselves. Billie secured a wood contract at the reservation, employed half a dozen men and teams, cleaned up a thousand dollars in a couple of months, and rode back to Los Portales in the late fall.

He had money in his pocket and youth in his heart. The day was waning as he rode up the street and in the sunlight the shadows of himself and his horse were attenuated to farcical lengths. Little dust whirls rose in the road, spun round in inverted cones like huge tops, and scurried out of sight across the prairie. Horses drowsed lazily in front of Tolleson's, anchored to the spot by the simple process of throwing the bridle to the ground. It all looked good to Billie. He had been hard at work for many months and he wanted to play.

A voice hailed him from across the street. "Hello, you Billie!"

Jim Clanton and Pauline Roubideau were coming out of a store. He descended from his horse and they fell upon him gayly.

" 'Jour, monsieur," the girl cried, and she gave him warmly both her hands.

The honest eyes of Billie devoured her. "Didn't know you were within a hundred miles of here. This is great."

"We've moved. We live about twenty miles from town now. But I'm in a good deal because Jean has bought the livery stable," she explained.

"I'm sure glad to hear that."

"You're to come and see us to-night. Supper will be ready in an hour. You bring him, Jim," ordered the girl. "I'll leave you boys alone now. You must have heaps to talk about."

The gaze of the cowpuncher followed her as

she went down the street light and graceful as a fawn. Not since spring had he seen her, though in the night watches he had often heard the sound of her gay voice, seen the flash of her bright eyes, and recalled the sweet and gallant buoyancy that was the dear note of her comradeship.

Billie looked after his horse and walked with Jim to the Proctor House. His mind was already busy appraising the changes in his friend. Clanton was now a "two-gun" man. From each hip hung a heavy revolver, the lower ends of the holsters tied down in order not to interfere with lightning rapidity of action. The young man showed no signs of nervousness, but his chill eyes watched without ceasing the street, doors and windows of buildings, the faces of passers-by and corner loafers. What Prince had foreseen was coming to pass. He was paying the penalty of his reputation as a bad man. Already incessant wariness was the price of life for him.

A second surprise awaited Billie at the Roubideau house. Polly was in the kitchen and looked out of the door only to wave a big spoon at them as they approached. Another young woman welcomed them. At sight of Billie a deep flush burned under her dark skin. It was, perhaps, because of this sign of emotion that her greeting was very cavalier.

196

"You're back, I see."

Prince ignored the hint of hostility in her manner. His big hand gripped her little one firmly.

"Yes, I'm back, Miss Lee, and right glad to see you lookin' so well. I'll never forget the last time we met."

Neither would she, but she did not care to tell him so. The memory of the adventure by the river-bank recurred persistently. This lean, sunbaked cowpuncher with the kind eyes and quiet efficiency of bearing had impressed himself upon her as no other man had. There was a touch of scorn in her feeling for herself, because she knew she wanted him for her mate more than anything else on earth. In the night, alone in the friendly darkness, her hot face pressed into the cool pillows, she confessed to herself that she loved him and longed for the sight of his strong, good-looking face with its smile of whimsical humor. But that was when she was safe from the eyes of the world. Now, to punish herself and to prevent him from suspecting the truth, she devoted her attention mainly to Clanton.

Jim was openly her admirer. He wanted Lee to know it and did not care who else observed his devotion. Pauline for one guessed the boy's state of mind and smiled at it, but Billie wondered whether the smile hid an aching heart. He knew that little Polly had a very tender feeling for the boy who had saved her life. More than once during supper it seemed to him that her soft eyes yearned for the reckless young fellow talking so gayly to Miss Snaith. The conviction grew in Prince — it found lodgment in his mind with a pang of despair — that the girl he cared for had given her love to his friend. He fought against the thought, tried resolutely to push it from him, but again and again it returned.

Not until supper was well under way did Jean Roubideau come in from the corral. He shook hands with Billie and at the same time explained to Polly his tardiness.

"Billie is not the only stranger in town to-night. Two or three blew in just before I left and kept me a few minutes. That Mysterious Pete Champa was one. You know him, don't you, Jim?"

The question was asked carelessly, casually, but Prince read in it a warning to his friend. It meant that he was to be ready for any emergency which might arise.

After they had eaten Billie went out to the porch to smoke with Jean.

"Is there goin' to be trouble between Mysterious Pete an' Jim?" he asked.

"Don't know. Wouldn't wonder if that was why Champa came to town. If I was Jim I'd keep an eye in the back of my head when I walked. It's a cinch Pete will try to get him — if he tries it at all — with all the breaks in his favor."

"Is it generally known that Jim was the man who killed Warren?"

"Yes." Jean stuffed and lit his pipe before he said anything more. "The kid can't get away from it now. Folks think of him as a killer. They watch him when he comes into a bar-room an' they're careful not to cross him. He's a bad man whether he wants to be or not."

Billie nodded. "I was afraid it would be that way, but I'm more afraid of somethin' else. The worst thing that can happen to any man, except to get killed himself, is to shoot another in cold blood. 'Most always it gives the fellow a cravin' to kill again. Haven't you noticed it? A kind of madness gets into the veins of a killer."

"Sure I've noticed it. He has to be watchin' — watchin' — watchin' all the time to make sure nobody gits him. His mind is on that one idea every minute. Consequence is, he's always ready to shoot. So as not to take any chances, he makes it a habit to be sudden death with a six-gun."

"That's it. Most of 'em are sure-thing killers. Jim's not like that. He's game as they

199

make 'em. But I'd give every cent I'm worth if he hadn't gone out an' got Peg-Leg."

"He never had any bringin' up, or at least he had the wrong kind." He listened a moment with a little smile. From the kitchen, where Jim was helping the young women wash the dishes, came a murmur of voices and occasionally a laugh. "Funny how all good women are mothers in their hearts. Polly's tryin' to save that boy from himself, an' I reckon maybe Miss Lee is too. In a way they got no business to have him here at all. I like him. That ain't the point. But he's got off wrong foot first. He's declared himself out of their class."

"And yore sister won't see it that way?"

"Not a bit of it. She's goin' to fight for his soul, as you might say, an' bring him back if she can do it. Polly's a mighty loyal little friend, if I am her brother that tells it."

"She's right," decided Prince. "It can't hurt her any. Nothin' that's wrong can do her any harm, because she's so fine she sees only the good. An' it's certainly goin' to do the kid good to know her."

"If he'd git out of here he might have a chance yet. But he won't. An' when he meets up with Champa or Dave Roush he's got to forget mighty prompt everything that Polly has told him."

"I heard Roush was on the mend. Is he up again?"

"Yes. He had a narrow squeak, but pulled through. Roush rode into town with Mysterious Pete to-night."

"Then they've probably come to gun Jim. I'll stay right with him for a day or two if I can."

"What for?" demanded Roubideau bluntly. "You're not in this thing. You've got no call to mix up in it. The boy saved Polly, an' I'll go this far. If I'm on the spot when he meets Champa or Roush — an' I'll try to be there — I won't let 'em both come at him without takin' a hand. But he has got to choose his own way in life. I can't stand between him an' the consequences of his acts. He's got to play his own hand."

"Did Dave Roush an' Mysterious Pete seem pretty friendly?"

"Thicker than three in a bed."

"Looks bad." Billie came to another phase of the situation. "How does it happen that Snaith's outfit have let Jim stay here without gettin' after him? Nothin' but a necktie party would suit 'em when we left in the spring."

"Times have changed," explained Roubideau. "This is quite a trail town now. The big outfits are bringin' in a good deal of money. Snaith can't run things with so high a

201

hand as he did. Besides, there are a good many of the trail punchers in town now. I reckon Wally Snaith has given orders not to start anything."

"Maybe Roush an' Champa have been given orders to take care of Jim."

Jean doubted this and said so. "Snaith doesn't play his hand under the table. But, of course, Sanders may have tipped 'em off to do it."

Clanton joined them presently and the three men walked downtown. The gay smile dropped from Jim's face the moment he stepped down from the porch. Already his eyes had narrowed and over them had come a kind of film. They searched every dark spot on the road.

"Let's go to Tolleson's," he proposed abruptly.

There was a moment of silence before Billie made a counter-proposition. "No, let's go back to the hotel."

"All right. You fellows go to the hotel. Meet you there later."

The eyes of Prince and Roubideau met. Not another word was spoken. Both of them knew that Clanton intended to show himself in public where any one that wanted him might find him. They turned toward Tolleson's, but took the precaution to enter

202

by the back door.

The sound of shuffling feet, of tinkling piano and whining fiddle, gave notice in advance that the dancers were on the floor. Clanton took the precaution to ease the guns in their holsters in order to make sure of a swift draw.

His forethought was unnecessary. Neither Roush nor Mysterious Pete was among the dancers, the gamblers, or at the bar. The three friends passed out of the front door and walked to the Proctor House. Clanton had done all that he felt was required of him and was willing to drop the matter for the night.

Chapter XX

Exit Mysterious Pete

In the cold, gray dawn of the morning after, Mysterious Pete straddled down the main street of Los Portales with a dark-brown taste in his mouth. He was feeling ugly. For he had imbibed a large quantity of liquor. He had gambled and lost. He had boasted of what he intended to do to one James Clanton, now generally known as "Go-Get-'Em Jim."

This last in particular was a mistake. More-over, it was quite out of accord with the usual custom of Mr. Champa. When he made up his mind to increase by one the number of permanent residents up on Boot Hill he bided his time, waited till the suspicions of his victim were lulled, and shot down his man without warning. The one fixed rule of his life was never to take an unnecessary chance. Now he was taking one.

Every chain has its weakest link. Mr. Champa drunk was a rock upon which Mr. Champa sober had more than once come to shipwreck. No doubt some busybody, seeking to curry favor with him, had run to this Clanton with the tale of how Mysterious Pete had sworn to kill him on sight.

The bad man was sour on the world this morning. He prided himself on being always a dead shot, but such a night as he had spent would not help his chances. There could be no doubt that his nerves were jumpy. What he needed was a few hours' sleep.

He would have taken a back street if he had dared, but to do so would have been a confession of doubt. The killer can afford to let nobody guess that he is afraid. When such a suspicion becomes current he might as well order his coffin. The men whom he holds in the subjection of fear will all be taking a chance with him.

So Mysterious Pete, bad man and murderer, coward at heart to the marrow, strutted toward his rooming-house with a heart full of hate to everybody. The pleasant morning sunshine was an offense to him. A care-free laugh on the breeze made him grit his teeth irritably. Particularly he hated Dave Roush. For Roush had led him into this cunningly by bribery and flattery. He had fed the jealousy of Pete, who could not brook the thought of a rival bad man in his own territory. He had hinted that perhaps Champa had better steer clear of this youth, whose reputation as a killer had grown so amazingly. Ever since Clanton had killed Warren the bad man had intended to "get him." But he had meant to do it without taking any risk. His idea was to pretend to be his friend, push a gun into his stomach, and down him before he could move. Now by his folly he had to take a fighting chance. Dave Roush, to save his own skin, had pushed him into danger. All this was quite clear to him now, and he raged at the knowledge.

Champa, too, was at another disadvantage. He was not sure that he would know Clanton when he saw him. He had set eyes on the young fellow once, on that occasion when he had gone with Warren to demand an inspection of the Flying V Y herd. But he had seen him only as one of a group of cowpunchers and not as an individual enemy, whereas it was quite certain that Go-Get-'Em Jim would recognize him.

From out of a doorway stepped a young fellow with his hand on his hip. Pete's six-gun flashed upward in a quarter curve even as the bullet crashed on its way. The youth staggered against the wall and sank together into a heap. Champa, every sense alert, fired again, then waited warily to make sure this was not a ruse of his victim.

Some one — a woman — darted from a building opposite, flew across the street, and dropped beside the crumpled figure. Her white skirt covered the body like a protecting flag.

The dark eyes in the white face lifted toward Champa were full of horror. "You murderer! You've killed little Bud Proctor!" cried the young woman.

He took an uncertain step or two toward her. Mysterious Pete knew that if this were true, his race was run.

"Goddlemighty, Miss Snaith! I swear I thought it was Clanton. He was drawing a gun on me."

Lee drew the boy to her bosom so that her body was between the killer and his victim. A swift, up-blazing, maternal fury seemed to leap from her face.

"Don't come any nearer! Don't you dare!" she cried.

The man's covert glance swept round. Already men were peering out of doors and windows to see what the shooting was about. Soon the street would be full of them, all full of deadly fury at him. He backed away, snarling, cut across a vacant lot, and ran to his room. The bolt in his door was no sooner closed than he knew it could not protect him. There comes a time in the career of a large percentage of bad men when some other hard citizen on behalf of the public puts a period to it. He is wiped out, not for what he has done only, but for fear also of what he may do. The only safety for him now was to get out of the country as fast as a horse could carry him. Instinctively Mysterious Pete recognized this now and cursed his folly for not going straight to a corral.

If he hurried he might still make his getaway. He reloaded his revolver, opened the door of his room, and listened. Cautiously he stole downstairs and out the back door of the building. A little girl was playing at keeping house in a corner of the yard. Scarcely more than a baby herself, she was vigorously spanking a doll.

"Be dood. You better had be dood," she admonished.

A crafty idea came into the cunning brain of the outlaw. She would serve as a protection against the bullets of his enemies. He caught her up and carried her, kicking and screaming, while he ran to the Elephant Corral.

"Saddle me a horse. Jump!" ordered the fugitive, his revolver out.

The trembling wrangler obeyed. He did not know the cause of Mysterious Pete's urgency. The fact was enough. He knew that this man with the bad record was flying in fear of his life. Tiny sweat beads stood out on his forehead. The fellow was in a blue funk and would shoot at the least pretext.

The saddle that the wrangler flung on the horse he had roped was a Texas one with double cinches. In desperate haste to be gone, Champa released the child a moment to tighten one of the bands.

A voice called to her. "Run, Kittie."

To the casual eye the child was all knobby legs and hair ribbons. She scudded for the stable, sobbing as she ran.

At sound of that voice Mysterious Pete leaped to the saddle and whirled his horse. He was too late. The man who had called to Kittie slammed shut the gate of the corral and laughed tauntingly.

"Better 'light, Mr. Champa. That caballo you're on happens to be mine."

Pete needed no introduction. This slight, devil-may-care young fellow at the gate was Clanton. He was here to fight. The only road of escape was over his body.

The gunman slid from the saddle. His instinct for safety still served him, for he came to the ground with the horse as a shield between him and his foe. The nine-inch barrel of his revolver rested on the back of the bronco as he blazed away. A chip flew from the cross-bar of the corral gate.

Clanton took no chances. The first shot from his forty-four dropped the cowpony. Pete backed away, firing as he moved. He flung bullet after bullet at the figure behind the gate. In his panic he began to think that his enemy bore a charmed life. Three times his lead struck the woodwork of the gate.

The retreating man whirled and dropped, his weapon falling to the dust. Clanton fired once more to make sure that his work was done, then moved slowly forward, his eyes focused on the body. A thin wisp of smoke rose from the revolver lying close to the still hand.

Mysterious Pete had died with his boots on after the manner of his kind.

Chapter XXI

Jim Receives and Declines an Offer

From the moment that Clanton walked out of the corral and left the dead gunman lying in the dust his reputation was established. Up till that time he had been on probation. Now he was a full-fledged killer. Nobody any longer spoke of him by his last name, except those friends who still hoped he might escape his destiny. "Go-Get-'Em Jim" was his title at large. Those on more familiar terms called him "Jimmie-Go-Get-'Em."

It was unfortunate for Clanton that the killing of Champa lifted him into instant popularity. Mysterious Pete had been too free with his gun. The community had been afraid of him. The irresponsible way in which he had wounded little Bud Proctor, whose life had been saved only by the courage of Lee Snaith, was the climax of a series of outrages committed by the man.

That Jim had incidentally saved Kittie McRobert from the outlaw was a piece of clean luck. Snaith came to him at once and buried the hatchet. In the war just starting, the cattleman needed men of nerve to lead his forces. He offered a place to Clanton, who jumped at the chance to get on the pay-roll of Lee's father.

"Bring yore friend Billie Prince to the store," suggested Snaith. "He's not workin' for Webb now. I can make a place for him, too."

Billie came, listened to the proposition of the grim old-timer, and declined quietly.

"Goin' to stick by Webb, are you?" demanded the chief of the opposite faction.

"Anything wrong with that? I've drawn a paycheck from him for three seasons."

"Oh, if it's a matter of sentiment."

As a matter of fact, Billie did not intend to go on the trail any more, though Webb had offered him a place as foreman of one of his herds. He had discovered in himself unsuspected business capacity and believed he could do better on his own. Moreover, he was resolved not to let himself become involved in the lawless warfare that was engulfing the territory.

It must be remembered that Washington County was at this time as large as the average Atlantic Coast State. It had become a sink for the riff-raff driven out of Texas by the Rangers, for all that wild and adventurous element which flocks to a new country before the law has established itself. The coming of the big cattle herds had brought money into the country, and in its wake followed the gambler and the outlaw. Gold and human life were the cheapest commodities at Los Portales. The man who wore a gun on his hip had to be one hundred per cent efficient to survive.

Lawlessness was emphasized by the peculiar conditions of the country. The intense rivalry to secure Government contracts for hay, wood, and especially cattle, stimulated unwholesome competition. The temptation to "rustle" stock, to hold up outfits carrying pay to the soldiers, to live well merely as a gunman for one of the big interests on the river, made the honest business of every-day life a humdrum affair.

None the less, the real heroes among the pioneers were the quiet citizens who went about their business and refused to embroil themselves in the feuds that ran rife. The men who made the West were the mule-skinners, the storekeepers, the farmers who came out in white-topped movers' wagons. For a time these were submerged by the more sensational gunman, but in the end they pushed to the top and wiped the "bad man" from the earth. It was this prosaic class that Billie Prince had resolved to join.

To that resolve he stuck through all the blood-stained years of the notorious Washington County War. He went about his private affairs with quiet energy that brought success. He took hay and grain contracts, bought a freighting outfit, acquired a small but steadily increasing bunch of cattle. Gradually he bulked larger in the public eye, became an anchor of safety to whom the people turned after the war had worn itself out and scattered bands of banditti infested the chaparral to prey upon the settlers.

This lean, brown-faced man walked the way of the strong. Men recognized the dynamic force of his close-gripped jaw, the power of his quick, steady eye, the patience of his courage. The eyes of women followed him down the street, for there was some arresting quality in the firm, crisp tread that carried the lithe, smooth-muscled body. With the passage of years he had grown to a full measure of mental manhood. It was inevitable that when Washington County set itself to the task of combing the outlaws from the mesquite it should delegate the job to Billie Prince.

The evening after his election as sheriff, Billie called at the home of Pauline Roubideau, who was keeping house for her brother. Jack Goodheart was leaving just as Prince stepped upon the porch. It had been two years now since Jack had ceased to gravitate in the direction of Lee Snaith. His eyes and his footsteps for many months had turned often toward Polly.

The gaze of the sheriff-elect followed the lank figure of the retreating man.

"I've a notion to ask that man to give up a good business to wear a deputy's star for me," he told Pauline.

"Oh, I wouldn't," she said quickly.

"Why not? He'd be a good man for the job. I want some one game — some one who will go through when he starts."

His questioning eyes rested on hers. She felt a difficulty in justifying her protest.

"I don't know — I just thought — "

"I'm waiting," said Prince with a smile.

"He wouldn't take it, would he?" she fenced.

"If it was put up to him right I think he would. Of course, it would be a sacrifice for him to make, but good citizens have to do that these days."

"He's had so much hard luck and been so long getting a start I don't think you ought to ask him." The color spilled over her cheeks like wine shaken from a glass upon a white cloth. Polly was always ardent on behalf of a friend.

"I can't help that. There's another man I

have in mind, but if I don't get him it will be up to Jack."

"Will it be dangerous?"

"No more than smoking a cigarette above an open keg of powder. But you don't suppose that would keep him from accepting the job, do you?"

"No," she admitted. "He would take it if he thought he ought. But I hope you get the other man."

"So do I."

Billie dismissed the subject and drew up a chair beside the hammock in which she was leaning back.

"This is my birthday, Polly," he told her. "I'm twenty-four years old."

"Good gracious! What a Methuselah!"

"I want a present, so I've come to ask for it."

With a sidelong tilt of her chin she flashed a look of quick eyes at him. Her voice did not betray the pulse of excitement that was beginning to beat in her blood.

"You've just been elected sheriff. Isn't that enough?" she evaded.

"That's a fine present to hand a man," he answered grimly. "An' I didn't notice you bubble with enthusiasm when I spoke of givin' half the glory to Goodheart."

"But I haven't a thing you'd care for. If I'd

215

only known in time I'd have sent to Vegas and got you something nice."

"You don't have to send to Vegas for it, Polly. The present I want is right here," he said simply.

She reached out a little hand impulsively. "Billie, I believe you're the best man I know — the very best."

"I hate to hear that. You're tryin' to let me down easy."

"I'm an ungrateful little idiot. Any other girl in town would jump at the chance to say, 'Thank you, kind sir.'"

"But you can't," he said gently.

"No, I can't."

He was not sure whether there was a flash of tears in her brown eyes, but he knew by that little trick of biting the lower lip that they were not far away. She was a tender-hearted little comrade, and it always hurt her to hurt others.

Billie drew a long breath. "That's settled, too, then. I asked you once before if there was some one else. I ask you again, but don't tell me if you'd rather not."

"Yes."

"You mean there is."

Again the scarlet splashed into her cheeks. She nodded her head three or four times quickly in assent.

"Not Jim Clanton?" he said, alarmed.

A faint, tender smile flashed on her lips. "I don't think I'll tell you who he is, Billie."

He hesitated. "That's all right, Polly. I don't want to pry into yore secret. But — don't do anything foolish. Don't marry a man with the notion of reformin' him or because he seems to you romantic. You have lots of sense. You'll use it, won't you?" he pleaded.

"I'll try to use it, Billie," she promised. Then, the soft eyes shining and the color still high in her cheeks, she added impulsively: "I don't know anybody that needs some one to love him more than that poor boy does."

"Mebbeso. But don't you be that some one, Polly." He hesitated, divided between loyalty to his friend and his desire for this girl's good. His brown, unscarred hand caught hers in a firm grip. "Don't you do it, little girl. Don't you. The woman that marries Jim Clanton is doomed to be miserable. There's no escape for her. She's got to live with her heart in her throat till the day they bring his dead body back to her."

She leaned toward him, and now there was no longer any doubt that her eyes were bright with unshed tears. "Perhaps a woman doesn't marry for happiness alone, Billie. That may come to her, or it may not. But she has to fulfill her destiny. I don't know how to say what

I mean, but she must go on and live her life and forget herself."

Prince rejected this creed flatly. "No! No! The best way to fulfill yore life is to be happy. That's what you've always done, an' that's why you've made other people happy. Because you go around singin' an' dancin', we all want to tune up with you. When I was out bossin' a freight outfit I used to think of you at night under the stars as a little Joybird. Now you've got it in that curly head of yours that you'd ought to be some kind of a missionary martyr for the sake of a man's soul. That's all wrong."

"Is it?" she asked him with a crooked, little, wistful smile. "How about you? Do you want to be sheriff? Is it going to make you so awfully happy to spend your time running down outlaws for the good of the country? Aren't you doing it because you've been called to it and not because you like it?"

"That's different," he protested. "When the community needs him a man's got to come through or be a yellow hound. But you've got no right to toss away yore life plumb foolishly just because you've got a tender heart." Billie stopped again, then threw away any scruples he might have on the score of friendship. "Jim is goin' to be what he is to the end of the chapter. You can't change him. Nobody can. In this Washington County War he's been a terror to the other side. You know that. For such a girl as you he's outside the pale."

"I heard Jean say once that Jim had never killed a man that didn't need killing," she protested.

"That may be true, too. But it wasn't up to him to do it. It isn't only killin' either. He's on the wrong track."

The young man could say no more. He could not tell her that Clanton was suspected of rustling and that his name had been mentioned in connection with robbery of the mail. These charges were not proved. Prince himself still loyally denied their truth, though evidence was beginning to pile up against the young gunman. He had warned Clanton, and Jim had clapped him on the shoulder, laughed, and invited him to take a drink with him. This was not quite the way in which Billie felt an innocent man would receive news that he was being furtively accused of crime.

"Yes, he's going wrong," agreed Pauline. "But we can't desert him, can we? You're his best friend. You know how brave he is, how generous, how at the bottom of his heart he loves people that are fine and true. If we stand by him we'll save him yet."

The young man's common sense told him that Clanton's future lay with himself and his attitude toward his environment, but he loved the spirit of this girl's gift of faith in her friends. It was so wholly like her to reject the external evidence and accept her own conviction of his innate goodness.

"I hope yore faith will work a miracle."

"I hate the things he does more than you do, Billie. It is horrible to me that he can take human life. I don't justify him at all, even though usually he is on the right side. But in spite of everything he has done Jim is only a wild boy. And he's so splendid some ways. Any day he would give his life for you or for me or for Lee Snaith. You feel that about him, don't you?"

"Yes."

He was not satisfied to let the subject drop, but for the present it had to be postponed. For a young man and a young woman were turning in at the gate. They were a handsome pair physically. Each of them moved with the lithe grace of a young puma. Pauline rose to meet them.

"I'm glad you came, Lee. Didn't know you were in town, Jim."

Clanton smiled. "I rode up from the Hondo to congratulate our new sheriff. Don't you let any of them outlaws escape, Billie."

Prince looked directly into his audacious eyes as he shook hands with him.

"Not if I can help it, Jim. I want you to be my chief deputy in cleanin' up the county. If you'll help me we'll make such a gather of bad men that it won't be safe for a crook to show his head here."

Pauline clapped her hands. "What a splendiferous idea! It's a great chance for you, Jim. You and Billie can do it too. I know you can."

The other young woman had recognized Prince only by a casual nod. It was her custom to ignore him as much as possible. Now her dark, velvety eyes jumped to meet his, then passed to Clanton. She recognized the significance of the moment. It was Jim's last opportunity to line up on the side of law and order. Lee, with Billie and Pauline, had stood his loyal friend against a growing public opinion. Would he justify their faith in him?

After a long silence Jim spoke. "No, I reckon not, Billie. I've got interests that will take all my time. Much obliged, old scout. I'd like to ride in couples with you like we used to do. I sure would, but I can't."

"That's all nonsense. It's no excuse at all," broke out Lee in her direct fashion. "Mr. Prince has more important affairs than you a good deal. He is dropping his to serve the people. You'll have to have a better reason than that to convince me."

Billie knew and Lee suspected what lay

back of the spoken word. The duty of the sheriff would be to hunt down the men with whom Clanton had lately been consorting. He felt that he could not desert his friends to line up against them. Some of these were a bad lot, the riff-raff of a wild country, but this would not justify him in his own mind for using his knowledge of their habits to run them to earth.

"No, I can't talk business with you, Billie," the young fellow said decisively.

"Why can't you?" demanded Lee.

Jim Clanton smiled. "You're certainly a right persistent young lady, but by advice of counsel I decline to answer."

Chapter XXII

The Rustlers' Camp

From Live-Oaks a breakneck trail runs up the side of the mountain, drops down into the valley beyond, and twists among the hills and through cañons to the Ruidosa. In the darkness a man followed this precarious path. His horse climbed it like a cat, without the least uncertainty or doubt. Both mount and rider had covered this ground often during the Washington County War. Joe Yankie expected to continue to use it as long as he found a profit in other men's cattle.

When he had reached the summit he swung to the right, dipped abruptly into a narrow gulch, skirted a clump of junipers, and looked down upon a little basin hidden snugly in the gorge. A wisp of pungent smoke rose to his nostrils. The pony began cautiously the sharp descent. The escarpment was of disintegrated granite which rang beneath the hoofs of the animal. A pebble rolled to the edge of the bluff and dropped into the black pit below.

From the gulf a challenging voice rose. "Hello, up there!"

"It's me — Joe," answered the rider.

"Time you were gettin' here," growled the other, as yet only a voice in the darkness.

Slowly the horse slid forward to a ribbon of trail that led less precipitously to the camp.

" 'Lo, Joe. Fall off an' rest," a one-armed man invited. By the light of the camp-fire he was a hard-faced, wall-eyed citizen with a jaw like a steel trap.

Yankie dismounted and straddled to the fire. "How-how; I'm heap hungry, boys. Haven't et since mornin'."

"We're 'most out of grub. Got nothin' but jerked beef an' hard-tack. How are things a-stackin', Joe?" asked a heavy-set, bow-legged man with a cold, fishy eye.

"Looks good, Dave. I'll lead the cattle to you. It'll be up to you an' Albeen an' Dumont to make a get-away with 'em."

"Don't you worry none about that. Onct I get these beeves on the trail there can't no shorthorn cattleman take 'em away from me."

"Oh, you're doin' this thing, are you?" drawled Albeen offensively. "There's been a heap of big I talk around here lately. First off, I want to tell you that when you call Homer Webb a shorthorn cattleman you've got another guess comin'. He's a sure enough old-timer. Webb knocked the bark off'n this country when it was green, an' you got to rise up early an' travel fast if you want to slip over anything on him."

"That's whatever," agreed Yankie. "I don't love the old man a whole lot. I've stood about all from him I'm intendin' to. One of these days it's goin' to be him or me. But the old man's there every jump of the road. He knew New Mexico when Los Portales was a whistlin' post in the desert. He's fought through this war an' come through richer than when he started. If I was lookin' for an easy mark I'd sure pass up Webb."

"He's got you lads buffaloed," jeered Roush. "Webb looks like anybody else to me.

I don't care if he's worth a million. If he fools with me he'll find I fog him quick."

"I've known fellows before that got all filled up with talk an' had to steam off about every so often," commented Albeen to the world at large.

"Meanin' me?"

Albeen carefully raked a live coal from the fire and pressed it down into the bowl of his pipe. The eyes in his leathery, brown face had grown hard as jade. For some time he and Dave Roush had been ready for an explosion. It could not come any too soon to suit the one-armed man.

"Meanin' you if you want to take it that way." Albeen looked straight at him with an unwinking gaze. "You're not the only man on the reservation that wears his gun low, Roush. Maybe you're a wolf for fair. I've sure heard you claim it right often. You're a two-gun man. I pack only one, seein' as I'm shy a wing. But don't git the notion you can ride me. I won't stand for it a minute."

"Sho! Dave didn't mean anything like that. Did you, Dave?" interposed Dumont hastily. "You was just kind o' jokin', wasn't you?"

"Well, I'm servin' notice right now that when any one drops around any jokes about me bein' buffaloed, he's foolin' with dynamite. No man alive can run a sandy on me an' git away with it."

The chill eyes of Albeen, narrowed to shining slits, focused on Roush menacingly. All present understood that he was offering Devil Dave a choice. He could draw steel, or he could side-step the issue.

The campers had been playing poker with white navy beans for chips. Roush, undecided, gathered up in his fingers the little pile of them in front of him and let them sift down again to the blanket on the edge of which he sat. Some day he and Albeen would have to settle this quarrel once for all. But not to-night. Dave wanted the breaks with him when that hour came. He intended to make a sure thing of it. Albeen was one of those fire-eaters who would play into his hand by his reckless courage. Better have patience and watch for his chance against the one-armed gunman.

"I ain't aimin' to ride you any, Albeen," he said sulkily.

"Lay off'n me, then," advised the other curtly.

Roush grumbled something inaudible. It might have been a promise. It might have been a protest. Yankie jumped into the breach and began to talk.

"I couldn't git away from the old man yesterday. I think he's suspicious about me. Anyhow, he acts like he is. I came in to Live-Oaks to-night without notifyin' him an' I got to be back in camp before mornin'. Here's my plan. I've got a new rider out from Kansas for his health. He's gun-shy. I'll leave him in charge of this bunch of stock overnight on the berrendo. He'll run like a scared deer at the first shot. Hustle the beeves over the pass an' keep 'em movin' till you come to Lost Cache."

Crouched over the blanket, they discussed details and settled them. Yankie rose to leave and Roush followed him to his horse.

"Don't git a notion I'm scared of Al-been, Joe," he explained. "No one-armed, hammered-down little runt can bluff me for a second. When I'm good an' ready I'll settle with him, but I'm not goin' to wreck this business we're on by any personal difficulty."

"That's right, Dave," agreed the foreman of the Flying V Y. "We all understand how you feel."

Yankie, busy fastening a cinch, had his forehead pressed against the saddle and could afford a grin. He knew that the courage of a killer is largely dependent on his physical well-being. If he is cold or hungry or exhausted, his nerve is at low ebb; if life is running strong in his arteries his grit is above par. For years Roush had been drinking to excess.

He had reached the point where he dared not face in the open a man like Albeen with nerves of unflawed steel. The declension of a gunman, if once it begins, is rapid and sure. One of those days, unless Roush were killed first, some mild-looking citizen would take his gun from him and kick him out of a bar-room.

The foreman traveled fast, but the first streaks of morning were already lighting the sky when he reached Rabbit Ear Creek, upon which was the Flying V Y Ranch No. 3 of which he was major-domo. He unsaddled, threw the bronco into the corral, and walked to the foreman's bunkhouse. Without undressing, he flung himself upon the bed and fell asleep at once. He awoke to see a long slant of sunshine across the bare planks of the floor.

Some one was hammerimg on the door. Webb opened it and put in his head just as the segundo jumped to his feet.

"Makin' up some lost sleep, Joe?" inquired the owner of the ranch amiably.

"I been out nights a good deal tryin' to check the rustlers," answered Yankie sullenly. He had been caught asleep in his clothes and it annoyed him. Would the old man guess that he had been in the saddle all night?

"Glad to hear you're gettin' busy on that job. They've got to be stopped. If you can't do it I'll have to try to find a man that can, Joe."

"Mebbe you think it's an easy job, Webb," retorted the other, a chip on his shoulder. "If you do it costs nothin' Mex to fire me an' try some other guy."

"I don't say you're to blame, Joe. Perhaps you're just unlucky. But the fact stands that I'm losin' more cattle on this range than at any one of my other three ranches or all of 'em put together."

"We're nearer the hills than they are," the foreman replied sulkily.

"I don't want excuses, but results, Joe. However, I came to talk about that gather of beeves for Major Strong."

Webb talked business in his direct fashion for a few minutes, then strolled away. The major-domo watched him walk down to the corral. He could not swear to it, but he was none the less sure that the Missourian's keen eye was fixed upon a sweat-stained horse that had been traveling the hills all night.

Chapter XXIII

Murder from the Chaparral

Webb was just leaving for one of his ranches lower down the river when a horseman galloped up. The alkali dust was caked on his unshaven face and the weary bronco was dripping with sweat.

The owner of the Flying V Y, giving some last instructions to the foreman, turned to listen to the sputtering rider.

"They — they done run off that bunch of beeves on the berrendo," he explained, trembling with excitement.

"Who?"

"I don't know. A bunch of rustlers. About a dozen of 'em. They tried to kill me."

Webb turned to Yankie. "You didn't leave this man alone overnight with that bunch of beeves for Major Strong?"

"Sure I did. Why not?" demanded the foreman boldly.

"We'll not argue that," said the boss curtly. "Go hunt you another job. You'll draw yore last pay-check from the Flying V Y to-day."

"If you're loaded up with a notion that some one else could do better — "

"It's not yore ability I object to, Yankie," cut in the ranchman.

"Say, what are you insinuatin'?" snarled the segundo.

"Not a thing, Yankie. I'm tellin' you to yore face that I think you're a crook. One of these days I'm goin' to land you behind bars at Santa Fe. No, don't make another pass like that, Joe. I'll sure beat you to it."

Wrayburn had ridden up and now asked the foreman a question about some calves.

"Don't ask me. Ask yore boss," growled Yankie, his face dark with fury.

"Don't ask me either," said Webb. "You're foreman of this ranch, Dad."

"Since when?" asked the old Confederate.

"Since right this minute. I've fired Yankie."

Dad chewed his cud of tobacco without comment. He knew that Webb would tell him all he needed to know.

"Says I'm a waddy! Says I'm a crook!" burst out the deposed foreman. "Wish you joy of yore job, Wrayburn. You'll have one heluva time."

"You will if Yankie can bring it about," amended the cattleman. He spoke coldly and contemptuously just as if the man were not present. "I've made up my mind, Dad, that he's in cahoots with the rustlers."

"Prove it! Prove it!" demanded the accused man, furious with anger at Webb's manner.

The ranch-owner went on talking to Wrayburn in an even voice. "I've suspected it for some time. Now I'm convinced. Yesterday mornin' I found him asleep in bed with his clothes on. His horse looked like it had been travelin' all night. I made inquiries. He went to Live-Oaks an' was seen to take the trail to the Ruidosa. Why?"

"You've been spyin' on me," charged Yankie. He was under a savage desire to draw his gun but he could not shake off in a moment the habit of subordination bred by years of service with this man.

"To let his fellow thieves know that he meant to leave a bunch of beef steers on the berrendo practically unguarded. That's why. I'd bet a stack of blues on it. You'll have to watch this fellow, Dad."

The new foreman took his cue from the boss. None the less, he meant just what he said. "You better believe I'll watch him. I've had misgivin's about him for a right smart time."

"He'll probably ride straight to his gang of rustlers. Well, he can't do us half as much harm there as here."

"I'll git you both. Watch my smoke. Watch

it." With a curse the rustler swung his horse round and gave it the spur. Poison hate churned in his heart. At the bend of the road he turned and shook a fist at them both.

"There goes one good horse an' saddle belongin' to me," said Webb, smiling ruefully. "But if I never get them back it's cheap at the price. I'm rid of one scoundrel."

"I wonder if you are, Homer," mused his friend. "Maybe you'd better have let him down easy. Joe Yankie is as revengeful as an Injun."

"Let him down easy!" exploded the cattleman. "When he's just pulled off a raw deal by which I lose a bunch of forty fat three-year-olds. I ought to have gunned him in his tracks."

"If you had proof, but you haven't. It's a right doubtful policy for a man to stir up a rattler till it's crazy, then to turn it loose in his bedroom."

The Missourian turned to the business of the hour. "We'll get a posse out after the rustlers right away, Dad. I'll see the boys an' you hustle up some rifles and ammunition."

Half an hour later they saw the dust of the cowpunchers taking the trail for the berrendo.

"I'll ride down an' get Billie Prince started after 'em. I can go with his posse as a deputy," suggested the ranchman.

To save Webb's time, Dad rode a few miles with him while the cattleman outlined to him the policy he wanted pursued.

The sun was high in the heavens when they met, not far from Ten Sleep, a rider. The cattleman looked at him grimly. In the Washington County War just ended, this young fellow had been the leading gunman of the Snaith-McRobert faction. If the current rumors were true he was now making an easy living in the chaparral.

The rider drew up, nodded a greeting to Wrayburn, and grinned with cool nonchalance at Webb. He knew from report in what esteem he was held by the owner of the Flying V Y brand.

"Yankie up at the ranch?" he asked.

"What do you want with him?" demanded Webb brusquely.

"I got a message for him."

"Who from?"

Clanton was conscious of some irritation against this sharp catechism. In point of fact Billie Prince had asked him to notify Yankie that he had heard of the rustling on the berrendo and was taking the trail at once. But Go-Get-'Em Jim was the last man in the world to be driven by compulsion. He had been ready to tell Webb the message Billie had given him for Yankie, but he was not ready to tell it until the Missourian moderated his tone.

"Mebbe that's my business — an' his, Mr. Webb," he said.

"An' mine too — if you've come to tell him how slick you pulled that trick on the berrendo."

Jim stiffened at once. "To Halifax with you an' yore cattle, Webb. Do you claim I rustled that bunch of beeves last night?"

"I see you know all about it?" retorted Webb with heavy sarcasm.

"Mebbeso. I'm not askin' yore permission to live — not just yet."

Webb flushed dark with anger. "You've got a nerve, young fellow, to go up to my ranch after last night's business. Unless you want to have yore pelt hung up to dry, keep away from any of the Flying V Y ranges. As for Yankie, if you go back to yore hole you'll likely find him. I kicked the hound out two hours ago."

"Like you did me three years ago," suggested Clanton, looking straight at the grizzled cowman. "Webb, you're the high mogul here since you fixed it up with the Government to send its cavalry to back yore play against our faction. You act like we've got to knock our heads in the dust three times when

235

we meet up with you. Don't you think it. Don't you think it for a minute. If I've rustled yore cattle, prove it. Until then padlock yore tongue, or you an' me'll mix it."

"You're threatenin' me, eh?"

"If that's what you want to call it."

"You're a killer, I'm told," flashed back Webb hotly. "Now listen to me. You an' yore kind belong in the penitentiary, an' that's where the honest folks of Washington County are goin' to send you soon. Give me half a chance an' I'll offer a reward of ten thousand dollars for you alive or dead. That's the way to get rid of gunmen."

"Is it?" Clanton laughed mockingly. "You advise the fellow that tries to collect that reward to get his life insured heavy for his widow."

If this was a boast, it was also a warning. Jimmie-Go-Get-'Em may not have been the best target shot on the border, but give him a man behind a spitting revolver as his mark and he could throw bullets with swifter, deadlier accuracy than any old-timer of them all. He did not take the time to aim; it was enough for him to look at his opponent as he fired.

The young fellow swung his horse expertly and cantered into the mesquite.

"I'll give you two months before you're

wiped off the map," the cattleman called after him angrily.

At the edge of a heavy growth of brush Clanton pulled up, flashed a six-shooter, and dropped two bullets in the dust at the feet of the horses in the road. Then, with a wave of his hand, he laughed derisively and plunged into the chaparral.

Webb, stung to irritable action, fired into the cholla and the arrowweed thickets. Shot after shot he sent at the man who had disappeared in the maze.

"Let him go, Homer. You're well quit of him," urged Wrayburn.

The words were still on his lips when out of the dense tangle of vegetation rang a shot. The owner of the Flying V Y clutched at his saddle-horn. A spasmodic shudder shook the heavy body and it began to sink.

Wrayburn ran to help. He was in time to catch his friend as he fell, but before he could lower the inert weight to the ground the life of Homer Webb had flickered out.

Chapter XXIV

Jimmie-Go-Get-'Em Leaves a Note

Prince and his posse were camped in a little park near the headquarters of Saco de Oro Creek when a trapper brought word to Billie of the death of Webb. The heart of the young sheriff sank at the news. It was not only that he had always liked and admired the bluff cattleman. What shocked him more was that Jim Clanton had killed him. Webb was one of the most popular ranchmen on the river. There would be an instant, widespread demand for the arrest and conviction of his slayer. Billie had taken an oath to uphold the law. His clear duty was to go out and capture Jim alive or dead.

Not for a moment did Billie doubt what he would do. He had pledged himself to blot out the "bad man," and he would go through no matter what the cost to his personal feelings.

A slow anger at Clanton burned in him. Why had he done this wanton and lawless thing? The boy he had known three years ago would never have shot down from cover a man like Webb. That he could have done it now marked the progress of the deterioration of his moral fiber. What right had he to ask those who remained loyal to him to sacrifice so often their sense of right in his favor?

The old intimacy between Billie and Jim had long since waned. They were traveling different roads these days. But though they were no longer chums their friendship endured. When they met, a warm affection lit the eyes of both. It had survived the tug of diverse interests, the intervention of long separations, the conflict born of the love of women. Would it stand without breaking this new test of its strength?

With a little nod to Goodheart the sheriff retired from the camp-fire. His deputy joined him presently on a hillside overlooking the creek.

"I'm goin' back to Live-Oaks to-night, Jack," announced Prince. "You'd better stay here a few days an' hunt through these gulches. Since that rain yesterday there's not one chance in fifty of runnin' down the rustlers, but you might happen to stumble on the place where they've got the cattle cached."

"You're goin' down about this Webb murder?"

"Yes. I'm goin' to work out some plans. It will take some strategy to land Clanton. He's

239

lived out in the hills for years an' he knows every foot of cover in the country."

Goodheart assented. To go blindly out into the mesquite after the young outlaw would have been as futile as to reach a hand toward the stars with the hope of plucking a gold-piece from the air.

"Watch the men he trains with. Keep an eye on the Elephant Corral an' check up on him when he rides in to Los Portales. Spot the tendejon at Point o' Rocks where he has a hang-out. Unless he has left the country he'll show up one of these days."

"That's what I think, Jack, an' I'm confident he hasn't gone. He has a reason for stayin' here."

Goodheart could have put a name to the reason. It was a fair enough reason to have held either him or the sheriff under the same circumstances.

"How about a reward? He trains with a crowd I'd hate to trust farther than I could throw a bull by the tail. Some of 'em would sell their own mothers for gold."

"I'll get in touch with Webb's family an' see if they won't offer a big reward for information leading to the arrest of the murderer."

Within the week every crossroads store in the county had tacked to it a placard offering a reward of five thousand dollars for the man who had killed Homer Webb.

No applications for it came in at first.

"Wait," said Goodheart, smiling. "More than one yellow dog has licked its jaws hungrily before that poster. Some dark night the yellowest one will sneak in here to see you."

On the main street of Los Portales one evening Billie met Pauline Roubideau. She came at him with a direct frontal attack.

"I've had a letter from Jim Clanton."

The sheriff did not ask her where it was postmarked. He did not want any information from Polly as to the whereabouts of her friend.

"You're one ahead of me then. I haven't," answered Prince.

"He says he didn't do it."

"Do what?"

"Shoot Mr. Webb. And I know he didn't if he says he didn't."

The grave eyes of the young man met hers. "But Dad Wrayburn was there. He saw the whole affair."

Pauline brushed this aside with superb faith. "I don't care. Jim never lied to me in his life. I know he didn't do it — and it makes me so glad."

The young man envied her the faith that could reject evidence as though it did not exist. The Jim Clanton she had once known would not have lied to her. Therefore the Jim

241

Clanton she knew now was worthy of perfect trust. If there was any flaw in that logic the sweet and gallant heart of the girl did not find it.

But Billie had talked with Dad Wrayburn. He had ridden out and gone over the ground with a fine-tooth comb. Webb had been killed by a bullet from a forty-four. Of his own knowledge Prince knew that Clanton was carrying a weapon of this caliber only three hours before the killing. There was no escape from the conviction of the guilt of his friend.

The sheriff walked back to the hotel where he was staying. On the way his mind was full of the young woman he had just left. He had never liked her better, never admired her more. But, somehow — and for the first time he realized it — there was no longer any sting in the thought of her. He did not have to fight against any unworthy jealousy because of her interest in Clanton. Of late he had been very busy. It struck him now that his mind had been much less preoccupied with the thought of her than it used to be. He supposed there was such a thing as falling out of love. Perhaps he was in process of doing that now.

Bud Proctor, a tall young stripling, met Prince on the porch of the hotel.

"Buck Sanders was here to see you, sheriff," the boy said.

Since the days when he had been segundo of the Snaith-McRobert outfit Sanders had declined in the world. Like many of his kind he had taken to drink, become bitten with the desire to get rich without working, and operated inconspicuously in the chaparral with a branding iron. Much water had poured down the bed of the Pecos in the past three years. The disagreement between him and Clanton had long since been patched up and they had lately been together a great deal.

Prince went up to his room, threw off his coat, and began to prepare some papers he had to send to the Governor. He was interrupted by a knock at the door.

Sanders opened at the sheriff's invitation, shoved in his head, looked around the room wanly, and sidled in furtively. He closed the door.

"Mind if I lock it?" he asked.

The sheriff nodded. His eyes fixed themselves intently on the man. "Go as far as you like."

The visitor hung his hat over the keyhole and moved forward to the table. His close-set eyes gripped those of the sheriff.

"What about this reward stuff?" he asked harshly.

An instant resentment surged up in Billie's heart. He knew now why this fellow had come

243

to see him secretly. It was his duty to get all the information he could about Clanton. He had to deal with this man who wanted to sell his comrade, but he did not relish the business.

"You can read, can't you, Sanders?" he asked ungraciously.

"Where's the money?" snarled his guest.

"It's in the bank."

"Sure?"

From his pocket-book Billie took a bank-deposit slip. He put it on the table where the other man could look it over.

"Would a man have to wait for the reward until Clanton was convicted?" the traitor asked roughly.

"A thousand would be paid as soon as the arrest was made, the rest when he was convicted," said Prince coldly.

"Will you put that in writin', Mr. Sheriff?"

The chill eyes of the officer drilled into those of the rustler. He drew a pad toward him and wrote a few lines, then shoved the tablet of paper toward Sanders. The latter tore off the sheet and put it in his pocket.

Sanders spoke again, abruptly. "Understand one thing, Prince. I don't have to take part in the arrest. I only tell you where to find him."

"And take me to the spot," added the sheriff. "I'll do the arrestin'."

"Whyfor must I take you there if I tell you where to go?"

"You want a good deal for your white alley, Sanders," returned the other contemptuously. "I'm to take all the chances an' you are to drag down the reward. That listens good. Nothin' to it. You'll ride right beside me; then if anything goes wrong, you'll be where I can ask you questions."

"Do you think I'm double-crossin' you? Is that it?" flushed the ex-foreman of the Lazy S M.

"I don't know. It might be Clanton you're double-crossin', or it might be me," said the sheriff with cynical insolence. "But if I'm the bird you've made a poor choice. In case we're ambushed, you'll be in nice, easy reach of my gun."

"Do I look like a fool?" snapped Sanders. "I'm out for the dough. I'm takin' you to Clanton because I need the money."

"Mebbeso. You won't need it long if you throw me down." Then abruptly, the sheriff dropped into the manner of dry business. "Get down to tacks, man. Where is Clanton's hang-out?"

Buck sat down and drew a sketch roughly on the tablet. "Cross the river at Blazer's Ford, cut over the hills to Ojo Caliente, an' swing to the east. He's about four miles from Round Top in an old dugout. Maybe you've heard of Saguaro Cañon. Well, he's holed up in a little gulch runnin' into it."

By daybreak next morning the sheriff's posse was in the saddle. In addition to Sanders, who rode beside Billie unarmed, Goodheart and two special deputies made up the party.

The sun was riding high when they reached Ojo Caliente. The party bore eastward, following a maze of washes, arroyos, and gorges. It was well into the afternoon when the informer ventured a suggestion.

"We're close enough. Better light here an' sneak forward on foot," the man said gruffly.

As he swung from the horse Billie smiled grimly. He had a plan of his own which he meant to try. Buck Sanders might not like it, but he was not in a position to make any serious objection.

They crept forward to a rim rock above a heavily wooded slope. A tongue-shaped grove ran down close to the edge of a narrow gulch.

Prince explained what he meant to do. "We'll all snake down closer. When I give the word you'll go forward alone, Sanders, an' call Jim out. Ask him to come forward an' look at yore bronco's hoof. That's all you'll have to do."

Sanders voiced a profane and vigorous

protest. "Have you forgot who this guy is you're arrestin'? Go-Get-'Em Jim is no tenderfoot kid. He's chain lightnin' on the shoot. If he suspects me one steenth part of a second, that will be long enough for him to gun me good."

"He'll not have a chance. We'll have him covered all the time."

"Say, we agreed you was goin' to make this arrest not me."

"I'll make it. All you've got to do is to call him out."

"All!" shrieked Sanders. "You know damned well I'm takin' the big risk."

"That's the way I intended it to be," the sheriff assured him coolly. "You're to get the reward, aren't you?"

The rustler balked. He polluted the air with low, vicious curses, but in the end he had to come to time.

They slipped through the grove till they could see on the edge of the ravine a dug-out. Prince flashed a handkerchief as a signal and Sanders rode down in the open skirting the timber. He swung from the saddle and shouted a "Hello, in the house!"

No answer came. Buck called a second and a third time. He waited, irresolute. He could not consult with Prince. At last he moved toward the house and entered. Presently he returned to the door and waved to the sheriff to come forward.

Very cautiously the posse accepted the invitation, but every foot of the way Billie kept the man covered.

Sanders ripped out a furious oath. "He's done made his get-away. Some one must 'a' warned him."

He held out to Prince a note scrawled on a piece of wrapping-paper. It was in Clanton's pell-mell, huddled chirography: —

Sorry I can't stay to entertain you, Billie. Make yourself at home. Bacon and other grub in a lard can by the creek. Help yourself.

Crack Sanders one on the bean with your six-gun on account for me.

JIMMIE-GO-GET-'EM.

Chapter XXV

The Mal-Pais

Billie Prince laughed. The joke was on him, but he was glad of it. As sheriff of Washington County it had been his duty to accept any aid that might come from the treachery of Sanders; but as a friend of Jim Clanton he did not want to win over him by using such weapons.

"Tickled to death, ain't you?" snapped the ex-foreman sourly. "Looks to me like you didn't want to make this arrest, Mr. Sheriff. Looks to me like some one else has been doin' some double-crossin' besides me."

"Naturally *you'd* think that," cut in Goodheart dryly. "The facts probably are that Go-Get-'Em Jim, knowin' his friends pretty well, had you watched, found out you called on the sheriff, an' guessed the rest. He's not a fool, you know."

"That's right. Git ready an alibi," Sanders snarled.

Casually Goodheart picked up the piece of wrapping-paper upon which the note had been written. He read aloud the last sentence.

" 'Crack Sanders one on the bean with your six-gun on account for me.' Seems to me if I was you, Buck, I'd alibi myself down the river into Texas as quick as I could jog a bronco along. But, of course, I don't know yore friend Go-Get-'Em as well as you do. Mebbe you'll be able to explain it to him. Tell him you were hard up an' needed the money."

The eyes of the rustler flashed from Goodheart to the sheriff. They were full of sinister suspicion. Had these men arranged to deliver him into the hands of Clanton? Was he himself going to fall into the pit he had dug?

"Gimme back my gun an' I'm not afraid of him or any of you," he bluffed.

"You'll get yore gun when we reach Los Portales," Prince told him. "I left it in my office."

"I ain't goin' to Los Portales."

"All right. Leave yore address and I'll send the gun by the buckboard driver."

All the baffled hate and cupidity of Sanders glared out of his wolfish face. "I'll let you know later where I'm at."

He straddled out of the house, pulled himself astride the waiting horse, and rode up the hill. Presently he disappeared over the crest."

"Much obliged, Jack," said Prince, smiling. "Exit Mr. Buck Sanders from New Mex-

250

ico. Our loss is Texas's gain. Chalk up one bad man emigrated from Washington County."

"He's sure goin' to take my advice," agreed the lank deputy. A little chuckle of amusement escaped from his throat. "To the day of his death he'll think we sent word to Go-Get-'Em Jim. I'll bet my next pay-check against a dollar Mex that he forgets to send you that address."

Billie availed himself of the invitation of Clanton to make himself at home. He and his posse spent the night in the dug-out and returned to Los Portales next day. For the better part of a week he was detained there on business, after which he took the stage to Live-Oaks.

News was waiting for Prince at the county seat that led him for a time to forget the existence of Clanton. The buckboard driver from El Paso reported the worst sandstorm he had ever encountered. It had struck him a mile or two this side of the Mal-Pais, as the great lava beds in the Tularosa Basin are commonly called. He had unhitched the horses, overturned the buckboard, and huddled in the shelter of the bed. There he had lain crouched for ten hours while the drifting sand, fine as powder, blotted out the world and buried him in drifts. He was an old plainsman, tough as leather, and he had weathered the storm

251

safely. A full day late he staggered into Live-Oaks a sorry sight.

The news that shook Live-Oaks into swift activity had to do with Lee Snaith. Just before the storm hit him the buckboard driver had met her riding toward the Mal-Pais.

Prince arrived to find the town upside down with the confusion of preparation. Swiftly he brought order out of the turmoil. He organized the rescue party, assigned leaders to the divisions, saw that each man was properly outfitted, and mapped off the territory to be covered by each posse. Outwardly he was cool, efficient, full of hopeful energy. But at his heart Billie felt an icy clutch of despair. What chance was there for Lee, caught unsheltered in the open, when the wiry, old Indian fighter, protected by his wagon, had barely won through alive?

Every horse in Live-Oaks that could be ridden was in the group that melted into the night to find Lee Snaith. Every living soul left in the little town was on the street to cheer the rescuers.

The sheriff divided his men. Most of them were to spend the night, and if necessary the next day and night, in combing the sand desert east of the Mal-Pais. Here Lee had last been seen, and here probably she had wandered round and round until the storm had beaten her down. It took little imagination to vision the girl, flailed by the sweeping sand, bewildered by it, choked at every gasping breath, hopelessly lost in the tempest.

Yet some bell of hope rang in Billie's breast. She might have reached the lava. If so, there was a chance that she might be alive. For though the wind had sweep enough here, the fine dust-sand of the alluvial plain could not be carried so densely into this rock-sea. Perhaps she had slipped into a fissure and found safety.

For fifty miles this great igneous bed stretches, a rough and broken sea of stone, across the thirsty desert. Its texture is like that of slag from a furnace. Once, in the morning of the world, it flowed from the crater along the line of least resistance, a vitreous river of fire. In a great molten mass it swept into the valleys, crawling like a great snake here and there, pushing fiery tongues into every crevice of the hills.

The margin of its flow is a cliff or steep slope varying in height from a few feet to that of a good-sized tree. Between the silt plain and the general level of its bed rises a terrace. In front of it Prince stopped and distributed the men he had reserved to search the lava bed. He gave definite, peremptory orders.

"We'll keep about two hundred yards

apart. Every twenty minutes each of you will fire his revolver. If any of you find Miss Snaith or any evidence of her, shoot three times in rapid succession. Each of you pass the signal down the line by firing four shots. Those who hear the three shots go in as fast as you can to the rescue. The others — those farther away, who hear the four shots only — will turn an' work back to the plain, continuing to fire once every twenty minutes. Do exactly as I tell you, boys. If you don't, some one will be lost an' may never get out alive. If any one of you gets out of touch with the rest of us, stay right where you are till mornin', then come out by the sun."

The horses were left in charge of a Mexican boy. The surface of the deposit is so broken that even a man on foot has difficulty in traversing it. Prince crawled forward from the terrace up the rough slope of the cliff which at this point bounded it. At the top of the rim he rose and came face to face with another man.

"A good deal like frozen hell, Billie," the other said casually.

"Where did you come from?" demanded the sheriff, amazed.

Jim Clanton laughed grimly. "I've been with yore party half an hour. Why shouldn't I be here when Lee Snaith is lost?"

"You were hiding in Live-Oaks?"

"Mebbeso. Anyway, I'm here. I'll take the right flank, Billie."

"Do you think there's a chance, Jim?" The voice of Prince shook with emotion. It was the first sign of distress he had given.

Clanton reflected just a moment before he answered. "I think there's just a chance. She saved our lives onct, Billie. If she's alive we'll find her, you an' me."

"By God, yes." Prince turned away. He could not talk about it without breaking down.

In the stress of a great shock Billie had made a vital discovery. The most important thing that would ever come to him in life was to find Lee Snaith alive. How blind he had been! He could see her now in imagination, as in reality he had seen her a hundred times, moving in the sun-pour with elastic tread, full-throated and deep-chested, athrob with life in every generous vein. How passionately she had loved things brave and true! How anger had flamed up in her like fire among tow at meanness and hypocrisy. Surely all the beauty of her person, the fineness of her character, could not be blotted out so wantonly. If there was any economy in his world God would never permit waste like that.

He wanted her. His soul cried out for her. Blindly and stormily he prayed that he might

255

find her alive and well, that the chance might still be given him to tell her how much he loved her.

Sometimes he covered small distances where the flow structure was comparatively smooth, broken only by minor irregularities. Again he came to abrupt pits, deep caverns, tumbled heaps of broken slabs, or jagged chunks of lava twisted into strange shapes. No doubt the volcanic flow had hardened to a crust on top, cracked, and sunk into the furnace below. This process must have gone on indefinitely.

He crept from slab to slab, pulled himself across chasms, worked slowly forward in the darkness. At intervals he fired and listened for an answer. Occasionally there drifted to him the sound of a shot from one of the other searchers. As the hours passed and brought to him no signal that the girl had been found, his hopes ebbed. It was very unlikely that she could have wandered so far into the bad lands as this.

He shuddered to think of her alone in this vast tomb of death. Suppose she were here and they never found her. Suppose she were asleep when he passed, worn out by terror and exhaustion. His voice grew hoarse from shouting. Sometimes, when the thought of her fate would become an agony to him, he could hardly keep his shout from rising to a scream.

Billie struck a match and looked at his watch. It was five minutes past three. A faint gray was beginning to sift into the sky. He had been nearly seven hours in the Mal-Pais. Out in God's country the world would soon be shaking sleep from its eyes. In this death zone there was neither waking nor sleeping. "Frozen hell," Clanton had called it. Prince shuddered.

The flare of the match had showed him that he was standing close to the edge of a fissure. In the darkness he could not see to the bottom of it.

A faint breath of a whimper floated to him. He grew rigid, every nerve taut. He dared not let himself believe it could be real. Of course he was imagining sounds. Presenly, no doubt, he would hear voices. In this devil's caldron a man could not stay quite sane.

Again, as if from below his feet, was lifted a strangled little sob.

"Lee!" he called huskily with what was left of his voice.

Something in the cavern moved. By means of outcropping spars of rock he lowered himself swiftly.

The darkness was Stygian. He struck another match.

257

From the gloom beyond the space lit by the small flame came the rustle of something stirring. The match burned out. He lit another and groped forward. His foot struck an impediment.

He looked down into the startled eyes and white face of Lee Snaith.

Chapter XXVI

A Dust-Storm

It had been a beautiful day of sunshine when Lee left Live-Oaks to ride to the Ninety-Four Ranch. Not a breath of wind stirred. The desert slept in a warm, golden bath. It was peaceful as old age.

But as the sun slipped past the meridian, gusts swept across the sands and whipped into the air inverted cones that whirled like vast tops in a wild race to nowhere. The air waves became more frequent and more furious. When Lee passed the buckboard driver, the whole desert seemed alive with stinging sand.

He called something to her that was lost in the wind. The girl waved at him a gauntleted hand. She had been out in dust-storms before and was not in the least alarmed. Across the lower part of her face she had tied a silk handkerchief to protect her mouth and nostrils from the sand.

The mail carrier had scarcely disappeared before the fury of the wind increased. It lashed the ground with heavy whips, raging and screaming in shrill, whistling frenzy, until the desert rose in terror and began to shift.

Lee bent her head to escape the sand that filled her eyes and nostrils and beat upon her cheeks so unmercifully. She thought perhaps the tempest would abate soon and she slipped from the saddle to crouch close to the body of the horse for protection. Instead of decreasing, the gale rose to a hurricane. It was as if the whole sand plain was in continuous, whirling motion.

The horse grew frightened and restless. It was a young three-year-old Jim Clanton had broken for her. Somehow — Lee did not know quite the way it happened — the bridle rein slipped from her fingers and the colt was gone.

She ran after the pony — called to it frantically — fought in pursuit against the shrieking blasts. The animal disappeared, swallowed in the whirlwind that encompassed her and it. Lee sank down, sheltering her face with her arms against the pelting sand sleet.

But years in the outdoor West had given Lee the primal virtue, courage. She scorned a quitter, one who lay down or cried out under punishment. Now she got to her feet and faced the storm. The closeness of her horizon — her outstretched arms could almost touch the limt of it — confused the mind of the girl. She no longer knew east from west, north from south. With a sudden sinking of the heart she realized that she was lost in this gray desert blizzard.

Blindly she chose a direction and plunged forward. At times the wind hit her like a moving wall and flung her to the ground. She would lie there panting for a few moments, struggle to her knees, and creep on till in a lull she could again find her feet.

How much of this buffeting, she wondered, could one endure and live? The air was so filled with dust that it was almost impossible to get a breath. Her muscles ached with the flogging they were receiving. She was so exhausted, her forces so spent, that the hinges of her knees buckled under her.

One of her feet struck against a rise in the ground and she stumbled. She lay there motionless for what seemed a long time before it penetrated her consciousness that one of her palms pained from a jagged cut the fall had caused. Her body lay on sharp-pointed rocks.

As far as they could reach, the groping fingers of the girl found nothing but hard, rough stone. Then, in a flash, the truth came to her. She had reached the Mal-Pais.

She crept across the lava in an effort to escape the strangling wind. Its rage followed her, drove the girl deeper into the bad lands. A renewal of hope urged her on. In its rough terrain she might find shelter from the tornado. In short stages, with rests between, she pushed into the vitreous lake, dragged herself up from the terrace, fought forward doggedly for what seemed to her an age.

A crevice barred the way. The fissure was too wide to step across and was perhaps ten feet deep. Lee slid into it, slipped, and fell the last step or two of the descent. She lay where she had fallen, too worn out to move.

It must have been almost at once that she fell asleep.

The stars were out when she awakened, her muscles stiff and aching from the pressure of her weight upon the rock. The girl lay for a minute wondering where she was. Above was a narrow bar of starlit sky. The walls of her pit of refuge were within touch of her finger tips. Then memory of the storm and her escape from it flashed back to her.

She climbed easily the rough side of the cavern and looked around. The wind had died

261

so that not even a murmur of it remained. As far as the eye could see the lava flow extended without a break. But she knew the cavern in which she had slept lay at a right angle to the line of her advance. All she had to do was to face forward and keep going till she reached the plain. The reasoning was sound, but it was based on a wrong premise. Lee had clambered out of the fissure on the opposite side from that by which she had entered. Every step she took now carried her farther into the bad lands.

Morning broke to find her completely at sea. Even the boasted weather of the Southwest played false. A drizzle of rain was in the air. Not until late in the afternoon did the sun show at all and by that time the wanderer was so deep in the Mal-Pais that when night closed down again she was still its prisoner.

She was hungry and fagged. The soles of her boots were worn out and her feet were badly blistered. Again she took refuge in a deep crevice for the night.

The loneliness appalled her. No living creature was to be seen. In all this awful desolation she was alone. Her friends at Live-Oaks would think she was at the Ninety-Four Ranch. Even if they searched for her she would never be found. After horrible suffering she would die of hunger and thirst. She broke down at last and wept herself to sleep.

Chapter XXVII

"A Lucky Guy"

Lee had the affrighted look of one roused suddenly from troubled dreams. The whimper that had drawn the attention of Prince must have come from her restless, tortured sleep. Not till his second match flared had she been really awake.

"Thank God!" he cried brokenly, all the pent emotion of the long night vibrant in his tremulous voice.

She began to sob, softly, pitifully.

The match went out, but even in the blackness of the pit he could not escape the look of suffering he had seen on her face. Her habit was to do all things with high spirit. He could guess how much she had endured to bring those hollow shadows under her dusky eyes. The woe of the girl touched his heart sharply, as if with the point of a rapier.

He stooped, liked her gently, and gathered her like a hurt child into his arms. "You poor lost lamb," he murmured. And again he cried, "Thank God, I came in time."

Her arms crept round his neck. She clung to him for safety, fearfully, lest even now he might vanish from her sight. Long, ragged sobs shook the body resting in his arms. He whispered words of comfort, stroked gently the dark head of blue-black hair, held her firmly so that she might know she had found a sure refuge from the fate that had so nearly devoured her.

The spasmodic quivering of the body died away. She dabbed at her eyes with a rag of a handkerchief and withdrew herself from his arms.

"I'm a nice baby," she explained with a touch of self-contempt. "But it's been rather awful, Billie. I . . . didn't know whether . . . "

"It's been the worst night of my life," he agreed. "I've been in hell for hours, dear. If — if anything had happened to you — "

The heart of the girl beat fast. She told herself he did not mean — could not mean what, with a sudden warmth of joy, her soul hunger had read into his words.

Prince uncorked his canteen and she drank. He gave her sandwiches and she devoured them. After he had helped her from the fissure he fired three shots. Faintly from the left came the answering bark of a revolver. What might almost have been an echo of it drifted from the right.

Lee Snaith was the most competent young woman the sheriff had ever met. He knew her self-reliance and had always guessed her sufficient to herself. Toward him especially he had sensed a suggestion of cool hostility. They had been friends, but with a distinct note of reservation on her part.

To-night the mask was off. She had come too close to raw reality to think of her pride. The morning light was sifting into the sky now. Billie could see the girl more clearly as she sat on a slab of rock waiting for the other searchers to join them. Was it his imagination that found in her an unwonted shyness of the dark eyes, a gentle timidity of manner when she looked at him?

His emotion still raced at high tide. What an incomparable mate she would be for any man! The rich contralto of her voice, the slow, graceful turn of the exquisite head, the vividness she brought to all her activities! How easy it was to light in her fine eyes laughter, indignation, the rare smile of understanding! Life with her would be an adventure into the hill-tops. With all his heart he yearned to take it beside her.

There were strange flashes in his eyes to-night that signaled to her a message she had despaired of ever receiving. The long lashes of the girl fell to the hot cheeks. A pulse of excitement beat in her blood. A few minutes before she had clung to him despairingly. Now she wanted to run away and hide.

He stepped close to her and let his hand fall lightly on her arm.

"I've been blind all these years, Lee," he told her. "It's you I love."

She stole a little look at him with shy, incredulous eyes. "Have you forgotten — Polly?"

"I haven't been in love with her for years, but I didn't know it till about the Christmas holidays. She was a habit with me. There never was a sweeter girl than Polly Roubideau. I'll always think a heap of her. But — well, she had more sense than I had — knew all the time we weren't cut out for each other." He laughed a little, flushing with embarrassment. It is not the easiest thing in the world to explain to a girl why you have neglected her in favor of another.

Lee trembled. The desire was strong in her to seize her happiness while she could. Surely she had waited long enough for it. But some impulse of fair play to him or of justice to herself held back the tide of love she longed to release.

"I think . . . you are impulsive," she said at last. "If you have anything you want to tell me, better wait until . . ."

"Not another moment!" he cried. "I've been in torment all night. I . . . I thought I'd lost you forever. You don't care for me, of course. You never have liked me very well, but — "

"Haven't I?" she breathed softly, not looking at him.

Love irradiated and warmed her. She forgot all she had suffered during the years she had waited for him to know his mind. She forgot the privations of the past two days. Her eyes were tender with the mist of unshed tears.

"It's going to be the biggest thing in my life. If there's any chance at all I'll wait as long as you like. Of course, the idea's new to you because you haven't ever thought of me that way — "

"You know so much about it," she replied, a faint smile in her dark eyes that had in it something of wistfulness, something of self-mockery. She looked directly at him and let him have it full in the face. "I ought to be ashamed of it, I suppose, but I'm not. I've thought of you — that way — lots of times. All girls do, when they meet a man they like."

"You like me?"

She might have told him that her heart had been his ever since that first week when she had met him and Clanton on the river. She might have added that all he had needed to do was to whisper "Come" and she would have galloped across New Mexico to meet him. But she made no such confession.

"Yes, I . . . like you," she said, a little tremor in her voice.

He noticed that she did not look at him. Her eyes had fallen to the fingers laced together on her lap. Under compulsion of his steady gaze she lifted her lashes at last. What he read there was beyond belief. The wonder of it lifted his feet from the earth.

"Lee!" he cried, joy and fear in the balance.

She answered his unspoken question with a little nod.

His hand shook. "I've been a blind idiot, dear. I never guessed such a thing."

"You were thinking about Polly all the time. I don't blame you. She's the sweetest thing I ever knew."

Billie sat down on the spar of rock beside her. His hand slipped down her arm till it covered hers. With the contact there came to him a flood of courage. He took her in his arms and kissed her with infinite tenderness.

Still unstrung from her adventures, she wept a little into his shoulder out of a full heart.

"D — don't mind me," she urged. "It's just because I'm so happy."

If Clanton, when he found them together a few minutes afterward, guessed what had happened, he gave no evidence of it but a grin, unless his later comment had a cryptic meaning. "I'll bet Billie is the glad lad at findin' you. He always was a lucky guy."

"I think I'm a little lucky too," Lee said with a grave smile.

Before starting, Prince examined the soles of the girl's boots. Out of his hat he fashioned a pair of overshoes and fastened them with strings to her feet.

"They'll help some," he promised. "I reckon you're not goin' to do much walkin' anyhow with three husky men along."

By this time the searcher on the other flank had joined them. The return trip was a long, hard one, but with Billie on one side of her and Jim on the other, Lee found it easy traveling. They aided her over the sharp rocks and lifted her across the rougher stretches of lava.

At the edge of the lava bed a buggy was waiting to take Lee to Live-Oaks in case she should be found. Prince helped Lee in and took the place of the boy who had driven it out.

Clanton put his foot on the hub of the wheel. "Just a minute, Billie. I'm wanted for the killin' of Homer Webb. I didn't shoot him an' I don't know who did. Somebody must have been lyin' there in the chaparral waitin' for him. I'll give myself up an' stand trial if you'll guarantee me fair play. No lynchin' bee. No packed jury. All the cards dealt fair an' honest above the table."

The sheriff had smiled at Pauline Roubideau's implicit faith in Jim Clanton's word. But now, face to face with his friend, he too believed and felt a load lift from his heart.

"That's a deal, Jim. You won't have to reckon with any mob or any hand-picked jury. I'll tell you the truth. I thought you did it. But if you say you didn't, that goes with me. I'll see you through."

"Good enough. I'll drop in to-morrow an' we can fix things up. I'd like to be tried outside of Washington County. There's too much prejudice here one way an' another. Well, take this little lady home an' scold her good for the way she's been actin'. She'd ought to get married to a man that will look after her an' not let her go buckin' into cyclones."

Billie smiled. "I'll talk to her about that, old scout."

Miss Snaith blushed furiously, but the best she could do was a bit of weak repartee. "I used to have hopes that you would ask me, Jim."

Jimmie-Go-Get-'Em laughed with friendly

malice. "I used to have hopes, too, in that direction, Lee, but I haven't any more. You be good to her or we also-rans will boil you in oil, Billie."

Chapter XXVIII

Sheriff Prince Functions

"Yippy yip yip yip!"

Old Reb, Quantrell's ex-guerrilla, now boss of mule-skinners for Prince, galloped down the street waving an old dusty white hat. Women and children and old men dribbled out from the houses, all eager for the news.

"Billie he found Miss Lee in the Mal-Pais. That boy sure had his lucky pants on to-day. She's all right too. I done seen her myself — just a mite tuckered out, as you might say," explained the former cowpuncher.

Live-Oaks shook hands with itself in exuberant joy. For an hour the school bell pealed out the good news. A big bonfire blazed in the court-house square. Wise dames busied themselves baking bread and frying doughnuts and roasting beef for the rescue party now homeward bound. It was a certainty that their men-folks would all be hungry and ready for a big feed.

By noon most of the searchers were back in town and the saloons were doing big business. When Prince drove down the main street of Live-Oaks an hour later, the road was jammed as for a Fourth-of-July celebration. Tired though she was, Lee had not the heart to disappoint these good friends. She went to the picnic ground at Frémont's Grove and was hugged and kissed by all the women at the dinner. She wept and was wept over till her lover decided she had had all the emotion that was good for her, whereupon he took her back to the home of her aunt and with all the newborn authority of his position ordered her to bed.

"But it's only three o'clock in the afternoon," Lee protested.

"Good-night" answered Billie inexorably.

She surrendered meekly. "If you say I must, my lord. I *am* awf'lly tired." Little globes of gladness welled up in her eyes. "Everybody's so good to me, Billie. I didn't know folks were so kind. I can't think what I can ever do to pay them back."

"I'll tell you how. You be good to yourself, honey," he told her with a sudden wave of emotion as he caught and held her tight in his arms. "You quit takin' chances with blizzards an' crazy gunmen an' — "

"— And horsethieves hidden in the chaparral?" she asked with a flash of demure eyes.

"You're goin' to take an awful big chance with one ex-horsethief. Lee, I'm the luckiest fellow on earth."

She nestled closer to him. Her lips trembled to his kiss.

"Billie, you're sure, aren't you?" she whispered. "It wasn't just pity for me."

He chose to reassure her after the fashion of a lover, in that wordless language which is as old as Eden.

His heart was full of her as he swung down the street buoyantly. He had known her saucy, scornful, and imperious. He had known her gay and gallant, had been the victim of her temper. Occasionally he had seen glimpses of tenderness toward Pauline and of motherliness toward Jim Clanton. But never until last night had he found her dependent and clinging. Her defense against him had been a manner of cool self-reliance. In the stress of her need that had been swept aside to show her flamy and yet shy, quick with innocent passion. She wanted him for a mate, just as he wanted her, and she made no concealment of it. In the candor of her love he exulted.

Lee slept round the clock almost twice and

appeared for a late breakfast. Her aunt told her some news with which Live-Oaks was buzzing.

Go-Get-'Em Jim had ridden into town, stopped at the sheriff's office and demanded cynically the thousand dollars offered by the Webb estate for his arrest.

"He'll come to no good end," prophesied Miss Snaith, senior.

"You don't quite understand him, aunt," protested Lee. "That's just his way. He likes to grand-stand, and he does it rather well. But he isn't half so bad as he makes out. He says he did not shoot Mr. Webb, and we feel sure he didn't."

"Of course he says so," replied the older women indignantly. "Why wouldn't he say so? But Dad Wrayburn was there and saw it all. There has been a lot too much promiscuous killing and he's one of the worst of the lot, your Jim Clanton is. Jimmie-Go-Get-'Em, indeed! I hope the law goes and gets him now it has a chance."

The opinion of Lee's aunt was in accord with the general sentiment. Washington County had within the past year suffered a change of heart. It had put behind its back the wild and reckless days of its youth when every man was a law to himself. Bar-room orators talked virtuously of law and order. They said it behooved the county to live down its evil reputation as the worst in the United States. Times had changed. The watchword now should be progress. It ought no longer to be a recommendation to a man that he could bend a six-gun surer and quicker than other folks. "Movers" in white-topped wagons were settling up the country. A railroad had pushed in to Live-Oaks. There was a lot of talk about Eastern capital becoming interested in irrigation and mining. It was high time to remember that Live-Oaks and Los Portales were not now frontier camps, but young cities.

Since Live-Oaks had been good for so short a time it wanted to prove by a shining example how it abhorred the lawlessness of its youth. At this inopportune moment Clanton gave himself up to be tried for the murder of Homer Webb.

When the news spread that Clanton had been given a change of venue and was to be tried at Santa Fé, the citizens of Live-Oaks were distinctly annoyed. It was known that the sheriff had always been a good friend of the accused man. The whisper passed that if he ever took Go-Get-'Em Jim out of the county the killer would be given a chance to escape.

Into town from the chaparral drifted the enemies Clanton had made during his career as a gunman. Yankie and Albeen and Dumont and Bancock moved to and fro in the crowds at the different gambling places and saloons. Even Roush, who in the past three years had never given young Clanton an opportunity to meet him face to face, stole furtively into the tendejons of the Mexcian quarter and spent money freely in treating. Among the natives Go-Get-'Em Jim was in ill-repute for shooting a bad man named Juan Ortez who had attempted to terrorize the town while on a spree.

"We're spendin' a lot of good money on this job. We'd ought it pull it off," Dumont whispered to Albeen.

"Whose money?" asked the one-armed man cynically.

It struck him as an ironic jest that the money they had got from the sale of Homer Webb's cattle should be spent to bring about the lynching of the man who had killed him.

Both the sheriff and his deputy were out of town rounding up a half-breed Mexican who had stabbed another at a dance. They reached Live-Oaks with their prisoner about the middle of the afternoon. Lee was waiting for them impatiently at the court-house.

"They're planning to lynch Jim," she told Prince abruptly.

"Who's goin' to do all that?" he asked.

"The riff-raff of the county are back of it, but the worst of it is that they've got a lot of good people in with them. Some of the Flying V Y riders are in town too. I never saw so much drinking before."

"When is it to be?"

"I don't know."

"Who told you?"

"Bud Proctor. He says Yankie and Albeen and that crowd are spending hundreds of dollars at the bars."

"I knew there was somethin' on foot soon as we hit town — felt it in the air." The sheriff looked at his watch. "We can just catch the afternoon train, Jack. Take this bird downstairs an' lock him up. I'll join you in a minute."

"What are you going to do?" asked Lee as soon as they were alone.

"Goin' to slip Jim aboard the train an' take him to Santa Fé."

"Can you do it without being seen?"

"I'll tell you that later," he answered with a grim smile. "Much obliged, honey. I'm goin' to be right busy now, but I'll tell you soon as I get back to town."

Lee nodded good-bye and went out. She liked it in him that just now he had no time even for her. From the door she glanced back. Already he was busy getting his guns ready.

Prince got his keys and unlocked the room where Clanton was. Jim was on the bed reading an old newspaper.

"Hello, Billie," he grinned.

"We're leaving on the afternoon train, Jim. Get a move on you an' hustle yore things together."

"Thought you weren't goin' till next week."

"Changed my mind. Jim, there's trouble afoot. Yore enemies are all in town. I want to get you away."

Clanton did not bat an eye. "Plannin' a necktie party, are they?"

"They've got notions. Mine are different."

"Do I get a gun if it comes to a showdown, Billie?"

"You do. I'll appoint you a deputy."

Jim laughed. "That sounds reasonable."

Goodheart joined them. The three men left the back door of the court-house and cut across the square. The station was three blocks distant. Before they had covered a hundred yards a boy on the other side of the street stopped, stared at them, and disappeared into the nearest saloon.

The prisoner looked at his friend and grinned gayly. "Somethin' stirrin' soon. We're liable to have a breeze in this neighborhood, looks like."

They reached the station without being mo-

278

lested, but down the street could be seen much bustle of men running to and fro. Prince looked at them anxiously.

"The clans are gathering," murmured Clanton nonchalantly, his hands in his pockets. "Don't you reckon maybe you'll have to feed me to the wolves after all, Billie?"

A saddled horse blinked in the sun beside the depot, the bridle rein trailing on the ground. Its owner sat on a dry-goods box and whittled. Jim glanced at the bronco casually. Jack Goodheart also observed the cowpony. He whispered to the sheriff.

Prince turned to his prisoner. "Jim, you can take that horse an' hit the dust, if you like."

"Meanin' that you can't protect me?"

The salient jaw of the sheriff tightened. He looked what he was, a man among ten thousand, quiet and forceful, strong as tested steel.

"You'll have exactly the same chance to weather this that we will."

A mob of men was moving down the street in loose formation. There was still time for a man to fling himself into the saddle and gallop away.

"You'd rather I'd stay, Billie."

"Yes. I'm sheriff. I'd like to show this drunken outfit they can't take a prisoner from me."

Clanton gave a little whoop of delight. "Go to it, son. You're law west of the Pecos. Let's see you make it stick."

Live-Oaks was as yet the terminus of the railroad. The train backed into the station just as the first of the mob arrived.

"Nothin' doin', Prince," announced Yankie, swaggering forward. "You're not goin' to take this fellow Clanton away. We've come to get him."

"That's right," agreed Albeen.

Jimmie-Go-Get-'Em grinned. "Makes twice now you've come to get me."

"We didn't make it go last time. Different now," said Bancock, moving forward.

"That's near enough," ordered Prince. "You've made a mistake, boys. I'm sheriff of Washington County, and this man's my prisoner."

"He's yore old side kick too, ain't he?" jeered Yankie.

Goodheart, following the orders he had received, moved forward to the engine and climbed into the cab beside the engineer and fireman. The sheriff and his prisoner backed to the seps of the smoking-car. Billie had had a word with the brakeman, his young friend Bud Proctor, who had at once locked the door at the other end of the smoker.

"Now," said Prince in a low voice.

280

Jim ran up lightly to the platform of the coach and passed inside. A howl of anger rose from the mob. There was a rush forward. Billie was on the lower step. His long leg lifted, the toe caught Yankie on the point of the chin, and the rustler went back head first into the crowd as though he had been shot from a catapult.

Instantly Prince leaped for the platform and whirled on the mob. He held now a gun in each hand. His eyes glittered dangerously as they swept the upturned faces. They carried to every man in the crowd the message that his prisoner could not be taken as long as the sheriff was alive.

Clanton threw open a window of the coach, rested his arms on the sill, and looked out. Again there was a roar of rage and a forward surge of the dense pack on the station platform.

"He ain't even got irons on the man's hands!" a voice shouted. "It's a frame-up to git him away from us!"

"Don't hide back there in the rear, Roush. Come right up to the front an' tell me that," called back Prince. "You're right about one thing. I don't need to handcuff Clanton. He has surrendered for trial, an' I'm here to see he gets a fair one. I'll do it if I have to put irons *in* his hands — shootin' irons."

Jim Clanton, his head framed in the window, laughed insolently. He was a picture of raffish, devil-may-care ease.

"Don't let Billie bluff you, boys. We can't bump off more 'n a dozen or so of you. Hop to it."

"You won't laugh so loud when the rope's round yore gullet," retorted Albeen.

"That rope ain't woven, yet," flung back the young fellow coolly.

Even as he spoke a lariat whistled through the air. Jim threw up a hand and the loop slid harmlessly down the side of the car. One of the riders of the Flying V Y had tried to drag the prisoner out with a reata.

"You mean well, but you'll never win a roping contest, Syd," jeered Clanton. "Good of you an' all my old friends to gather here to see me off. I see you back there, Roush. It's been some years since we met, an' me always lookin' for you to say to you a few well-chosen words. I'll shoot straighter next time."

The vigilantes raised a howl of fury. They were like a wolf pack eager for the kill. Between them and their prey stood one man, cool, indomitable, steady as a rock. He held death in each hand, and every man present knew it. They could get Clanton if they were willing to pay the price, but though there were game men in the mob, not one of them wanted to be the first to put his foot on the lower step of the coach.

From the other end of the car came the sudden noise of hammering. Some one had found a sledge in the baggage-room and with a dozen armed men back of him was trying to break down the door.

Prince called to his prisoner. "You've got to get in this, Jim. I appoint you deputy sheriff. Unstrap this belt from my waist. Take the other end of the car an' hold it. No shootin' unless it comes to a showdown. Understand?"

Clanton nodded. His eyes gleamed. "I'll behave proper, Billie."

Five seconds later the beating on the door stopped. The eyes of the big blacksmith with the hammer popped out with a ludicrous terror. Go-Get-'Em Jim was standing in the aisle grinning at him with a six-gun in each hand. With a wild whoop the horseshoer dropped the sledge and turned. He flung himself down the steps carrying with him half a dozen others. Not till he was safe in his own shop two blocks away did he stop running.

A shrill whistle rang out from the side of the train farthest from the station. The wheels began to move slowly. There was a rush for the engine. Jack Goodheart stood in the door of the cab ready for business.

"No passengers allowed here, boys," he announced calmly. "Take the coaches in the rear."

A dozen revolvers cracked. There was a rattle of breaking windows. The engine, baggage-car, and smoker moved forward, leaving the rest of the train on the track.

Men, swarming like ants, had climbed to the top of the cars, evidently with some idea of getting at their victim from above. Some of these were on the forward coaches. They began to drop off hurriedly as the station fell to the rear.

The wheels turned faster. Bud Proctor swung aboard and joined the sheriff.

"I cut off the other cars and gave the signal to start," he explained triumphantly.

"Good boy, Bud. Knew I could tie to you," Prince answered with the warm smile that always won him friends.

They passed into the car together. Clanton was leaning far out of the window waving a mocking hand of farewell to the crowd on the platform. He drew his head in and handed the weapons back to his friend.

"Don't I make a good deputy, Billie? I didn't fire even once."

Chapter XXIX

"They Can't Hang Me If I Ain't There"

The jury brought in a verdict of murder in the first degree. Clanton was sentenced to be hanged at Live-Oaks four weeks after the day the trial ended. Prince himself had been called back to Washington County to deal with a band of rustlers who had lately pulled off a series of bold, wholesale cattle thefts. He left Goodheart to bring the prisoner back with him in case of a conviction.

The deputy sheriff left the train at Las Vegas, to which point Prince had sent a man with horses to meet Jack and the convicted murderer. It was not likely that the enemies of Clanton would make another attempt to frustrate the law, but there was a chance that they would. Goodheart did not take the direct road to Live-Oaks, but followed the river valley toward Los Portales.

The party reached the Roubideau ranch at dusk of the third night. Pauline had been at the place three months keeping house for her father. She flew to meet Jim, her eyes filled with a divine pity. Both hands went out to his manacled ones impulsively. Her face glowed with a soft, welcoming warmth.

"You poor boy! You poor, poor boy!" she cried. Then, flaming, she turned on Goodheart: "Bel et bien! Why do you load him down with chains? Are you afraid of him?"

The deputy flushed. "I have no right to take any chances of an escape. You know that."

"I know he is innocent. Why did they find him guilty?"

"I had no evidence," explained Jim simply. "Dad Wrayburn swore I shot twice at Webb just before I disappeared in the brush. Then a shot came out of the chaparral. It's not reasonable to suppose some one else fired it, especially when the bullet was one that fitted a forty-four."

"But you didn't fire it. You told me so in your letter."

"My word didn't count with the jury. I'd have to claim that, anyhow, to save my life. My notion is that the bullet didn't come from a six-gun at all, but from a seventy-three rifle. But I can't prove that either."

"It isn't fair. It — it's an outrage." Polly burst into tears and took the slim young fellow into her arms. "They ought to know you wouldn't do that. Why didn't your friends tell them so?"

He smiled, a little wistfully. "A gunman doesn't have friends, Polly. Outside of you an' Lee an' Billie I haven't any. All the newspapers in the territory an' all the politicians an' most of the decent people have been pullin' for a death sentence. Well, they've got it." He stroked her hair softly. "Don't you worry, girl. They won't get a chance to hang me."

Pauline released him, dabbed at her eyes, and ran, choking, into the house.

"You've got to be in trouble to make a real hit with Miss Roubideau," suggested the lank deputy, a little bitterly. "I'll take those bracelets off now, Clanton. You can wash for supper."

Polly saw to it, anyhow, that the prisoner had the best to eat there was in the house. She made a dinner of spring chicken, mashed potatoes, hot biscuits, jelly, and apple pie.

A rider for the Flying V Y dropped in after they had eaten and bridled like a turkey cock at sight of Clanton.

"Don't you let him git away from you, Jack," he warned the officer. "We're allowin' to have a holiday on the sixth up at our place so as to go to the show. It *is* the sixth, ain't it?" he jeered, turning to the handcuffed man on the lounge.

"The sixth is correct," answered Jim

coolly, meeting him eye to eye.

"You wouldn't talk that way if Clanton was free," said Goodheart. "You're taggin' yoreself a bully an' a cheap skate when you do it."

"Say, is that any of yore business, Mr. Deputy Sheriff?"

"It is when you talk to my prisoner. Cut it out, Swartz."

"All right."

The cowpuncher turned to Pauline, who had come to the door and stood there. "You'll be goin' to the big show on the sixth, Miss Roubideau. Live-Oaks will be a sure-enough live town that day."

The young woman walked straight up to the big cowpuncher. Her eyes blazed. "Get out of this house. Don't ever come here again. Don't speak to me if you meet me."

The Flying V Y rider was taken aback. Like a good many young fellows within a radius of a hundred miles, he was a candidate for the favor of Pierre Roubideau's daughter.

"Why, I — I — " he stammered. "I didn't aim for to offend you. This fellow bushwhacked my boss. He — "

"That isn't true," she interrupted. "He didn't do it."

"Sure he did it. Go-Get-'Em Jim is a killer. A girl like you, Miss Roubideau, has got no business stickin' up for a bad man who — "

"Didn't you hear me? I told you to go."

"You've been invited to remove yoreself from the place an' become a part of the outdoor scenery, Swartz," cut in Goodheart, a snap to his jaw. "I'd take that invite pronto if I was you."

The cowpuncher picked up his hat and walked out. The drawling voice of the prisoner followed him.

"Don't you worry, Polly. They can't hang me if I ain't there, can they?"

The deputy guessed that Pauline wished to talk alone with Clanton. Presently he arose and sauntered to the door. "I want to see yore father about some horses Billie needs. Back soon."

He gave them a half-hour, but he took pains to see that his assistant covered the back door while he watched the front of the house. The prisoner was handcuffed, but Jack did not intend to take any chances. Personally he believed that Clanton was guilty, but whether he was or not it was his duty to bring the convicted man safely to Live-Oaks. This he meant to do.

Chapter XXX

Polly Has a Plan

Pauline moved across the room and sat down beside Jim. An eager light shone in her soft, brown eyes.

"Listen!" she ordered in a low voice. "I've got a plan. There's a chance that it will work, I think. But tell me first about your sleeping arrangements. Does Jack or the other guard sit up and watch you all the time?"

"No. The champion roper of New Mexico, Arizona, an' Texas throws the diamond hitch on yours truly. He does an expert job, tucks me up, an' says good-night. He knows I'm perfectly safe till mornin', especially since both he an' Brad sleep in the same room with me."

"Well, I'm going to give you dad's room." She leaned forward and whispered to him steadily for five minutes.

The sardonic mockery had vanished from the face of the prisoner. He listened, every nerve and fiber of him at alert attention. Occasionally he asked a question. Carefully she explained the plan, going over each detail of it again and again.

Jim Clanton was efficient. In those days it was a necessary quality for a bad man if he wished to continue to function. He offered a suggestion or two which Pauline incorporated in her proposed campaign of action. At best her scheme was hazardous. It depended upon all things dovetailing properly. But he was in no place to pick and choose. All he asked was a chance and an even break of luck.

"You dandy girl!" he cried softly, and took her two hands between the palms of his fettered ones. "I'm a scalawag, Polly. But if you pull this off for me, I'll right-about-face. That's a promise. Somehow I've never acted like I wanted to. I've done a heap of wild an' foolish things, an' I've killed whenever it was put up to me. I don't reckon any woman that married me would be real happy. But if you'll take a chance I'll go away from here an' we'll make a fresh start. You're the only girl there is for me."

A faint smile lay in her eyes. "You used to think Lee was the only girl, didn't you?"

"Well, I don't know. I like Polly Roubideau better."

Abruptly she flung at him a statement that was a question. "You didn't kill Mr. Webb."

"No. I never killed but one man without

givin' him an even break. That was Peg-Leg Warren, an' he was a cold-blooded murderer."

A troubled little frown creased her forehead. "I've thought for more than a year now that you — liked me that way. And I've had it in my mind a great deal as to what I ought to do if you spoke to me about it. I wish you had a good wife, Jim. Maybe she could save you from yourself."

"Mebbe she could, Polly."

The lashes of her eyelids fell. She looked down at the bands of iron around his small wrists. "I — I've prayed over it, Jim. But I'm not clear that I've found an answer." Her low voice broke a little. "I don't know what to say."

"Is it that you are afraid of what I'm goin' to be? Can't you trust yore life with me? I shouldn't think you could."

Her eyes lifted and met his bravely. "I think that wouldn't stop me if — if I cared for you that way."

"It's Billie Prince, then, is it?"

"No, it isn't Billie Prince. Never mind who it is. What I must decide is whether I can make you the kind of wife you need without being exactly — "

"In love with me," he finished for her.

"Yes. I've always liked you very much.

You've been good to me. I love you like a brother, I think. Oh, I don't know how to say it."

"Let's get this straight, Polly. Is there some one else you love?"

A tide of color flooded her face to the roots of the hair. She met his steady look reluctantly.

"We needn't discuss that, Jim."

"Needn't we?" He laughed a little, but his voice was rough with feeling. "You're the blamedest little pilgrim ever I did see. What kind of a fellow do you think I am? I ain't good enough for you — not by a thousand miles. Even if you felt about me the way I do about you, it would be a big risk for you to marry me. But now — Sho, little missionary, I ain't so selfish as to let you sacrifice yore life for me."

"If I marry you it will be because I want to, Jim."

"You'll want to because you're such a good little Christian you think it's up to you to save a brand from the burning. But I won't let you do any such foolishness. You go marry that other man. If he's a good, square, decent fellow, you'll be a whole lot better off than if you tied up with a ne'er-do-well like me."

They heard a step on the porch.

"Don't forget. Three taps if you're alone in

the room," she said in a whisper.

Goodheart came into the parlor with Pierre Roubideau. "Expect we'd better turn in, Clanton. We've got to make an early start to-morrow."

The prisoner rose at once. Pauline had drawn her father aside and was giving him some instructions. The old Frenchman nodded, smiling. He understood her little feminine devices and was a cheerful victim of them.

The young woman found a chance for a word alone with the deputy.

"I want to see you to-night, Jack, about — something." Her eyes were very bright and the color in the soft cheeks high. She spoke almost in a whisper.

The lank young sheriff had the soul of an inarticulate poet. Beneath the tan of his leathery face the blood burned. This was the first really kind word he had had from her since their arrival. All her solicitation had been for the condemned youth in his care. Perhaps all she wanted now was to ask some favor for Clanton, but hope leaped in his heart.

He made arrangements for the night in his usual careful way. It was not pleasant to have to watch the prisoner as a cat does a mouse, but Goodheart was thorough in whatever he undertook. Skillfully he tied Clanton in such a way as to allow him enough freedom of motion to change position without giving him enough to make it possible for him to untie himself.

"Back after a while," he told Jim.

The young man on the bed grunted sleepily and the deputy returned to the parlor.

Pauline, still in her kitchen apron, smiled in at the door upon him and her father.

"You two go out on the porch and smoke your pipes," she said. "I have to finish my work in the kitchen, then I have to go down to the cellar and take care of the milk. I'll not be long."

Pierre, an obedient parent, rose and moved toward the porch. Before he left the room Goodheart took the precaution to lock the bedroom door and pocket the key. He was a little ashamed of this, but he knew that Go-Get-'Em Jim was a very competent and energetic person. Convicted and sentenced though he was, Clanton still boasted with cool aplomb that there would be no hanging on the sixth. The deputy strolled round to the back of the house to make sure his assistant was still on the job. After a few words with the man he returned to the porch. He was satisfied there was no possible chance of an escape. The prisoner lay handcuffed and tied to a bed by the champion roper of the Southwest. The door of the room was locked. Both exits from the house were guarded. Jack felt that he could safely enjoy a smoke.

Chapter XXXI

Goodheart Makes a Promise and Breaks It

Pauline was a singularly honest little soul, but she now discovered in herself unsuspected capacity for duplicity. She went singing about her work, apparently care-free as a lark. Presently, still humming a French chanson, she appeared on the porch swinging a key, passed the two men with a gay little nod, and disappeared around the corner of the house to the cellar.

The rancher apologized for the key. "We've had to lock the cellar lately since so many movers have been going through on this road. Eh bien! Our hams — they took wings and flew."

Polly rattled the milk pans for a moment or two and then listened. From above there came to her the sound of three faint raps on the woodwork of the bed. She crept up the stairs that led from the cellar into the house. At the top of them was a trapdoor. Very slowly and carefully she pushed this up. Through the opening she passed into a bedroom.

Softly the girl stole to the bed. From the cellar she had brought a butcher knife and with this she sawed at the rope which bound the prisoner.

"But your handcuffs. What can we do about them?" she whispered.

Clanton stretched his stiff muscles. He made no answer in words. For a moment or two his arms writhed, then from out of the iron bracelet his long slender hand slowly twisted. Soon the second wrist was also free.

"I've had a lot of fun poked at my girl hands, but they come in useful sometimes," he murmured.

"I'll have to hurry back or I'll be missed," she told him. "You'll find a saddled horse in the aspens."

He caught her by the shoulders and held her fast. "You've been the truest little friend ever a man had. You've stuck by me an' believed in me even when I didn't believe in myself any longer. No matter what folks said about me or about you for takin' an interest in such a scamp, you never quit fightin' to keep me decent. I've heard tell of guardian angels — well, that's what you've been to me, little pilgrim."

"I haven't forgotten the boy who rode up Escondido Cañon to save me from death and dishonor," Pauline cried softly.

"You've paid that debt fifty times. I owe you more than I can tell. I wisht I knew a way to pay it."

Her soft and dusky eyes clung to his pleadingly. "If you get away, Jim, you *will* be good, won't you?"

"I'll be as good as I've got it in me to be. I don't know how good that is, Polly. But I'll do my level best."

"Oh, I'm so glad," she whispered. "Good luck — heaps of it."

He was not quite sure whether it was his privilege to kiss the parted red lips upturned to him, but he took a chance and was not rebuked.

Pauline went noiselessly down the steps again into the cellar while Clanton held the trapdoor. He lowered it inch by inch so that it would not creak, then spread over it the Navajo rug that had been there before the entrance of the girl.

Pierre Roubideau was still on his first pipe when Polly came round the corner of the house and stopped at the porch steps.

"I want to show you our new colt, Jack," she said to the deputy. This matter-of-fact statement came a little shyly and a little

298

tremulously from her lips. Her heart was beating furiously.

The officer rose at once. "Just a minute," he said, and went into the house.

He unlocked the door of the room where Clanton was and glanced in. The prisoner lay on the bed in the moonlight, the blankets drawn over him. From his deep, regular breathing Jack judged him to be asleep. He relocked the door and joined Pauline.

The face of the girl was very white in the moonlight. Her big eyes flashed at him a question. Had he discovered that his prisoner was free?

They walked slowly toward the corral. From it Goodheart could see the front of the house, but not the cellar entrance at the side. Neither of them spoke until they reached the fence. He turned and leaned his elbows against it, facing the house.

Pauline was under great nervous tension. Her lips were dry and her throat parched. If the guard at the rear caught sight of the prisoner while he was escaping, Clanton would certainly be shot down. She knew Jim better than to hope that he would let himself be taken again alive.

The conscience of the girl troubled her too. She was doing this to save the life of a friend, but it was impossible not to feel a sense of treachery toward this other friend whose approval was so much more vital to her happiness. Would Jack think that she had conspired against his honor in an underhanded way? He was a man of strict principles. Would he cast her off and have no more to do with her?

She woke from her worries to discover that an emotional climax was imminent. Jack was telling her, in awkward, broken phrases, of his love for her. Polly had waited a long time for his confession, but coming at this hour it filled her with shame and distress. What an evil chance that he should be blurting out the story of his faith and trust in her while she was in the act of betraying him!

"Don't, Jack, don't!" she begged.

"It's all right," he said gently. "I know you don't care for me. But I had to tell you. Just had to do it. Couldn't keep still any longer. It's all right, Polly. I can stand it. I didn't go for to worry you."

She wept.

Her tears distressed him. He urged her to forget his presumption. She had been so good to him that he had spoken in spite of himself.

Pauline found she could not let him deceive himself. If she let him go now, perhaps he might never come back.

"You goose!"

Though the words came smothered through her handkerchief, he gained incredible comfort from them.

"Polly!" he cried.

"Don't you say a word, Jack," she ordered. "Let me do the talking."

"If you'll tell me that — that — you care anything for — for — "

" — For a big stupid who is too modest ever to think enough of himself," she completed. "Well, I do. I care a great deal for him."

"You don't mean — "

"I do, too. That's just what I mean. No, you keep back there till I'm through, Jack. I want to find out if you love me as much as I do you."

"Polly!" he cried a second time.

Her small face was very serious and white in the moonshine.

"Suppose we don't agree about something. Say I do a thing that seems right to me, but it doesn't seem right to you. What then?"

"It'll seem right to me if you do it," he answered.

"That's just a compliment."

"No, it's the truth. Whatever you do seems right to me."

"But suppose I do something that you think is wrong. Perhaps it may seem to you disloyal."

"If you do it because you think you ought to I'll not find it disloyal."

"Sure, Jack?"

"Certain sure," he answered.

"It's a promise?"

"It's a promise."

Little imps of mischief bubbled into the brown eyes. "Then why don't you kiss me, goose?"

He caught her to him with a fierce rapture.

There came to them the sudden sound of drumming hoofs. A shot rang out in the night. Goodheart, with the first kiss of his sweetheart almost on his lips, flung Pauline aside and ran to the house.

The other guard met him at the front steps. "By God, he's gone!" the man cried.

"Clanton?"

"Yep."

"Can't be. He was handcuffed, tied to the bed, and locked in. I've got the key in my pocket."

The deputy sheriff took the steps at one bound, flung himself across the parlor, and unlocked the door. One glance showed him the empty bed, the displaced rug, and the trapdoor. He stepped forward and picked up the bits of rope and the handcuffs.

"Some one cut the rope and freed him," he said, confounded at the impossibility of the thing that had occurred.

"Must of slipped his hands out of the cuffs, looks like," the guard suggested.

"He got me to give him a bigger size — complained they chafed his wrists."

"Some trick that, if he *has* got kid hands."

The chill eyes of Goodheart gimleted into those of his assistant. "Did you do this, Brad? God help you if you did."

A light step sounded on the threshold. Pauline came into the room. "I did it, Jack," she said.

"You!"

"I came up through the trapdoor when I was in the cellar. I cut the rope and told him there was a horse saddled in the aspens."

Thoughts raced in his bewildered mind. She had planned all this carefully. Almost under his very eyes she had done it. Then she had lured him from the house to give Clanton a better chance. She had let him make love to her so that she could keep him at the corral while the prisoner escaped. It was all a trick. Even now she was laughing up her sleeve at the way she had made a fool of him.

"You saddled the horse and left it there." His statement was a question, too.

"Yes. I had to save him. I knew he was innocent."

All the explanations she had intended

shriveled up before the scorn in his eyes. He brushed past her without a word and strode out of the house.

Pauline went to her room and flung herself on the bed. After a time her father came in and sat down beside the girl. He put a gentle hand on her shoulder.

"I know what you think, dad," she said without turning her head. "But I couldn't help it. I had to do it."

"It may make you trouble, ma petite."

"I can't help that. Jim didn't kill Mr. Webb. I know it."

"After a fair trial a jury said he did, Polly. We have to take their word for it."

"You think I did wrong then."

"You did what you think was right. In my heart is no blame for you."

He comforted her as best he could and left her to sleep. But she did not sleep. All through the night she lay and listened. She was miserably unhappy. Her head and her heart ached. Jack had promised that she should be the judge of what was right for her to do, and at the first test he had failed her. She made excuses for him, but the hurt of her disappointment could not be assuaged.

In the early morning she heard the clatter of horses' hoofs in the yard. During the night she had not undressed. Now she rose and went out to meet her lover. He was at the stable, a gaunt figure, hollow-eyed, dusty, and stern. He had failed to recapture his prisoner.

"Jack," she pleaded, reaching out a hand timidly toward him.

Again he rejected her advance in grim silence. Swinging to the saddle, he rode out of the gate and down the road toward Live-Oaks.

With a little whimper Polly moved blindly to the house through her tears.

Chapter XXXII

Jim Takes a Prisoner

After Goodheart left the room where his prisoner was confined, Clanton waited a few moments till the sound of his footsteps had died away. He rose, moved noiselessly across the floor, and raised the trapdoor slowly. The creaking of the rusty hinges seemed to Jim to be shouting aloud the news of his escape. The young fellow descended into the cellar and stood there without moving till his eyes became accustomed to the darkness. He groped his way to the door, which Pauline had left open an inch or two. Carefully he edged through and crouched in the gloom at the foot of the steps.

Not far away some one was whistling cheerfully. Clanton recognized the tune as the usual musical offertory of Brad. He was giving "Uncle Ned" to an unappreciative world.

The fugitive crept up the steps and peered over the top. Brad was sitting on a bench against the wall. Evidently he was quite comfortable and had no intention of moving. The guard was so near that it would not be a fair risk to try to make a dash across the moonlit open for the aspen grove. He was so far that before the prisoner could reach him his gun would be in action. There was nothing to do but wait. Jim huddled against the sustaining wall while with the passing minutes his chance of escape slipped away.

Pierre Roubideau came round the corner of the house and joined Brad. The guard made room for him on the bench. If Roubideau sat down, the man in the shadow knew he was lost. They would sit there and chat till Goodheart came back and discovered his absence.

The rancher hesitated while he felt for his pipe. "Reckon I left it in the kitchen," he said.

Brad followed him round the corner of the house. Clanton waited no longer. They might return, or they might not. He did not intend to stay to find out.

Swiftly he ran toward the aspens. Half the distance he had covered when a voice called sharply to halt. The guard had turned and caught sight of him.

The feet of the running man slapped the ground faster. As he dodged into the trees a bullet flew past him. Yet a moment, and he had flung himself astride the bronco waiting there and had electrified that sleepy animal into life.

The pony struck its stride immediately. It took the rising ground at a gallop, topped the hill, and disappeared over the brow. The rider plunged into the thick mesquite. He knew that Goodheart would pursue, but he knew, too, that the odds were a hundred to one against capture if he could put a mile or two between him and the Roubideau ranch. A man could vanish in any one of fifty draws. He could find a temporary hiding-place up any gulch under cover of the matted brush. Therefore he turned toward the mountains.

Since he was unarmed, it was essential that Clanton should get into touch with his associates of the chaparral at once. Until he had a six-gun strapped to his side and a carbine under his leg he would not feel comfortable. All night he traveled, winding in and out of cañons, crossing divides, and dipping down into little mountain parks. He knew exactly where he wanted to go, and he moved toward his destination in the line of greatest economy.

Morning found him descending from a mountain pass to the Ruidosa.

"Breakfast soon, you wall-faced old Piute," Jim told his mount. "You're sure a weary caballo, but we got to keep hitting the trail till we cross that hogback."

A thin film of smoke rose from a little valley to the left. Clanton drew up abruptly. He had no desire to meet now any strangers whose intentions had not been announced.

Swiftly, with a pantherish smoothness of motion, he slid from the cowpony and moved to the edge of a bluff that looked down into the arroyo below. He crept forward and peered through a clump of cactus growing at the edge of the escarpment.

The camp-fire was at the very foot of the bluff. A man was stooped over it cooking breakfast.

The heart of the fugitive lost a beat, then raced wildly. The camper was Devil Dave Roush. A rifle lay beside him. His revolver was in a cartridge belt that had been tossed on a boulder within reach of his hand.

Clanton wriggled back without a sound

from the edge of the cliff and rose to his feet. A savage light of triumph blazed in his eyes. The enemy for whom he had long sought was delivered into his hands. He ran back to the bronco and untied the reata from the tientos. Deftly he coiled the rope and adjusted the loop to suit him. Again he stole to the rim rock and waited with the stealthy, deadly patience of the crouched cougar.

Roush rose. His arms fell to his sides. Instantly the rope dropped, uncoiling as it flew. With perfect accuracy the loop descended upon its victim and tightened about his waist, pinning the arms close to the body.

Clanton hauled in the rawhide swiftly. Dragged from his feet, Roush could make no resistance. Before he could gather his startled wits, he found himself dangling in midair against the face of the rock wall.

The man above fastened the end of the rope to the roots of a scrub oak and ran down the slope at full speed. In less than half a minute he was standing breathless in front of his prisoner.

Already shaken with dread, Roush gave way to panic fear at sight of him.

"Goddlemighty! It's Clanton!" he cried.

Jim buckled on the belt and appropriated the rifle His grim face told Roush all he needed to know.

There had been a time when Roush, full of physical life and energy, had boasted that he feared no living man. In his cups he still bragged of his bad record, of his accuracy as a gunman, of his gameness. But he knew, and his associates suspected, that Devil Dave had long since drunk up his courage. His nerves were jumpy and his heart bad. Now he begged for his life abjectly. If he had been free from the rope that held him dangling against the wall, he would have crawled like a whipped cur to the feet of his enemy.

At a glance Clanton saw Roush had been camping alone. The hobbled horse, the blankets, the breakfast dishes, all told him this. But he took no chances. First he saddled the horse and brought it close to the camp-fire. When he sat down to eat the breakfast the rustler had cooked, it was with his back to the bluff and the rifle across his knees.

"This here rope hurts tur'ble — seems like my wrists are on fire," whined the man. "You let me down, Mr. Clanton, and I'll explain eve'ything. I want to be yore friend. I sure do. I don't feel noways onfriendly to you. Mebbe I used to be a bad lot, but I'm a changed man now."

Go-Get-'Em Jim said nothing. He had not spoken once, and his silence filled the roped man with terror. The shifting eyes of Devil

Dave read doom in the cold, still ones of his enemy.

Sometimes Roush argued in a puling whimper. Sometimes his terror rose to the throat and his entreaties became shrieks. He died a dozen deaths while his foe watched him with a chill stillness more menacing than any threats.

The first impulse of Clanton had been to stamp out the life of this man just as he would that of a diamond-backed rattlesnake; but he meant to take his time about it and to see that the fellow suffered. Not until he was halfway through the meal did the memory of his pledge to Pauline jump to his mind. Quickly he pushed it from him. He had not meant to include Roush in his promise. As soon as he had made an end of this ruffian he would turn over a new leaf. But not yet. Roush was outside the pale. His life belonged to Jim. He would be a traitor to the memory of his sister if he let the villain go.

The lust for vengeance swelled in the young man's blood like a tide. It was his right to kill; more, it was his duty. So he tried to persuade himself. But deep within him a voice was making itself heard. It whispered that if he killed Roush now, he could never look Pauline Roubideau in the face again. She had fought gallantly for his soul, and at last he had pledged his honor to a new course. Now twelve hours ago she had risked her reputation to save his life. If he failed her now, it would be a betrayal of all the desires and purposes that had of late been stirring in him.

Clammy beads of sweat stood on his forehead. He had been given a new chance, and it warred with every inherited instinct of his nature. The fight within was cruel and bitter. But when he rose, his breakfast forgotten, it was won. He would let Roush go unhurt. He would do it for the sake of Polly Roubideau, who had been such a good friend to him.

Devil Dave, ghastly with fear, was still pleading for his life. Clanton, who had heard nothing of what the fellow had been saying in the past ten minutes, came to a sudden alert attention.

"I'll go into court an' swear it if you'll let me be. I'll tell the jedge an' the jury that Joe Yankie told me an' Albeen an' Dumont that he bushwhacked Webb an' then cut his stick so that you-all got the blame. Honest to God, I will, Mr. Clanton. Jest you trust me an' see."

"When did Yankie tell you that?"

"He done told us at the camp-fire one night. He made his brags how you got the blame for it an' would have to hang."

"Albeen heard him say it — an' Dumont too?"

"Tha's right, Mr. Clanton. An' I'll sure take my Bible oath on it."

Go-Get-'Em Jim whipped out the forty-five from its holster and fired. Roush dropped screaming to the ground. He thought he had been shot. The bullet had cut the rope above his head.

"Get up," ordered Clanton in disgust.

Roush rose stiffly.

Jim swung to the saddle of the horse beside him. "Hit the dust," he told his captive.

The rider followed the footman to the top of the bluff. Here Roush was instructed to mount the horse Clanton had been astride all night. Riding behind the tame bad man, Jim cut across the hills to a gulch and followed it till the ravine ran out in a little valley. He crossed this and climbed a stiff pass from the other side of which he looked down on Live-Oaks a thousand feet below.

The young man tied the hands of his prisoner behind him. From a coat pocket he drew a looking-glass, caught the sun's rays, and flung them upon a house in the suburbs of the town.

Out of the house there presently came a man. He stood in the doorway a moment before going down the street. A flash of hot sunlight caught him full in the face. He moved. The light danced after him. Then he woke up.

From the cliff far above friends of his had been wont to heliograph signals during the late Washington County War.

He read the light flashes and at once saddled a horse. A few minutes later he might have been seen on the breakneck trail that leads across the mountains to the Ruidosa. After a stiff climb he reached the summit and swung sharply along the ridge to the right. A voice hailed him.

"Hello, Reb!"

"Hello, Go-Get-'Em! Thought Goodheart was bringin' you back a prisoner." Quantrell's old guerrilla looked with unconcealed surprise at the bound man. He knew the story of Clanton's deep-rooted hatred of the Roush clan.

"I didn't sign any bond to stay his prisoner," Jim answered dryly. Then, sharply, he turned upon Roush. "Spill out yore story about Yankie."

Reluctantly Roush told once more his tale. He spoke only under the pressure of imminent peril, for he knew that if this ever got back to the men in the chaparral they would kill him with no more compunction than they would a coyote.

"Take this bird down to Billie Prince, Reb. Tell him I jumped Roush on the Ruidosa an' he peached to save his hide. This fellow is a

314

born liar, but I reckon he's tellin' the truth this time. If he rues back on his story, tell Billie to put an advertisement in the Live-Oaks 'Round-Up' and I'll drop in to town an' have a séance with Mr. Roush."

Reb scratched his sunburnt head. "I don't aim to be noways inquisitive, Go-Get-'Em, but howcome you to wait long enough to take this hawss-thief captive? I'd 'a' bet my best mule team against a dollar Mex that you'd have gunned him on sight."

"I'll tell you why, Reb. He had one rifle an' one six-gun. I didn't have either the one or the other, so I had to borrow his guns before I talked turkey. By that time I'd changed my mind about bumpin' him off right now. When Yankie finds out what he's been sayin' he'll do the trick for me."

"You're right he will. Good job, too. I hate a sneak like I do a side-winder." Reb turned to his prisoner. "Git a move on you, Roush. I want this job over with. I'm no coyote herder."

Chapter XXXIII

The Round-Up

Dumont had been on the grill for three hours. He had taken refuge in dogged silence. He had been badgered into lies. He had broken down at last and told the truth. Sheriff Billie Prince, keen as a hound on the scent, persistent as a bulldog, peppered the man's defense with a machine-gun fire of questions. Back of these loomed the shadow of a long term in the penitentiary.

For Dumont had been caught with his iron hot. The acrid smell of burnt flesh was still in the air when an angry cattleman and two of his riders came on the man and the rustled calf. Fortunately for the thief the sheriff happened to be in the neighborhood. He had rescued the captured waddy from the hands of the incensed ranchers and brought him straight to Live-Oaks.

The rustler was frightened. There had been a bad quarter of an hour when it looked as though he might be the central figure in a lynching. Even after this danger had been weathered, the outlook was full of gloom. He had to choose between a long prison sentence and the betrayal of his comrades. Dumont had no iron in his blood. He dodged and evaded and bluffed — and at last threw up his hands. If the sheriff would protect him from the vengeance of the gang, he would give any information wanted or do anything he was told to do.

The arrival of Reb and his prisoner interrupted the quiz. Prince had Dumont returned to his cell and took up the new business of Roush and his story. The sheriff knew he would be blamed for the escape of Clanton and he thought it wise to have the whole matter opened up before witnesses. Wallace Snaith and Dad Wrayburn both happened to be in town and Billie sent the boss muleskinner to bring them. To these men he turned over the examination of Roush.

They wrung from him, a scrap at a time, the story Yankie had told his confederates at the camp-fire. A statement of the facts was drawn up and signed by Roush under protest. It was witnessed by the four men present.

Devil Dave was locked up and Dumont brought back to the office of the sheriff. Taken by surprise at the new form of the questionnaire, already broken in spirit and therefore eager to conciliate these powerful citizens, the rustler at once corroborated the story of Roush. He, too, signed a statement drawn up by Prince.

"Just shows, doggone it, how a man can be too blamed sure," commented Wrayburn. "I'd 'a' bet my life Go-Get-'Em Jim killed Webb. But he didn't. It's plain enough now. After his rookus with the old man, Yankie must have got a seventy-three an' waited in the chaparral. It just happened he was lyin' hid close to where we met Clanton. It beats the Dutch."

"An' if Jim hadn't escaped he'd have been hanged for killin' Webb."

"That's right, sheriff. On my testimony, too. Say, let me go to the Governor with these papers an' git the pardon. I'd like to give it to the boy myself, jest to show him there's no hard feelin's," urged Wrayburn.

"That's all right, Dad. I'm goin' to be right busy this next week, I shouldn't wonder. I've got business up in the hills."

"If you're goin' on a round-up, I hope you make a good gather, Prince," said Snaith, smiling.

Not in the history of Washington County had there been another such a round-up as this one of which Sheriff Prince was the boss. He made his plans swiftly and thoroughly. His posses were to sweep the country between

Saco de Oro Creek and Caballero Cañon. Every gap was to be stopped, every exit guarded. Dumont, much against his will, rode beside the sheriff as guide. Goodheart had charge of the first party that went out. His duty was to swing round and close the gulches to the north. Here he would wait until the hunted men were driven into the trap he had set. Old Reb, with a second posse, started next morning for the headwaters of Seven-Mile Creek. An hour later the sheriff himself took the road. He left town sooner than he had intended because Roush had escaped during the night and was probably on his way into the hills to warn the rustlers.

Get them in a talkative mood and old-timers who took part in it will still tell the story of that man-drive in the mountains. Riders combed the draws and the buttes, eyes and ears alert for those who might lie hidden on the rim rocks or in the cactus. It was grim business. Driven out of their holes, the rustlers fought savagely. One, trapped in a hill pocket, stood off a posse till he was shot to death. A second was wounded, captured, and sent back with two other suspects to Live-Oaks. At the end of a week Prince had the remnant of the band surrounded in a mountain park close to Caballero Cañon.

The country into which the outlaws had

been driven was an ideal terrain for defense. The brush was thick and tall. Two wooded arroyos gashed the rim of the valley and ran down into the basin. An attack against determined men here was bound to prove costly.

Billie knew that three men lay in the chaparral and he believed that one of them at least was wounded. Old Reb had jumped them up from a fireless camp, and in their hurry to escape the outlaws had left all their provisions and two of their horses. They left, too, one of the posse with a bullet hole in his forehead. The sheriff's plan was to tighten the lines gradually and starve out the rustlers.

But though Prince would not let his men advance to a general assault, he made up his mind to find out more as to the condition of the men he had surrounded. He wanted to make sure they had not slipped past his guards into Caballero Cañon. In the back of his head, too, was the feeling that if he could get into touch with them, perhaps he might arrange for a surrender.

He called Goodheart to one side. "As soon as it's dark I'm goin' in to find out what's doin'. We haven't heard a murmur from these birds for hours. Perhaps they've flown. Anyhow, I'm goin' to find out."

"How many of us are goin'?"

"Just one of us — Billie Prince."

"If two of us went — "

"It would double the chances of discovery. No, I'm goin' alone. Maybe I can have a talk with Albeen or Yankie. I don't want to take 'em dead, but alive."

"They'll probably get you while you're in there, Prince."

"I don't think it. But if I'm not back by mornin' you are in charge of this hunt. Use yore judgment."

The deputy ventured one more protest, but his chief vetoed it. Billie had decided what to do and argument did not touch him.

He did not take a rifle. In the thick brush it would be hard to handle noiselessly and the snapping of a twig might mean the difference between life and death. The sheriff slipped into the tangle of cat-claw, prickly pear, and mesquite, vanishing into the gloom from the sight of Goodheart.

On the back of an envelope Dumont had drawn for him a rough map of the valley. It showed that the wooden arroyos ran together like the spokes of a wheel. The judgment of Prince was that he must look for the men he wanted close to the angle of intersection. Up one or the other of these draws it was likely they would make their dash for freedom, since otherwise they would have to emerge into the open. Therefore, they would hold the base of the V in order not to be cut off from the chance of getting out of the trap.

The sheriff snaked forward, most of the time on his stomach or on hands and knees, for what seemed an interminable period. Each least movement had to be planned and executed with precision. He dared not risk the cracking of a dead branch or the rustle of dry foliage. As silently as an Apache he wriggled through the grass.

Billie became aware of a sound to the left. He listened. It presently defined itself as a wheezing rattle halfway between a cough and a groan.

Toward it Prince deflected. He knew himself to be now in the acute danger zone, and he increased if possible his precautions. The moaning continued intermittently. Billie wondered why, if this were the camp of the outlaws, no other sound broke the stillness. Closer, inch by inch, making the most of every bunch of yucca and cholla, the officer slowly crept.

The figure of a man lay in the sand, the head resting on a folded slicker. From time to time it moved slightly, and always the restlessness was accompanied by the little throat rattle that had first attracted the attention of the sheriff. The face, lying full in the moonlight, was of a ghastly pallor.

Prince lay crouched behind a piñon till he was sure the man was alone. It was possible that his confederates might return at any moment, but Billie could not let him suffer without aid. He stepped forward, revolver in hand, every sense ready for instant response.

The wounded man was Joe Yankie. The experienced eyes of Prince told him that the rustler had not long to live. He was already in that twilight region which is the border land between the known and the unknown. Billie spoke his name, and for a moment the eyes of the man cleared.

"Yore boys got me when they jumped our camp," he explained feebly.

"Sorry, Joe. You were firin' when they hit you."

The wounded man nodded. " 'S all right. Streak o' bad luck. Gimme water. I'm on fire."

The officer unbuckled his canteen, lifted the head of the dying man, and let the water trickle down his throat. Gently he lowered the head again to the pillow.

Then he asked a question. "Where are Albeen and — Roush?"

The last name was a shot in the dark, but it hit the bull's eye.

"Left — hours ago."

Yankie closed his eyes wearily, but by sheer strength of will Prince recalled him from the doze into which he was slipping.

"Did you kill Homer Webb?"

"Yes."

"Had Clanton anything to do with it?"

"No."

A film gathered over the eyes of the dying man. The lids closed. Billie adjusted the pillow a little more comfortably and rose. He could do no more for him at present and he must set about his work. For though the net of the round-up had gathered hundreds of stolen cattle and most of those engaged in the business of brand-blotting, Prince knew his job would not be finished if Roush and Albeen escaped.

He quartered over the ground foot by foot. The camp of the rustlers had been here and the footsteps showed there had been three. Yankie was accounted for. That left Roush and Albeen. The sheriff discovered the place where they had been sleeping.

His eyes lit with the eagerness of the hunter who has come on the spoor. He had found two sets of tracks leading from the bed-ground. One of these showed no heel marks and the deep impress of toes in the soft sand. The other presented a more sharply defined print with a greater distance between the steps.

They told Billie a story of a man tiptoeing away in breathless silence, and of another man, wakened by some sound or by some premonition, pursuing him in reckless haste.

The imagination of the trailer built up a web of cause and effect. Two men, with only one horse, were caught in a trap from which both were in a desperate hurry to escape. Each, no doubt, was filled with suspicion of the other while they waited for darkness to fall that they might try to slip through the cordon of watchers. One of the two, at least, was unknown. If he could make a getaway, *and leave no witness behind*, there would be no proof positive that he was one of the rustlers. The situation was ripe for tragedy.

In the back of the sheriff's mind rose thoughts of something sinister that had happened in the early hours of darkness. A chill ran down his spine. He expected presently to stumble across something cold and chill that only a little while ago had been warm with life.

Prince recognized a weakness in his theory. If Roush was the man who had tiptoed toward the horse in the pines, why had he not made sure first by shooting Albeen while he slept? There was no absolute answer to that. But it might be that the one-armed man had been dozing lightly and that Roush had not the nerve to take a chance. For if his first shot failed to kill, the betrayed man could still drop him.

The trailer had no doubt in his mind that Roush was the man who had tried to slip away to the horse. Albeen was a gun-fighter, quick on the shoot, hasty of temper, but with the reputation of being both game and stanch. It would not be in character for him to leave a companion in the lurch.

In the scrub pines at the foot of the arroyo Prince found the place where a horse had been tied. The footprints had diverged sharply toward a cluster of big boulders that rose in the grove. Billie did not at once follow them. He wanted to make sure of another point first.

Every sense alert against a possible surprise, he studied the ground around the spot where the bronco had been fastened. One set of tracks came straight from the big rocks to the hitching tree. Here all tracks ended, except those of a galloping horse and the ones made by the man who had originally left the animal here.

One man had gone up the arroyo to slip through or to fight his way out of the trap. The other man had stayed here. The officer knew what he would find lying among the big rocks.

The body lay face down, a revolver close to

the still hand. Three chambers of it had been fired. Prince turned over the heavy torso and looked into the contorted face of Dave Roush.

The man had fallen a victim to his own treachery.

Chapter XXXIV

Primrose Paths

When Billie Prince had finished the job that had been given him to do, he went back quietly to Live-Oaks without knowing that he had led the last campaign of a revolution in the social life of Washington County. Because a strong, determined man had carried law into the mesquite, citizens could henceforth go about their business without fear or dread.

The rule of the "bad man" was over. Revolvers were no longer a part of the necessary wearing apparel of gentlemen of spirit. Life became safe and humdrum. The frontier world gave itself to ploughing fields and building fences and digging irrigation ditches and planting orchards. As a corollary it married and reared children and built little red schoolhouses.

But before all this came to pass some details had to be arranged in the lives of certain young people of the country. In one instance, at least, Lee Snaith appointed herself adjuster in behalf of Cupid.

Goodheart reached town a few hours earlier than his chief. Lee met him just before supper in front of the court-house.

"Where's Billie?" she asked with characteristic directness.

"He's on his way back. A wounded man couldn't be moved an' he had to stay with him a while. The man was Joe Yankie. A messenger just got in to say he died."

"Billie isn't wounded?"

"No. Not his fault, though. When we had the rustlers cornered, he crawled in through the brush to their camp. Fool business, I told him. Never saw anything gamer. Lucky for him Albeen had made his get-away."

The eyes on the girl thanked the deputy for this indirect praise. Little patches of red burned in her dusky cheeks. The way to make a life friend of her was to be fond of Billie.

Lee changed the subject abruptly. "Jack, you haven't half the sense I thought you had."

"Much obliged," he answered sardonically. She was looking straight at him and he knew what was in her mind.

"If I was a man — and if the nicest girl in

328

the world was in love with me — I'd try not to be as stiff as a poker."

"I'm as stiff as a poker, am I?"

"Yes." The dark eyes of the young woman were eager pools of light. "She's the truest-hearted girl I ever saw — the best friend, the loyalest comrade. I should think you'd be ashamed to set yourself up to judge her."

"Of course, you're not settin' yourself up to judge *me*, Lee?"

"I'm going to tell you what I think. The others are afraid of you because you can put on that high-and-mighty, stand-offish air. Well, I'm not."

"I see you're not."

"She told me all about it. Since she was Polly Roubideau she had to help Jim escape. Can't you see that? She knew he was innocent, and it turned out she was right. Suppose she made a mistake — and I don't admit it for a minute. Can't you make allowance for other folks' judgment being different from yours? Are you never wrong yourself?"

"It isn't a question of judgment."

He hesitated and decided to say no more. How could he tell Lee that Pauline had deliberately misled him to give Clanton a better chance of escape? He had fought it out a hundred times in his mind, but he could not escape the conviction that she had

329

made a tool of his love.

The girl went to the heart of the matter. "Polly loves you, and she is breaking her heart because of your wretched pride. If you don't go straight to her and beg her pardon for your want of faith in her, you're not half the man I think you are, Jack Goodheart."

A warm glow of hope flushed through his blood.

"How do you know she loves me?"

"Because — because — " Lee stopped. She did not intend to betray any confidences. "I know it. That's enough."

He threw away impulsively the prudent pride that he had been nourishing. "Where can I find Polly?"

"You're being invited to supper at my aunt's this evening. I'll not be home for half an hour, but if you go right up, maybe you can find some one to entertain you."

He buried her little hand in his big paw and strode away. She watched him, a soft tenderness shining in her eyes. Lee was a lover herself, and she wanted everybody in the world to be as happy as she was.

Two horsemen rode down the street toward her. She looked up. One of them was Billie Prince, the other Jim Clanton.

The younger man gave a shout of gay greeting. "Yip-ee yippy yip." He leaned from the cowpony and gave her his gloved hand. "I've brought him back to you. He sure did make a good clean-up. I'm the only bad man left in Washington County."

She met his impudent little smile with friendly eyes. "Dad Wrayburn's back from Santa Fé with the pardon, Jim. I'm so glad."

"I'm some glad myself. Do you want me to shut my eyes whilst you an' Billie — "

The sheriff knocked the rest of the sentence out of him with a vigorous thump on the back.

While Lee and her lover shook hands their eyes held fast to each other.

"Good to see you, Billie," she said.

"Same here, Lee."

"When you and Jim have put up your horses I want you to come up to aunt's for supper."

"We'll be there."

It was not a very gay little supper. Pauline and Jack Goodheart had very little to say for themselves, but in their eyes were bright pools of happiness. Clanton sustained the burden of the talk, assisted in a desultory fashion by Lee and Billie. But there was so much quiet joy at the table that for years the hour was one fenced off from all the others of their lives. Even Jim, who for the first time felt himself almost an outsider, since he did not belong to the close communion of lovers, could find plenty for which to be thankful.

He made an announcement before he left. "There's no room here for me now that you lads are marryin' all my girls. I'm goin' to hit the trail. It's Texas for me. I've got a letter in my pocket offerin' me a job as a Ranger an' I'm goin' to take it."

They shook hands with him in warm congratulation. Their friend was no longer a killer. He had definitely turned his back on lawlessness and would henceforth walk with the law. The problem of what was to become of Go-Get-'Em Jim was solved.

As to the problem of their own futures, that did not disturb these happy egoists in the least. Life beckoned them to primrose paths. It is the good fortune of lovers that their vision never pierces the shadows in which lie the sorrows of the years and the griefs that wear them gray.

The employees of THORNDIKE PRESS hope you have enjoyed this Large Print book. All our Large Print titles are designed for easy reading, and all our books are made to last. Other Thorndike Large Print books are available at your library, through selected bookstores, or directly from us. For more information about current and upcoming titles, please call or mail your name and address to:

THORNDIKE PRESS
PO Box 159
Thorndike, Maine 04986
800/223-6121
207/948-2962

'Lindy had met Dave Roush at a dance up on Lonesome where she had no business to be. At the time she had been visiting a distant cousin in a cove adjacent to that creek. Some craving for adventure, some instinct of defiance, had taken her to the frolic where she knew the Roush clan would be in force. From the first sight of her Dave had wooed her with a careless bravado that piqued her pride and intrigued her interest. The girl's imagination translated in terms of romance his insolence and audacity. Into her starved existence he brought color and emotion.

Did she love him? 'Lindy was not sure. He moved her at times to furious anger, and again to inarticulate longing she did not understand. For though she was heritor of a life full-blooded and undisciplined, every fiber of her was clean and pure. There were hours when she hated him, glimpsed in him points of view that filled her with vague distrust. But always he attracted her tremendously.

"You're goin' with me, gal," he urged.

Close to her hand was a little clump of forget-me-nots which had pushed through the moss. 'Lindy feigned to be busy picking the blossoms.

"No," she answered sulkily.

"Yes. To-night — at eleven o'clock, 'Lindy, — under the big laurel."

9

While she resented his assurance, it none the less coerced her. She did not want a lover who groveled in the dust before her. She wanted one to sweep her from her feet, a young Lochinvar to compel her by the force of his personality.

"I'll not be there," she told him.

"We'll git right across the river an' be married inside of an hour."

"I tell you I'm not goin' with you. Quit pesterin' me."

His devil-may-care laugh trod on the heels of her refusal. He guessed shrewdly that circumstances were driving her to him. The girl was full of resentment at her father's harsh treatment of her. Her starved heart craved love. She was daughter of that Clanton who led the feud against the Roush family and its adherents. Dave took his life in his hands every time he crossed the river to meet her. Once he had swum the stream in the night to keep an appointment. He knew that his wildness, his reckless courage and contempt of danger, argued potently for him. She was coming to him as reluctantly and surely as a wild turkey answers the call of the hunter.

The sound of a shot, not distant, startled them. He crouched, wary as a rattlesnake about to strike. The rifle seemed almost to leap forward.

10

Prologue

A girl sat on the mossy river-bank in the dappled, golden sunlight. Frowning eyes fixed on a sweeping eddy, she watched without seeing the racing current. Her slim, supple body, crouched and tense, was motionless, but her soul seethed tumultuously. In the bosom of her coarse linsey gown lay hidden a note. Through it destiny called her to the tragic hour of decision.

The foliage of the young pawpaws stirred behind her. Furtively a pair of black eyes peered forth and searched the opposite bank of the stream, the thicket of rhododendrons above, the blooming laurels below. Very stealthily a handsome head pushed out through the leaves.

" 'Lindy," a voice whispered.

The girl gave a start, slowly turned her head. She looked at the owner of the voice from steady, deep-lidded eyes. The pulse in her brown throat began to beat. One might have guessed her with entire justice a sullen lass, untutored of life, passionate, and high-spirited, resentful of all restraint. Hers was such beauty as lies in rich blood beneath dark col-

7

oring, in dusky hair and eyes, in the soft, warm contours of youth. Already she was slenderly full, an elemental daughter of Eve, primitive as one of her fur-clad ancestors. No forest fawn could have been more sensuous or innocent than she.

Again the man's glance swept the landscape cautiously before he moved out from cover. In the country of the Clantons there was always an open season on any one of his name.

"What are you doin' here, Dave Roush?" the girl demanded. "Are you crazy?"

"I'm here because you are, 'Lindy Clanton," he answered promptly. "That's a right good reason, ain't it?"

The pink splashed into her cheeks like spilled wine.

"You'd better go. If dad saw you — "

He laughed hardily. "There'd be one less Roush — or one less Clanton," he finished for her.

Dave Roush was a large, well-shouldered man, impressive in spite of his homespun. If he carried himself with a swagger there was no lack of boldness in him to back it. His long hair was straight and black and coarse, a derivative from the Indian strain in his blood.

"Git my note?" he asked.

She nodded sullenly.

8

ARIZONA GUNS

WILLIAM MacLEOD RAINE

ARIZONA GUNS

Thorndike Press • Thorndike, Maine

Library of Congress Cataloging in Publication Data:

Raine, William MacLeod, 1871-1954.
Arizona guns / William MacLeod Raine.
  p. cm.
ISBN 1-56054-215-2 (alk. paper : lg. print)
1. Large type books. I. Title.
[PS3535.S385A87   1992]   91-19459
813'.52—dc20   CIP

Thorndike Press Large Print edition published in 1992
by arrangement with Houghton Mifflin Company.

Cover design by Harry Swanson.

The tree indicium is a trademark of Thorndike Press.

This book is printed on acid-free, high opacity paper.

"Hit's Bud — my brother Jimmie." She pushed him back toward the pawpaws. "Quick! Burn the wind!"

"What about to-night? Will you come?"

"Hurry. I tell you hit's Bud. Are you lookin' for trouble?"

He stopped stubbornly at the edge of the thicket. "I ain't runnin' away from it. I put a question to ye. When I git my answer mebbe I'll go. But I don't 'low to leave till then."

"I'll meet ye there if I kin git out. Now go," she begged.

The man vanished in the pawpaws. He moved as silently as one of his Indian ancestors.

'Lindy waited, breathless lest her brother should catch sight of him. She knew that if Jimmie saw Roush there would be shooting and one or the other would fall.

A rifle shot rang out scarce a hundred yards from her. The heart of the girl stood still. After what seemed an interminable time there came to her the sound of a care-free whistle. Presently her brother sauntered into view, a dead squirrel in his hand. The tails of several others bulged from the game bag by his side. The sister did not need to be told that four out of five had been shot through the head.

"Thought I heard voices. Was some one with you, sis?" the boy asked.

11

"Who'd be with me here?" she countered lazily.

A second time she was finding refuge in the forget-me-nots.

He was a barefoot little fellow, slim and hard as a nail. In his hand he carried an old-fashioned rifle almost as long as himself. There was a lingering look of childishness in his tanned, boyish face. His hands and feet were small and shapely as those of a girl. About him hung the stolid imperturbability of the Southern mountaineer. Times were when his blue eyes melted to tenderness or mirth; yet again the cunning of the jungle narrowed them to slits hard as jade. Already, at the age of fourteen, he had been shot at from ambush, had wounded a Roush at long range, had taken part in a pitched battle. The law of the feud was tempering his heart to implacability.

The keen gaze of the boy rested on her. Ever since word had reached the Clantons of how 'Lindy had "carried on" with Dave Roush at the dance on Lonesome her people had watched her suspiciously. The thing she had done had been a violation of the hill code and old Clay Clanton had thrashed her with a cowhide till she begged for mercy. Jimmie had come home from the still to find her writhing in passionate revolt. The boy had been furious at his father; yet had admitted the substantial justice of the punishment. Its wisdom he doubted. For he knew his sister to be stubborn as old Clay himself, and he feared lest they drive her to the arms of Bad Dave Roush.

"I reckon you was talkin' to yo'self, mebbe," he suggested.

"I reckon."

They walked home together along a path through the rhododendrons. The long, slender legs of the girl moved rhythmically and her arms swung like pendulums. Life in the open had given her the litheness and the grace of a woodland creature. The mountain woman is cheated of her youth almost before she has learned to enjoy it. But 'Lindy was still under eighteen. Her warm vitality still denied the coming of a day when she would be a sallow, angular snuff-chewer.

Within sight of the log cabin the girl lingered for a moment by the sassafras bushes near the spring. Some deep craving for sympathy moved her to alien speech. She turned upon him with an imperious, fierce tenderness in her eyes.

"You'll never forgit me, Bud? No matter what happens, you'll — you'll not hate me?"

Her unusual emotion embarrassed and a

little alarmed him. "Oh, shucks! They ain't anything goin' to happen, sis. What's ailin' you?"

"But if anything does. You'll not hate me — you'll remember I allus thought a heap of you, Jimmie?" she insisted.

"Doggone it, if you're still thinkin' of that scalawag Dave Roush — " He broke off, moved by some touch of prescient tragedy in her young face. " 'Course I ain't ever a-goin' to forgit you none, sis. Hit ain't likely, is it?"

It was a comfort to him afterward to recall that he submitted to her impulsive caress without any visible irritability.

'Lindy busied herself preparing supper for her father and brother. Ever since her mother died when the child was eleven she had been the family housekeeper.

At dusk Clay Clanton came in and stood his rifle in a corner of the room. His daughter recognized ill-humor in the grim eyes of the old man. He was of a tall, gaunt figure, strongly built, a notable fighter with his fists in the brawling days before he "got religion" at a camp meeting. Now his Calvinism was of the sternest. Dancing he held to be of the devil. Card-playing was a sin. If he still drank freely, his drinking was within bounds. But he did not let his piety interfere with the feud. Within the year, pillar of the church though

14

he was, he had been carried home riddled with bullets. Of the four men who had way-laid him two had been buried next day and a third had kept his bed for months.

He ate for a time in dour silence before he turned harshly on 'Lindy.

"You ain't havin' no truck with Dave Roush are you? Not meetin' up with him on the sly?" he demanded, his deep-set eyes full of menace under the heavy, grizzled brows.

"No, I ain't," retorted the girl, and her voice was sullen and defiant.

"See you don't, lessen yo' want me to tickle yore back with the bud again. I don't allow to put up with no foolishness." He turned in ex-planation to the boy. "Brad Nickson seen him this side of the river to-day. He says this ain't the fustest time Roush has been seen hangin' 'round the cove."

The boy's wooden face betrayed nothing. He did not look at his sister. But suspicions began to troop through his mind. He thought again of the voices he had heard by the river and he remembered that it had become a habit of the girl to disappear for hours in the after-noon.

'Lindy went to her room early. She nursed against her father not only resentment, but a strong feeling of injustice. He would not let her attend the frolics of the neighborhood be-

15

cause of his scruples against dancing. Yet she had heard him tell how he used to dance till daybreak when he was a young man. What right had he to cut her off from the things that made life tolerable?

She was the heritor of lawless, self-willed, passionate ancestors. Their turbulent blood beat in her veins. All the safeguards that should have hedged her were gone. A wise mother, an understanding father, could have saved her from the tragedy waiting to engulf her. But she had neither of these. Instead, her father's inhibitions pushed her toward that doom to which she was moving blindfold.

Before her cracked mirror the girl dressed herself bravely in her cheap best. She had no joy in the thing she was going to do. Of her love she was not sure and of her lover very unsure. A bell of warning rang faintly in her heart as she waited for the hours to slip away.

A very little would have turned the tide. But she nursed her anger against her father, fed her resentment with the memory of all his wrongs to her. When at last she crept through the window to the dark porch trellised with wild cucumbers, she persuaded herself that she was going only to tell Dave Roush that she would not join him.

Her heart beat fast with excitement and dread. Poor, undisciplined daughter of the hills though she was, a rumor of the future whispered in her ears and weighted her bosom.

Quietly she stole past the sassafras brake to the big laurel. Her lover took her instantly into his arms and kissed the soft mouth again and again. She tried to put him from her, to protest that she was not going with him. But before his ardor her resolution melted. As always, when he was with her, his influence was paramount.

"The boat is under that clump of bushes," he whispered.

"Oh, Dave, I'm not goin'," she murmured.

"Then I'll go straight to the house an' have it out with the old man," he answered.

His voice rang gay with the triumph of victory. He did not intend to let her hesitations rob him of it.

"Some other night," she promised. "Not now — I don't want to go now. I — I'm not ready."

"There's no time like to-night, honey. My brother came with me in the boat. We've got horses waitin' — an' the preacher came ten miles to do the job."

Then, with the wisdom born of many flirtations, he dropped argument and wooed her ardently. The anchors that held the girl to safety dragged. The tug of sex, her desire of

17

love and ignorance of life, his eager and passionate demand that she trust him: all these swelled the tide that beat against her prudence.

She caught his coat lapels tightly in her clenched fists.

"If I go I'll be givin' up everything in the world for you, Dave Roush. My folks'll hate me. They'd never speak to me again. You'll be good to me. You won't cast it up to me that I ran away with you. You'll — you'll — " Her voice broke and she gulped down a little sob.

He laughed. She could not see his face in the darkness, but the sound of his laughter was not reassuring. He should have met her appeal seriously.

The girl drew back.

He sensed at once his mistake. "Good to you!" he cried. " 'Lindy, I'm a-goin' to be the best ever."

"I ain't got ary mother, Dave." Again she choked in her throat. "You wouldn't take advantage of me, would you?"

He protested hotly. Desiring only to be convinced, 'Lindy took one last precaution.

"Swear you'll do right by me always."

He swore it.

She put her hand in his and he led her to the boat.

Ranse Roush was at the oars. Before he

18

had taken a dozen strokes a wave of terror swept over her. She was leaving behind forever that quiet, sunny cove where she had been brought up. The girl began to shiver against the arm of her lover. She heard again the sound of his low, triumphant laughter.

It was too late to turn back now. No hysterical request to be put back on her side of the river would move these men. Instinctively she knew that. From to-night she was to be a Roush.

They found horses tied to saplings in a small cove close to the river. The party mounted and rode into the hills. Except for the ring of the horses' hoofs there was no sound for miles. 'Lindy was the first to speak.

"Ain't this Quicksand Creek?" she asked of her lover as they forded a stream.

He nodded. "The sands are right below us — not more'n seven or eight steps down here Cal Henson was sucked under."

After another stretch ridden in silence they turned up a little cove to a light shining in a cabin window. The brothers alighted and Dave helped the girl down. He pushed open the door and led the way inside.

A man sat by the fireside with his feet on the table. He was reading a newspaper. A jug of whiskey and a glass were within reach of his hand. Without troubling to remove his boots

19

from the table, he looked up with a leer at the trembling girl.

Dave spoke at once. "We'll git it over with. The sooner the quicker."

'Lindy's heart was drenched with dread. She shrank from the three pairs of eyes focused upon her as if they had belonged to wolves. She had hoped that the preacher might prove a benevolent old man, but this man with the heavy thatch of unkempt, red hair and furtive eyes set askew offered no comfort. If there had been a single friend of her family present, if there had been any woman at all! If she could even be sure of the man she was about to marry!

It seemed to her that the preacher was sneering when he put the questions to which she answered quaveringly. Vaguely she felt the presence of some cruel, sinister jest of which she was the sport.

After the ceremony had been finished the three men drank together while she sat white-faced before the fire. When at last Ranse Roush and the red-headed preacher left the cabin, both of them were under the influence of liquor. Dave had drunk freely himself.

'Lindy would have given her hopes of heaven to be back safely in the little mud-daubed bedroom she had called her own.

Three days later 'Lindy wakened to find a

broad ribbon of sunshine across the floor of the cabin. Her husband had not come home at all the night before. She shivered with self-pity and dressed slowly. Already she knew that her life had gone to wreck, that it would be impossible to live with Dave Roush and hold her self-respect.

But she had cut herself off from retreat. All of her friends belonged to the Clanton faction and they would not want to have anything to do with her. She had no home now but this, no refuge against the neglect and insults of this man with whom she had elected to go through life. To her mind came the verdict of old Nance Cunningham on the imprudent marriage of another girl: " 'Randy's done made her bed; I reckon she's got to lie on it."

A voice hailed the cabin from outside. She went to the door. Ranse Roush and the red-haired preacher had ridden into the clearing and were dismounting. They had with them a led horse.

"Fix up some breakfast," ordered Ranse.

The young wife flushed. She resented his tone and his manner. Like Dave, he too assumed that she had come to be a drudge for the whole drunken clan, a creature to be sneered at and despised.

Silently she cooked a meal for the men. The girl was past tears. She had wept herself out.

While they ate the men told of her father's fury when he had discovered the elopement, of how he had gone down to the mill and cast her off with a father's curse, renouncing all relationship with her forever. It was a jest that held for them a great savor. They made sport of him and of the other Clantons till she could keep still no longer.

"I won't stand this! I don't have to! Where's Dave?" she demanded, eyes flashing with contempt and anger.

Ranse grinned, then turned to his companion with simulated perplexity. "Where is Dave, Brother Hugh?"

"Damfino," replied the red-headed man, and the girl could see that he was gloating over her. "Last night he was at a dance on God-Forgotten Crick. Dave's soft on a widow up there, you know."

The color ebbed from the face of the wife. One of her hands clutched at the back of a chair till the knuckles stood out white and bloodless. Her eyes fastened with a growing horror upon those of the red-headed man. She had come to the edge of an awful discovery.

"You're no preacher. Who are you?"

"Me?" His smile was cruel as death. "You done guessed it, sister. I'm Hugh Roush — Dave's brother."

"An' — an' — my marriage was all a lie?"

22

"Did ye think Dave Roush would marry a Clanton? He's a bad lot, Dave is, but he ain't come that low yet."

For the first and last time in her life 'Lindy fainted.

Presently she floated back to consciousness and the despair of a soul mortally stricken. She saw it all now. The lies of Dave Roush had enticed her into a trap. He had been working for revenge against the family he hated, especially against brave old Clay Clanton who had killed two of his kin within the year. With the craft inherited from savage ancestors he had sent a wound more deadly than any rifle bullet could carry. The Clantons were proud folks, and he had dragged their pride in the mud.

If the two brothers expected her to make a scene, they were disappointed. Numb with the shock of the blow, she made no outcry and no reproach.

"Git a move on ye, gal," ordered Ranse after he had finished eating. "You're goin' with us, so you better hurry."

"What are you goin' to do with me?" she asked dully.

"Why, Dave don't want you any more. We're goin' to send you home."

"I reckon yore folks will kill the fatted calf for you," jeered Hugh Roush. "They tell me you always been mighty high-heeled, 'Lindy

23

Clanton. Mebbe you won't hold yore head so high now."

The girl rode between them down from the hills. Who knows into what an agony of fear and remorse and black despair she fell? She could not go home a cast-off, a soiled creature to be scorned and pointed at. She dared not meet her father. It would be impossible to look her little brother Jimmie in the face. Would they believe the story she told? And if they were convinced of its truth, what difference would that make? She was what she was, no matter how she had become so.

On the pike they met old Nance Cunningham returning from the mill with a sack of meal. The story of that meeting was one the old gossip told after the tragedy to many an eager circle of listeners.

"She jes' lifted her han' an' stopped me, an' if death was ever writ on a human face it shorely wuz stomped on hers. 'I want you to tell my father I'm sorry,' she sez. 'He swore he'd marry me inside of an hour. This man hyer — his brother — made out like he wuz a preacher an' married us. Tell my father that an' ask him to forgive me if he can.' That wuz all she said. Ranse Roush hit her horse with a switch an' sez, 'Yo' kin tell him all that yore own self soon as you git home.' I reckon I wuz the lastest person she spoke to alive."

24

They left the old woman staring after them with her mouth open. It could have been only a few minutes later that they reached Quicksand Creek.

'Lindy pulled up her horse to let the men precede her through the ford. They splashed into the shallows on the other side of the creek and waited for her to join them. Instead, she slipped from the saddle, ran down the bank, and plunged into the quicksand.

"Goddlemighty!" shrieked Ranse. "She's a-drownin' herself in the sands."

They spurred their horses back across the creek and ran to rescue the girl. But she had flung herself forward face down far out of their reach. They dared not venture into the quivering bog after her. While they still stared in a frozen horror, the tragedy was completed. The victim of their revenge had disappeared beneath the surface of the morass.

Chapter I

"Call Me Jimmie-Go-Get-'Em"

The boy had spent the night at a water-hole in a little draw near the foot of the mesa. He had supped on cold rations and slept in his blanket without the comfort of glowing piñon knots. For yesterday he had cut Indian signs and after dark had seen the shadow of Apache camp-fires reflected in the clouds.

After eating he swung to the bare back of his pony and climbed to the summit of the butte. His trained eyes searched the plains. A big bunch of antelope was trailing down to water almost within rifle-shot. But he was not looking for game.

He sniffed the smoke from the pits where the renegades were roasting mescal and judged the distance to the Apache camp at close to ten miles. His gaze swept toward the sunrise horizon and rested upon a cloud of dust. That probably meant a big herd of cattle crossing to the Pecos Valley on the Chisum Trail that led to Fort Stanton. The riders were likely just throwing the beeves from the bedground to

26

the trail. The boy waited to make sure of their line of travel.

Presently he spoke aloud, after the fashion of the plainsman who spends much time alone in the saddle. "Looks like they'll throw off to-night close to the 'Pache camp. If they do hell's a-goin' to pop just before sunup to-morrow. I reckon I'll ride over and warn the outfit."

From a trapper the boy had learned that a band of Mescalero Apaches had left the reservation three weeks before, crossed into Mexico, gone plundering down the Pecos, and was now heading back toward the Staked Plains. Evidently the drover did not know this, since he was moving his cattle directly toward the Indian camp.

The young fellow let his cowpony pick its way down the steep shale hill to the draw. He saddled without a wasted motion, packed his supplies deftly, mounted, and was off. In the way he cut across the desert toward the moving herd was the certainty of the frontiersman. He did not hurry, but he wasted no time. His horse circled in and out among the sand dunes, now topped a hill, now followed a wash. Every foot of the devious trail was the most economical possible.

At the end of nearly an hour's travel he pulled up, threw down his bridle reins, and studied the ground carefully. He had cut Indian sign. What he saw would have escaped the notice of a tenderfoot, and if it had been pointed out to him none but an expert trailer would have understood its significance. Yet certain facts were printed here on the desert for this boy as plainly as if they had been stenciled on a guide-post. He knew that within forty-eight hours a band of about twenty Mescalero bucks had returned to camp this way from an antelope hunt and that they carried with them half a dozen pronghorns. It was a safe guess that they were part of the large camp the smoke of which he had seen.

Long before the young man struck the drive, he knew he was close by the cloud of dust and the bawling of the cattle. His course across country had been so accurate that he hit the herd at the point without deflecting.

An old Texan drew up, changed his weight on the saddle to rest himself, and hailed the youngster.

"Goin' somewheres, kid, or just ridin'?" he asked genially.

"Just takin' my hawss out for a jaunt so's he won't get hog-fat," grinned the boy.

The Texan chewed tobacco placidly and eyed the cowpony. The horse had been ridden so far that he was a bag of bones.

"Looks some gaunted," he commented.

"Four Bits is so thin he won't throw a shadow," admitted the boy.

"Come a right smart distance, I reckon?"

"You done said it."

"Where you headin' for?"

"For Deaf Smith County. I got an uncle there. Saw your dust an' dropped over to tell you that a big bunch of 'Paches are camped just ahead of you."

The older man looked at him keenly. "How do you know, son?"

"Smelt their smoke an' cut their trail."

"Know Injuns, do you?"

"I trailed with Al Sieber 'most two years."

To have served with Sieber for any length of time was a certificate of efficiency. He was the ablest scout in the United States Army. Through his skill and energy Geronimo and his war braves were later forced to give themselves up to the troops.

" 'Nuff said. Are these 'Paches liable to make us any trouble?"

"Yes, sir. I think they are. They're a bunch of broncos from the reservation an' they have been across the line stealin' horses an' murderin' settlers. They will sure try to stampede your cattle an' run off a lot of 'em."

"Hmp! You better go back an' see old man Webb about it. What's yore name, kid?"

For just an eye-beat the boy hesitated. "Call

29

me Jim Thursday."

A glimmer of a smile rested in the eyes of the Texan. He was willing to bet that this young fellow would not have given him that name if to-day had not happened to be the fifth day of the week. But it was all one to the cowpuncher. To question a man too closely about his former residence and manner of life was not good form on the frontier.

"I'll call you Jim from Sunday to Saturday," he said, pulling a tobacco pouch from his hip pocket. "My name is Wrayburn — Dad Wrayburn, the boys call me."

The Texan shouted to the man riding second on the swing. "Oh, you, Billie Prince!"

A tanned, good-looking young fellow cantered up.

"Meet Jimmie Thursday, Billie," the old-timer said by way of introduction. "This boy says there's heap many Injuns on the war-path right ahead of us. I reckon I'll let you take the point while I ride back with him an' put it up to the old man."

The "old man" turned out to be a short, heavy-set Missourian who had served in the Union Army and won a commission by intelligence and courage. Wherever the name of Homer Webb was known it stood for integrity and square-dealing. His word was as good as a signed bond.

30

Webb had come out of the war without a cent, but with a very definite purpose. During the last year of the Confederacy, while it was tottering to its fall, he had served in Texas. The cattle on the range had for years been running wild, the owners and herdsmen being absent with the Southern army. They had multiplied prodigiously, so that many thousands of mavericks roamed without brand, the property of any one who would round them up and put an iron on their flanks. The money value of them was very little. A standard price for a yearling was a plug of tobacco. But Webb looked to the future. He hired two riders, gathered together a small remuda of culls, and went into the cattle business with energy. To-day the Flying V Y was stamped on forty thousand longhorns.

The foreman of the Flying V Y was riding with the owner of the brand at the drag end of the herd. He was a hard-faced citizen known as Joe Yankie. When Wrayburn had finished his story, the foreman showed a row of tobacco-stained teeth in an unpleasant grin.

"Same old stuff, Dad. There always is a bunch of bucks off the reservation an' they're always just goin' to run our cattle away. If you ask me there's nothin' to it."

Young Thursday flushed. "If you'll ride out with me I'll show you their trail."

31

Yankie looked at him with a sneer. He guessed this boy to be about eighteen. There was a suggestion of effeminacy about the lad's small, well-shaped hands and feet. He was a slender, smooth-faced youth with mild blue eyes. It occurred to Webb, too, that the stranger might have imagined the Apaches. But in his motions was something of the lithe grace of the puma. It was part of the business of the cattleman to judge men and he was not convinced that this young fellow was as inoffensive as he looked.

"Where you from?" asked the drover.

"From the San Carlos Agency."

"Ever meet a man named Micky Free out there?"

"I've slept under the same tarp with him many's the time when we were followin' Chiricahua 'Paches. He's the biggest daredevil that ever forked a horse."

"Describe him."

"Micky's face is a map of Ireland. He's got only one eye; a buck punched the other out when he was a kid. His hair is red an' he wears it long."

"Any beard?"

"A bristly little red mustache."

"That's Micky to a T." Webb made up his mind swiftly. "The boy's all right, Yankie. He'll do to take along."

"It's your outfit. Suits me if he does you." The foreman turned insolently to the newcomer. "What'd you say your name was, sissie?"

The eyes of the boy, behind narrowed lids, grew hard as steel.

"Call me Jimmie-Go-Get-'Em," he drawled in a soft voice, every syllable distinct.

There was a moment of chill silence. A swift surprise had flared into the eyes of the foreman. The last thing in the world he had expected was to have his bad temper resented so promptly by this smooth-faced little chap. Since Yankie was the camp bully he bristled up to protect his reputation.

"Better not get on the prod with me, young fellow me lad. I'm liable to muss up your hair. Me, I'm from the Strip, where folks grow man-size."

The youngster smiled, but there was no mirth in that thin-lipped smile. He knew, as all men did, that the Cherokee Strip was the home of desperadoes and man-killers. The refuse of the country, driven out by the law of more settled communities, found here a refuge from punishment. But if the announcement of the foreman impressed him, he gave no sign of it.

"Why didn't you stay there?" he asked with bland innocence.

Yankie grew apoplectic. He did not care to discuss the reasons why he had first gone to the Strip or the reasons why he had come away. This girl-faced boy was the only person who had asked for a bill of particulars. Moreover, the foreman did not know whether the question had been put in child-like ignorance of any possible offense or with an impudent purpose to enrage him.

"Don't run on the rope when I'm holdin' it, kid," he advised roughly. "You're liable to get thrown hard."

"And then again I'm liable not to," lisped the youth from Arizona gently.

The bully looked the slim newcomer over again, and as he looked there rang inside him some tocsin of warning. Thursday sat crouched in the saddle, wary as a rattlesnake ready to strike. A sawed-off shotgun lay under his leg within reach of his hand, the butt of a six-gun was even closer to those smooth, girlish fingers. In the immobility of his figure and the steadiness of the blue eyes was a deadly menace.

Yankie was no coward. He would go through if he had to. But there was still time to draw back if he chose. He was not exactly afraid; on the other hand, he did not feel at all easy.

He contrived a casual, careless laugh. "All

right, kid. I don't have to rob the cradle to fill my private graveyard. Go get your Injuns. It will be all right with me."

Webb drew a breath of relief. There was to be no gunplay after all. He had had his own reasons for not interfering sooner, but he knew that the situation had just grazed red tragedy.

"I'm goin' to take the boy's advice," he announced to Yankie. "Ride forward an' swing the herd toward that big red butte. We'll give our Mescalero friends a wide berth if we can."

The foreman hung in the saddle a moment before he turned to go. He had to save his face from a public backdown. "Bet you a week's pay there's nothin' to it, Webb."

"Hope you're right, Joe," his employer answered.

As soon as Yankie had cantered away, Dad Wrayburn, ex-Confederate trooper, slapped his hand on his thigh and let out a modulated rebel yell.

"Dad burn my hide, Jimmie-Go-Get-'Em, you're all right. Fustest time I ever saw Joe take water, but he shorely did splash some this here occasion. I wouldn't 'a' missed it for a bunch of hog-fat yearlin's."

Webb had not been sorry to see his arrogant foreman brought up with a sharp turn, but in the interest of discipline he did not care to say so.

"Why can't you boys get along peaceable with Joe, I'd like to know? This snortin' an' pawin' up the ground don't get you anything."

"I reckon Joe does most of the snortin' that's done," Wrayburn answered dryly. "I ain't had any trouble with him, because he spends a heap of time lettin' me alone. But there's no manner of doubt that Joe rides the boys too hard."

The drover dismissed the subject and turned to Thursday.

"Want a job?"

"Mebbe so."

"I need another man. Since you sabe the ways of the 'Paches I can use you to scout ahead for us."

"What you payin'?"

"Fifty a month."

"You've hired a hand."

"Good enough. Better pick one of the boys to ride with you while you are out scoutin'."

"I'll take Billie Prince," decided the new rider at once.

"You know Billie?"

"Never saw him before to-day. But I like his looks. He's a man to tie to."

"You're right he is."

The drover looked at his new employee with a question in his shrewd eyes. The boy was either a man out of a thousand or he was a first-class bluffer. He claimed to have cut Indian sign and to know exactly what was written there. At a single glance he had sized up Prince and knew him for a reliable side partner. Without any bluster he had served notice on Yankie that it would be dangerous to pick on him as the butt of his ill-temper.

In those days, on the Pecos, law lay in a holster on a man's thigh. The individual was a force only so far as his personality impressed itself upon his fellows. If he made claims he must be prepared to back them to a fighting finish.

Was this young Thursday a false alarm? Or was he a good man to let alone when one was looking for trouble? Webb could not be sure yet, though he made a shrewd guess. But he knew it would not be long before he found out.

Chapter II

Shoot-a-Buck Cañon

Webb sent for Billie Prince.

"Seems there's a bunch of bronco 'Paches camped ahead of us, Billie. Thursday here trailed with Sieber. I want you an' him to scout in front of us an' see we don't run into any ambush. You're under his orders, y' understand."

Prince was a man of few words. He nodded.

"You know the horses that the boys claim. Well, take Thursday to the remuda an' help him pick a mount from the extras in place of that broomtail he's ridin'," continued the drover. "Look alive now. I don't want my cattle stampeded because we haven't got sense enough to protect 'em. No 'Paches can touch a hoof of my stock if I can help it."

"If they attack at all it will probably be just before daybreak, but it is just as well to be ready for 'em," suggested Thursday.

"I brought along some old Sharps an' some Spencers. I reckon I'll have 'em loaded an' distribute 'em among the boys. Billie, tell

38

Yankie to have that done. The rifles are racked up in the calf wagon."

Billie delivered the orders of the drover to the foreman as they passed on their way to the remuda. Joe gave a snort of derision, but let it go at that. When Homer Webb was with one of his trail outfits he was always its boss.

While Thursday watched him, Prince roped out a cinnamon horse from the remuda. The cowpuncher was a long-bodied man, smooth-muscled and lithe. The boy had liked his level eye and his clean, brown jaw before, just as now he approved the swift economy of his motions.

Probably Billie was about twenty years of age, but in that country men ripened young. Both of these lads had been brought up in that rough-and-ready school of life which holds open session every day of the year. Both had already given proofs of their ability to look out for themselves in emergency. A wise, cool head rested on each of these pairs of young shoulders. In this connection it is worth mentioning that the West's most famous outlaw, Billie the Kid, a killer with twenty-one notches on his gun, had just reached his majority when he met his death some years later at the hands of Pat Garrett.

The new rider for the Flying V Y outfit did not accept the judgment of Prince without confirming it. He examined the hoofs of the horse and felt its legs carefully. He looked well to its ears to make sure that ticks from the mesquite had not infected the silky inner flesh.

"A good bronc, looks like," he commented.

"One of the fastest in the remuda — not very gentle, though."

Thursday picked the witches' bridles from its mane before he saddled. As his foot found the stirrup the cinnamon rose into the air, humped its back, and came down with all four legs stiff. The quirt burned its flank, and the animal went up again to whirl round in the air. The boy stuck to the saddle and let out a joyous whoop. The battle was on.

Suddenly as it had begun the contest ended. With the unreasoning impulse of the half-broken cowpony the cinnamon subsided to gentle obedience.

The two riders cantered across the prairie in the direction of the Indian camp. That the Apaches were still there Thursday thought altogether likely, for he knew that it takes a week to make mescal. No doubt the raiders had stopped to hold a jamboree over the success of their outbreak.

The scouts from the cattle herd deflected toward a butte that pushed out as a salient into the plain. From its crest they could get a sweeping view of the valley.

"There's a gulch back of it that leads to old man Roubideau's place," explained Prince. "Last time we were on this Pecos drive the boss stopped an' bought a bunch of three-year-olds from him. He's got a daughter that's sure a pippin, old man Roubideau has. Shoot, ride, rope — that girl's got a lot of these alleged bullwhackers beat a mile at any one of 'em."

Thursday did not answer. He had left the saddle and was examining the ground carefully. Billie joined him. In the soft sand of the wash were tracks of horses' hoofs. Patiently the trailer followed them foot by foot to the point where they left the dry creek-bed and swung up the broken bank to a swale.

"Probably Roubideau and his son Jean after strays," suggested Prince.

"No. Notice this track here, how it's broken off at the edge. When I cut Indian sign yesterday, this was one of those I saw."

"Then these are 'Paches too?"

"Yes."

"Goin' to the Roubideau place." The voice of Billie was low and husky. His brown young face had been stricken gray. Bleak fear lay in the gray eyes. Hi companion knew he was thinking of the girl. "How many of 'em do you make out?"

41

"Six or seven. Not sure which."

"How old?"

"They passed here not an hour since."

It was as if a light of hope had been lit in the face of the young man. "Mebbe there's time to help yet. Kid, I'm goin' in."

Jim Thursday made no reply, unless it was one to vault to the saddle and put his horse to the gallop. They rode side by side, silently and alertly, rifles across the saddle-horns in their hands. The boy from Arizona looked at his new friend with an increase of respect. This was, of course, a piece of magnificent folly. What could two boys do against half a dozen wily savages? But it was the sort of madness that he loved. His soul went out in a gush of warm, boyish admiration to Billie Prince. It was the beginning of a friendship that was to endure, in spite of rivalry and division and misunderstanding, through many turbid years of trouble. This was no affair of theirs. Webb had sent them out to protect the cattle drive. They were neglecting his business for the sake of an adventure that might very well mean the death of both of them. But it was characteristic of Thursday that it never even occurred to him to let Prince take the chance alone. Even in the days to come, when his name was anathema in the land, nobody ever charged that he would not go through with a comrade.

There drifted to them presently the faint sound of a shot. It was followed by a second and a third.

"The fight's on," cried Thursday.

Billie's quirt stung the flank of his pony. Near the entrance to the cañon his companion caught up with him. From the rock walls of the gulch came to them booming echoes of rifles in action.

"Roubideau must be standin' 'em off," shouted Prince.

"Can we take the 'Paches by surprise? Is there any other way into the cañon?"

"Don't know. Can't stop to find out. I'm goin' straight up the road."

The younger man offered no protest. It might well be that the ranchman was in desperate case and in need of immediate help to save his family. Anyhow, the decision was out of his hands.

The horses pounded forward and swept round a curve of the gulch into sight of the ranch. In a semicircle, crouched behind the shelter of boulders and cottonwoods, the Indian line stretched across the gorge and along one wall. The buildings lay in a little valley, where an arroyo ran down at a right angle and broke the rock escarpment. A spurt of smoke came from a window of the stable as the rescuers galloped into view.

One of the Apaches caught sight of them and gave a guttural shout of warning. His gun jumped to the shoulder and simultaneously the bullet was on its way. But no living man could throw a shot quicker than Jim Thursday, if the stories still told of him around camp-fires are true. Now he did not wait to take sight, but fired from his hip. The Indian rose, half-turned, and fell forward across the boulder, his naked body shining in the sun. By a hundredth part of a second the white boy had outspeeded him.

The riders flung themselves from their horses and ran for cover.

The very audacity of their attack had its effect. The Indians guessed these two were the advance guard of a larger party which had caught them in a trap. Between two fires, with one line of retreat cut off, the bronco Apaches wasted no time in deliberation. They made a rush for their horses, mounted, and flew headlong toward the arroyo, their bodies lying low on the backs of the ponies.

The Indians rode superbly, their bare, sinewy legs gripping even to the moccasined feet the sides of the ponies. Without saddle or bridle, except for the simple nose rope, they guided their mounts surely, the brown bodies rising and falling in perfect accord with the motion of the horses.

A shot from the stable hit one as he galloped past. While his horse was splashing through the creek the Mescalero slid slowly down, head first, into the brawling water.

Billie took a long, steady aim and fired. A horse stumbled and went down, flinging the rider over its head. With a "Yip — Yip!" of triumph Thursday drew a bead on the man as he rose and dodged forward. Just as the boy fired a sharp pain stung his foot. One of the escaping natives had wounded him.

The dismounted man ran forward a few steps and pulled himself to the back of a pony already carrying one rider. Something in the man's gait and costume struck Prince.

"That fellow's no Injun," he called to his friend.

"Look!" Thursday was pointing to the saddleback between two peaks at the head of the arroyo.

A girl on horseback had just come over the summit and stood silhouetted against the sky. Even in that moment while they watched her she realized for the first time her danger. She turned to fly, and she and her horse disappeared down the opposite slope. The Mescaleros swept up the hill toward her.

"They'll git her! They'll sure git her!" cried Billie, making for his horse.

45

The younger man ran limping to his cinnamon. At every step he winced, and again while his weight rested on the wounded foot as he dragged himself to the saddle. A dozen yards behind his companion he sent his horse splashing through the creek.

The cowponies, used to the heavy going in the hills, took the slope in short, quick plunges. Neither of the young men used the spur, for the chase might develop into a long one with stamina the deciding factor. The mesquite was heavy and the hill steep, but presently they struck a cattle run which led to the divide.

Two of the Apaches stopped at the summit for a shot at their pursuers, but neither of the young men wasted powder in answer. They knew that close-range work would prove far more deadly and that only a chance hit could serve them now.

From Billie, who had reached the crest first, came a cry of dismay. His partner, a moment later, knew the reason for it. One of the Apaches, racing across the valley below, was almost at the heels of the girl.

The cowpunchers flung their ponies down the sharp incline recklessly. The animals were sure-footed as mountain goats. Otherwise they could never have reached the valley right side up. It was a stretch of broken shale with much loose rubble. The soft sandstone farther along had eroded and there was a great deal of slack débris down which the horses slipped and slid, now on their haunches and again on all fours.

The valley stretched for a mile before them and terminated at a rock wall into which, no doubt, one or more cañons cut like sword clefts. The cowpunchers had picked mounts, but it was plain they could not overhaul the Apaches before the Indians captured the girl.

Billie, even while galloping at full speed, began a long-distance fire upon the enemy. One of the Mescaleros had caught the bridle of the young woman's horse and was stopping the animal. It looked for a moment as if the raiders were going to make a stand, but presently their purpose became clear to those in pursuit. The one that Billie had picked for a renegade white dropped from the horse upon which he was riding double and swung up behind the captive. The huddle of men and ponies opened up and was in motion again toward the head of the valley.

But though the transfer had been rapid, it had taken time. The pursuers, thundering across the valley, had gained fast. Rifles barked back and forth angrily.

The Indians swerved sharply to the left for the mouth of a cañon. Here they pulled up to check the cowboys, who slid from their saddles to use their ponies for protection.

"That gorge to the right is called Escondido Cañon," explained Prince. "We combed it for cattle last year. About three miles up it runs into the one where the 'Paches are. Don't remember the name of that one."

"I'll give it a new name," answered the boy. He raised his rifle, rested it across the back of his pony, and took careful aim. An Indian plunged from his horse. "Shoot-a-Buck Cañon — how'll that do for a name?" inquired Thursday with a grin.

Prince let out a whoop. "You got him right. He'll never smile again. Shoot-a-Buck Cañon goes."

The Indians evidently held a hurried consultation and changed their minds about holding the gorge against such deadly shooting as this.

"They're gun-shy," announced Thursday. "They don't like the way we fog 'em and they're goin' to hit the trail, Billie."

After one more shot Prince made the mistake of leaving the shelter of his horse too soon. He swung astride and found the stirrup. A puff of smoke came from the entrance to the gulch. Billie turned to his friend with a puzzled, sickly smile on his face. "They got me, kid."

"Bad?"

The cowboy began to sag in the saddle. His friend helped him to the ground. The wound was in the thigh.

"I'll tie it up for you an' you'll be good as new," promised his friend.

The older man looked toward the gorge. No Indians were in sight.

"I can wait, but that little girl in the hands of those devils can't. Are you game to play a lone hand, kid?" he asked.

"I reckon."

"Then ride hell-for-leather up Escondido. It's shorter than the way they took. Where the gulches come together be waitin' an' git 'em from the brush. There's just one slim chance you'll make it an' come back alive."

The boy's eyes were shining. "Suits me fine. I'll go earn that name I christened myself — Jimmie-Go-Get-'Em."

Billie, his face twisted with pain, watched the youngster disappear at a breakneck gallop into Escondido.

Chapter III

Ranse Roush Pays

Jim Thursday knew that his sole chance of success lay in reaching the fork of the cañons before the Indians. So far he had been lucky. Three Apaches had gone to their happy hunting ground, and though both he and Billie were wounded, his hurt at least did not interfere with accurate rifle-fire. But it was not reasonable to expect such good fortune to hold. In the party he was pursuing were four men, all of them used to warfare in the open. Unless he could take them at a disadvantage he could not by any possibility defeat them and rescue their captive.

His cinnamon pony took the rising ground at a steady gallop. Its stride did not falter, though its breathing was labored. Occasionally the rider touched its flank with the sharp rowel of a spur. The boy was a lover of horses. He had ridden too many dry desert stretches, had too often kept night watch over a sleeping herd, not to care for the faithful and efficient animal that served him and was a companion

50

to his loneliness. Like many plainsmen he made of his mount a friend.

But he dared not spare his pony now. He must ride the heart out of the gallant brute for the sake of that life he had come to save. And while he urged it on, his hand patted the sweat-stained neck and his low voice sympathized.

"You've got to go to it, old fellow, if it kills you," he said aloud. "We got to save that girl for Billie, ain't we? We can't let those red devils take her away, can we?"

It was a rough cattle trail he followed, strewn here with boulders and there tilted down at breakneck angle of slippery shale. Sometimes it fell abruptly into washes and more than once rose so sharply that a heather cat could scarce have clambered up. But Thursday flung his horse recklessly at the path, taking chances of a fall that might end the mad race. He could not wait to pick a way. His one hope lay in speed, in reaching the fork before the enemy. He sacrificed everything to that.

From the top of a sharp pitch he looked down into the twin cañon of Escondido. A sharp bend cut off the view to the left, so that he could see for only seventy-five or a hundred yards. But his glance followed the gulch up for half a mile and found no sign of life. He was in time.

Swiftly he made his preparations. First he led the exhausted horse back to a clump of young cottonwoods and tied it safely. From its place beside the saddle he took the muley gun and with the rifle in his other hand he limped swiftly back to the trail. Every step was torture, but he could not stop to think of that now. His quick eye picked a perfect spot for an ambush where a great rock leaned against another at the edge of the bluff. Between the two was a narrow opening through which he could command the bend in the trail below. To enlarge this he scooped out the dirt with his fingers then reloaded the rifle and thrust it into the crevice. The sawed-off shotgun lay close to his hand.

Till now he had found no time to get nervous, but as the minutes passed he began to tremble violently and to whimper. In spite of his experience he was only a boy and until today had never killed a man.

"Doggone it, if I ain't done gone an' got buck fever," he reproached himself. "I reckon it's because Billie Prince ain't here that I'm so scairt. I wisht I had a drink, so as I'd be right when the old muley gun gits to barkin'."

A faint sound, almost indistinguishable, echoed up the gulch to him. Miraculously his nervousness vanished. Every nerve was keyed up, every muscle tense, but he was cool as water in a mountain stream.

The sound repeated itself, a faint tinkle of gravel rolling from a trail beneath the hoof of a horse. At the last moment Thursday changed his mind and substituted the shotgun for the rifle.

"Old muley she spatters all over the State of Texas. I might git two at once," he muttered.

The light, distant murmur of voices reached him. His trained ear told him just how far away the speakers were.

An Apache rounded the bend, a tall, slender young brave wearing only a low-cut breech-cloth and a pair of moccasins. Around his waist was strapped a belt full of cartridges and from it projected the handle of a long Mexican knife. The brown body of the youth was lithe and graceful as that of a panther. He was smiling over his shoulder at the next rider in line, a heavy-set, squat figure on a round-bellied pinto. That smile was to go out presently like the flame of a blown candle. A third Mescalero followed. Like that of the others, his coarse, black hair fell to the shoulders, free except for a band that encircled the forehead.

Still the boy did not fire. He waited till the last of the party appeared, a man in fringed buckskin breeches and hickory shirt riding pillion behind a young woman. Both of these were white.

The sawed-off gun of Thursday covered the second rider carefully. Before the sound of the shot boomed down the gorge the Apache was lifted from the bare back of the pony. The heavy charge of buckshot had riddled him through and through.

Instantly the slim, young brave in the lead dug his heels into the flank of his pony, swung low to the far side so that only a leg was visible, and flew arrow-straight up the cañon for safety. Thursday let him go.

Twice his rifle rang out. At that distance it was impossible for a good shot to miss. One bullet passed through the head of the third Mescalero. The other brought down the pony upon which the whites were riding.

The fall of the horse flung the girl free, but the foot of her captor was caught between the saddle and the ground. Thursday drew a bead on him while he lay there helpless, but some impulse of mercy held his hand. The man was that creature accursed in the border land, a renegade who has turned his face against his own race and must to prove his sincerity to the tribe out-Apache an Apache at cruelty. Still, he was white after all — and Jim Thursday was only eighteen.

Rifle in hand the boy clambered down the

jagged rock wall to the dry river-bed below. The foot of his high-heeled boot was soggy with blood, but for the present he had to ignore the pain messages that throbbed to his brain. The business on hand would not wait.

While Thursday was still slipping down from one outcropping ledge of rock to another, a plunge of the wounded horse freed the regenade. The man scrambled to his feet and ran shakily for the shelter of a boulder. In his hurry to reach cover he did not stop to get the rifle that had been flung a few yards from him when he fell.

The boy caught one glimpse of that evil, fear-racked face. The blood flushed his veins with a surge of triumph. He was filled with the savage, primitive exultation of the head-hunter. For four years he had slept on the trail of this man and had at last found him. The scout had fought the Apaches impersonally, without rancor, because a call had come to him that he could not ignore. But now the lust of blood was on him. He had become that cold, implacable thing known throughout the West as a "killer."

The merciless caution that dictates the methods of a killer animated his movements now. Across the gulch, nearly one hundred and fifty yards from him, the renegade lay crouched. A hunched shoulder was just visible.

Thursday edged carefully along the ledge. He felt for holds with his hand and feet, for not once did his gaze lift from that patch of hickory shirt. The eyes of the boy had narrowed to slits of deadly light. He was wary as a hungry wolf and as dangerous. That the girl had disappeared around the bend he did not know. His brain functioned for just one purpose — to get the enemy with whom he had come at last to grips.

As the boy crept along the rock face for a better view of his victim, the minutes fled. Five of them — ten — a quarter of an hour passed. The renegade lay motionless. Perhaps he hoped that his location was unknown.

The man-hunter on the ledge flung a bullet against the protecting boulder. His laugh of cruel derision drifted across the cañon.

"Run to earth at last, Ranse Roush!" he shouted, "I swore I'd camp on your trail till I got you — you an' the rest of yore poison tribe."

From the trapped wretch quavered back a protest.

"Goddlemighty, I ain't done nothin' to you-all. Lemme explain."

"Before you do any explainin' mebbe you'd better guess who it is that's goin' to send yore cowardly soul to hell inside of five minutes."

"If you're some kin to that gal on the hawss with me, why, I'll tell you the honest-to-God truth. I was aimin' to save her from the 'Paches when I got a chanct. Come on down an' let's we-uns talk it over reasonable."

The boy laughed again, but there was something very far from mirth in the sound of that chill laughter. "If you won't guess I'll have to tell you. Ever hear of the Clantons, Ranse Roush? I'm one of 'em. Now you know what chance you got to talk yoreself out of this thing."

"I — I'm glad to meet up with you-all. I got to admit that the Roush clan is dirt mean. Tha's why I broke away from 'em. Tha's why I come out here. You Clantons is all right. I never did go in for this bushwhackin' with Dave an' Hugh. I never — "

"You're a born liar like the rest of yore wolf tribe. You come out here because the country got too hot to hold you after what you did to 'Lindy Clanton. I might 'a' knowed I'd find you with the 'Paches. You allus was low-mixed Injun." The boy had fallen into the hill vernacular to which he had been born. He was once more a tribal feudist of the border land.

"I swear I hadn't a thing to do with that," the man cried eagerly. "You shore done got that wrong. Dave an' Hugh done that. They're a bad lot. When I found out about

57

'Lindy Clanton I quarreled with 'em an' we-all split up company. Tha's the way of it."

"You're ce'tainly in bad luck then," the boy shouted back tauntingly. "For I aim to stomp you out like I would a copperhead." Very distinctly he added his explanation. "I'm 'Lindy Clanton's brother."

Roush begged for his life. He groveled in the dust. He promised to reform, to leave the country, to do anything that was asked of him.

"Go ahead. It's meat an' drink to me to hear a Roush whine. I got all day to this job, but I aim to do it thorough," jeered Clanton.

A bullet flattened itself against the rock wall ten feet below the boy. In despair the man was shooting wildly with his revolver. He knew there was no use in pleading, that his day of judgment had come.

Young Clanton laughed in mockery. "Try again, Roush. You ain't quite got the range."

The man made a bolt for the bend in the cañon a hundred yards away. Instantly the rifle leaped to the shoulder of the boy.

"Right in front of you, Roush," he prophesied.

The bullet kicked up the dust at the feet of the running man. The nerve of Roush failed him and he took cover again behind a scrub live-oak. A memory had flashed to him of the day when he had seen a thirteen-year-old boy named Jim Clanton win a turkey shoot against the best marksmen of the hill country.

The army Colt spit out once more at the boy on the ledge. Before the echo had died away the boom of an explosion filled the cañon. Roush pitched forward on his face.

Jim Clanton lowered his rifle with an exclamation. His face was a picture of amazement. Some one had stolen his vengeance from him by a hair's breadth.

Two men came round the bend on horseback. Behind them rode a girl. She was mounted on the barebacked pinto of the Indian Clanton had killed with the shotgun.

The boy clambered down to the bed of the gulch and limped toward them. The color had ebbed from his lips. At every step a pain shot through his leg. But in spite of his growing weakness anger blazed in the light-blue eyes.

"I waited four years to git him. I kept the trail hot from Tucson to Vegas an' back to Santone. An' now, doggone it, when my finger was on the trigger an' the coyote as good as dead, you cut in an' shoot the daylights out of him. By gum, it ain't fair!"

The older man looked at him in astonishment. "But he iss only a child, Polly! Cela me passe!"

"Mebbe I am only a kid," the boy retorted

resentfully. "But I reckon I'm man enough to handle any Roush that ever lived. I wasn't askin' for help from you-uns that I heerd tell of."

The younger man laughed. He was six or seven years older than the girl, who could not have been more than seventeen. Both of them bore a marked likeness to the middle-aged man who had spoken. Jim guessed that this was the Roubideau family of whom Billie Prince had told him.

"Just out of the cradle, by Christmas, and he's killed four 'Paches inside of an hour an' treed a renegade to boot," said young Roubideau. "I'd call it a day's work, kid, for it sure beats all records ever I knew hung up by one man."

The admiration of the young rancher was patent. He could not take his eyes from the youthful phenomenon.

"He's wounded, father," the girl said in a low voice.

The boy looked at her and his anger died away. "Billie sent me up the gulch when he was shot. He 'lowed it was up to me to git you back from those devils, seein' as he couldn't go himself."

Polly nodded. She seemed to be the kind of girl that understands without being told in detail.

Before Thursday could protect himself, Roubideau, senior, had seized him in his arms, embraced him, and kissed first one cheek and then the other. "Eh bien! But you are the brave boy! I count it honor to know you. My little Polly, have you not save her? Ah! But I forget the introductions. Myself, I am Pierre Roubideau, à tout propos at your service. My son Jean. Pauline — what you call our babie."

"My real name is Jim Clanton," answered the boy. "I've been passin' by that of 'Thursday' so that none of the Roush outfit would know I was in the country till I met up face to face with 'em."

"Clanton! It iss a name we shall remember in our prayers, n'est-ce pas, Polly?" Pierre choked up and wrung fervently the hand of the youngster.

Clanton was both embarrassed and wary. He did not know at what moment Roubideau would disgrace him by attempting another embrace. There was something in the Frenchman's eye that told of an emotion not yet expended fully.

"Oh, shucks; you make a heap of fuss about nothin'," he grumbled. "Didn't I tell you it was Billie Prince sent me? An' say, I got a pill in my foot. Kindness of one of them dadgummed Mescaleros. I hate to walk on that laig. I wish yore boy would go up on the bluff an' look after my horse. I 'most rode it to death, I reckon, comin' up the cañon. An' there's a sawed-off shotgun. He'll find it . . . "

For a few moments the ground had been going up and down in waves before the eyes of the boy. Now he clutched at a stirrup leather for support, but his fingers could not seem to find it. Before he could steady himself the bed of the dry creek rose up and hit him in the head.

Chapter IV

Pauline Roubideau Says "Thank You"

Jimmie Clanton slid back from unconsciousness to a world the center of which was a girl sitting on a rock with his rifle across her knees. The picture did not at first associate itself with any previous experience. She was a brown, slim young thing in a calico print that fitted snugly the soft lines of her immature figure. The boy watched her shyly and wondered at the quiet self-reliance of her. She was keeping guard over him, and there was about her a cool vigilance that went oddly with the small, piquant face and the tumbled mass of curly chestnut hair that had fallen in a cascade across her shoulders.

"Where are yore folks?" he asked presently.

She turned her head slowly and looked at him. Southern suns had sprinkled beneath her eyes a myriad of powdered freckles. She met his gaze fairly, with a boyish directness and candor.

"Jean has ridden out to tell your friends about you and Mr. Prince. Father has gone back to the house to fix up a travois to carry you."

"Sho! I can ride."

"There's no need of it. You must have lost a great deal of blood."

He looked down at his foot and saw that the boot had been cut away. A bandage of calico had been tied around the wound. He guessed that the girl had sacrificed part of a skirt.

"And you stayed here to see the 'Paches didn't play with me whilst yore father was gone," he told her.

"There wasn't any danger, of course. The only one that escaped is miles away from here. But we didn't like to leave you alone."

"That's right good of you."

Her soft, brown eyes met his again. They poured upon him the gift of passionate gratitude she could not put into words. It was from something much more horrible than death that he had snatched her. One moment she had been a creature crushed, leaden despair in her heart. Then the miracle had flashed down from the sky. She was free, astride the pinto, galloping for home.

"Yes, you owe us much." There was a note of light sarcasm in her clear, young voice, but the feeling in her heart swept it away in an emotional rush of words from the tongue of her father. "Vous avez pris le fait et cause pour moi. Sans vous j'étais perdu."

"You're French," he said.

"My father is, not my mother. She was from Tennessee."

"I'm from the South, too."

"You didn't need to tell me that," she answered with a little smile.

"Oh, I'm a Westerner now, but you ought to have heerd me talk when I first came out." He broached a grievance. "Say, will you tell yore dad not to do that again? I'm no kid."

"Do what?"

"You know." The red flamed into his face. "If it got out among the boys what he'd done, I'd never hear the last of it."

"You mean kissed you?"

"Sure I do. That ain't no way to treat a fellow. I'm past eighteen if I am small for my age. Nobody can pull the pat-you-on-the-head-sonny stuff on me."

"But you don't understand. That isn't it at all. My father is French. That makes all the difference. When he kissed you it meant — oh, that he honored and esteemed you because you fought for me."

"I been tellin' you right along that Billie Prince is to blame. Let him go an' kiss Billie an' see if he'll stand for it."

A flash of roguishness brought out an unexpected dimple near the corner of her insubordinate mouth. "We'll be good, all of us, and never do it again. Cross our hearts."

Young Clanton reddened beneath the tan. Without looking at her he felt the look she tilted sideways at him from under the long, curved lashes. Of course she was laughing at him. He knew that much, even though he lacked the experience to meet her in kind. Oddly enough, there pricked through his embarrassment a delicious little tingle of delight. So long as she took him in as a partner of her gayety she might make as much fun of him as she pleased.

But the owlish dignity of his age would not let him drop the subject without further explanation. "It's all right for yore dad to mush you. I reckon a girl kinder runs to kisses an' such doggoned foolishness. But a man's different. He don't go in for it."

"Oh, doesn't he?" asked Polly demurely. She did not think it necessary to mention that every unmarried man who came to the ranch wanted to make love to her before he left. "I'm glad you told me, because I'm only a girl and I don't know much about it. And since you're a man, of course you know."

"That's the way it is," he assured her, solemn as a pouter.

She bit her lip to keep from laughing out, but on the heels of her mirth came a swift reproach. In his knowledge of life he might be a boy, but in one way at least he had proved himself a man. He had taken his life in his hands and ridden to save her without a second thought. He had fought a good fight, one that would be a story worth telling when she had become an old woman with grandchildren at her knee.

"Does your foot hurt you much?" she asked gently.

"It sort o' keeps my memory jogged up. It's a kind of forget-me-not souvenir, for a good boy, compliments of a Mescalero buck, name unknown, probably now permanently retired from his business of raisin' Cain. But it might be a heap worse. They would've been glad to collect our scalps if it hadn't been onconvenient, I expect."

"Yes," she agreed gravely.

He sat up abruptly. "Say, what about Billie? I left him wounded outside. Did yore folks find him?"

"Yes. It seems the Apaches trapped them in the stable. They roped horses and came straight for the cañon. They found Mr. Prince, but they had no time to stop then. Father is looking after him now. He said he was going to take him to the house in the buckboard."

"Is he badly hurt?"

"Jean thinks he will be all right. Mr. Prince told him it was only a flesh wound, but the muscles were so paralyzed he couldn't get around."

"The bullet did not strike an artery, then?"

"My brother seemed to think not."

"I reckon there's no doctor near."

Her eye twinkled. "Not very near. Our nearest neighbor lives on the Pecos one hundred and seventeen miles away. But my father is as good as a doctor any day of the week."

"Likely you don't borrow coffee next door when you run out of it onexpected. But don't you get lonesome?"

"Haven't time," she told him cheerfully. "Besides, somebody going through stops off every three or four months. Then we learn all the news."

Jimmie glanced at her shyly and looked

quickly away. This girl was not like any woman he had known. Most of them were drab creatures with the spirit washed out of them. His sister had been an exception. She had had plenty of vitality, good looks and pride, but the somber shadow of her environment had not made for gayety. It was different with Pauline Roubideau. Though she had just escaped from terrible danger, laughter bubbled up in her soft throat, mirth rippled over her mobile little face. She expressed herself with swift, impulsive gestures at times. Then again she suggested an inheritance of slow grace from the Southland of her mother.

He did not understand the contradictions of her and they worried him a little. Billie had told him that she could rope and shoot as well as any man. He had seen for himself that she was an expert rider. Her nerves were good enough to sit beside him at quiet ease within a stone's throw of three sprawling bodies from which she had seen the lusty life driven scarce a half-hour since. Already he divined the boyish *camaraderie* that was so simple and direct an expression of good-will. And yet there was something about her queer little smile he could not make out. It hinted that she was really old enough to be his mother, that she was heiress of wisdom handed down by her sex through all the generations. As yet he had not found out that he was only a boy and she was a woman.

Chapter V

No Four-Flusher

Pauline Roubideau knew the frontier code. She evinced no curiosity about the past of this boy-man who had come into her life at the nick of time. None the less she was eager to know what connection lay between him and the renegade her brother had killed. She had heard Jim Clanton say that he had waited four years for his revenge and had followed the man all over the West. Why? What motive could be powerful enough with a boy of four-teen to sway so completely his whole life to-ward vengeance?

She set herself to find out without asking. Inside of ten minutes the secret which had been locked so long in his warped soul had been confided to her. The boy broke down when he told her the story of his sister's death. He was greatly ashamed of himself for his emotion, but the touch of her warm sympathy melted the ice in his heart and set him sobbing.

Quickly she came across to him and knelt down by his side.

"You poor boy! You poor, poor boy!" she murmured.

Her arm crept round his shoulders with the infinitely tender caress of the mother that lies, dormant or awake, in all good women.

"I — I — I'm nothing but a baby," he gulped, trying desperately to master his sobs.

"Don't talk foolishness," she scolded to comfort him. "I wouldn't think much of you if you didn't love your sister enough to cry for her."

There were tears in her own eyes. Her lively young imagination pictured vividly the desolation of the young hill girl betrayed so cruelly, the swift decline of her stern, broken-hearted father. The thought of the half-grown boy following the betrayers of his sister across the continent, his life dedicated for years to vengeance, was a dreadful thing to contemplate. It shocked her sense of all that was fitting. No doubt his mission had become a religion with him. He had lain down at night with that single purpose before him. He had risen with it in the morning. It had been his companion throughout the day. From one season to another he had cherished it when he

70

should have been filled with the happy, healthy play impulses natural to his age.

The boy told the story of that man-hunt without a suspicion that there was anything in it to outrage the feelings of the girl.

"If it hadn't been for old Nance Cunningham, I reckon Devil Dave an' his brothers would have fixed up some cock an' bull story about how 'Lindy was drowned by accident. But folks heard Nance an' then wouldn't believe a word they said. Dad swore us Clantons to wipe out the whole clan of 'em. Every last man in the hills that was decent got to cussin' the Roush outfit. Their own friends turned their backs on all three. Then the sheriff come up from the settlemint an' they jest naturally lit out.

"I heerd tell they were in Arizona an' after dad died I took after 'em. But seemed like I had no luck. When I struck their trail they had always just gone. To-day I got Ranse — leastways I would 'a' got him if yore brother hadn't interfered. I'll meet up with the others one o' these times. I'll git 'em too."

He spoke with quiet conviction, as if it were a business matter that had to be looked after.

"Did you ever hear this: 'Vengeance is mine; I will repay, saith the Lord'?"

He nodded. "Dad used to read that to me. There's a heap in the Bible about killin' yore

71

enemies. Dad said that vengeance verse meant that we-all was the Lord's deputies, like a sheriff has folks to help him, an' we was certainly to repay the Roushes an' not to forgit interest neither."

The girl shook her head vigorously. "I don't think that's what it means at all. If you'll read the verses above and below, you'll see it doesn't. We're to feed our enemies when they are hungry. We're to do them good for evil."

"That's all right for common, every-day enemies, but the Roush clan ain't that kind," explained the boy stubbornly. "It shore is laid on me to destroy 'em root an' branch, like the Bible says."

By the way he wagged his head he might have been a wise little old man. The savage philosophy of the boy had been drawn in with his mother's milk. It had been talked by his elders while as a child he drowsed before the big fireplace on winter nights. After his sister's tragic death it had been driven home by Bible texts and by a solemn oath of vengeance. Was it likely that anything she could say would have weight with him? For the present the girl gave up her resolve to convert him to a more Christian point of view.

The sun had sunk behind the cañon wall when Pierre Roubideau arrived with a travois which he had hastily built. There was no wagon-road up the gulch and it would have been difficult to get the buckboard in as far as the fork over the broken terrain. As a voyageur of the North he had often seen wounded men carried by the Indians in travois across the plains. He knew, too, that the tribes of the Southwest use them. This one was constructed of two sixteen-foot poles with a canvas lashed from one bar to the other. The horse was harnessed between the ends of the shafts, the other ends dragging on the ground.

Clanton looked at this device distastefully. "I'm no squaw. Whyfor can't I climb on its back an' ride?"

"Because you are seeck. It iss of the importance that you do not exert yourself. Voyons! You will be comfortable here. N'est-ce pas, Polly?" Pierre gesticulated as he explained volubly. He even illustrated the comfort by lying down in the travois himself and giving a dramatic representation of sleep.

The young man grumbled, but gave way reluctantly.

"How's Billie Prince?" he asked presently from the cot where he lay.

"He will hafe a fever, but soon he will be well again. I, Pierre, promise it. For he iss of a good strength and sound as a dollar."

Pauline, rifle in hand, scouted ahead of the travois and picked the smoothest way down the rough ravine. The horse that Roubideau drove was an old and patient one. Its master held it to a slow, even pace, so that the wounded boy was jolted as little as possible. When they had reached the entrance to the gorge, travel across the valley became less bumpy.

The young girl walked as if she loved it. The fine, free swing of the hill woman was in her step. She breasted the slope with the light grace of a forest faun. Presently she dropped back to a place beside the conveyance and smiled encouragement at him.

"Pretty bad, is it?"

He grinned back. "It's up to me to play the hand I've been dealt."

That he was in a good deal of pain was easy to guess.

"We're past the worst of it," Pauline told him. "Up this hill — down the other side — and then we're home."

The bawling of thirsty cattle and the blatting of calves could be heard now.

"It iss that Monsieur Webb has taken my advice to drive the herd up the cañon and into the park for the night," explained Roubideau. "There iss one way in, one way out. Guard the entrances and the 'Paches cannot stampede the cattle. Voilà!"

From the hill-top the leaders of the herd could be seen drinking at the creek. Cattle behind were pushing forward to get at the water, while the riders on the point and at the swing were directing the movement of the beeves, now checking the steady pressure from the rear and now hastening the pace of those dawdling in the stream. To add to the confusion cows were mooing loudly for their off-spring not yet unloaded from the calf wagon.

Near the summit Jean with the buckboard met the party from the cañon. He helped Clanton to the seat and drove to the house.

Webb cantered up. "What's this I hear about you, Jimmie-Go-Get-'Em? They tell me you've made four good Injuns to-day, shot up a renegade, rescued this young lady here, 'most rode one of my horses to death, an' got stove up in the foot yore own self. It certainly must have been yore busy afternoon."

The drover looked at him with a new respect. He had found the answer to the question he had put himself a few hours earlier. This boy was no four-flusher. He not only knew how and when to shoot, was game as a bulldog, and keen as a weasel; he possessed, too, that sixth sense so necessary to a gunfighter, the instinct which shows him how to take advantage of every factor in the situation so as to come through safely.

"I didn't do it all," answered Clanton, flushing. "Billie helped, and the Roubideaus got two of 'em."

"That's not the way Billie tells it. Anyhow, you-all made a great gather between you. Six 'Paches that will never smile again ought to give the raiders a pain."

"Don't you think we'd better get him to bed?" said Pauline gently.

"You're shoutin', ma'am," agreed Webb. "Roubideau, the little boss says Jimmie-Go-Get-'Em is to be put ιο bed. I'll tote him in if you'll give my boys directions about throwin' the herd into yore park and loose-herdin' 'em there."

The Missourian picked up the wounded boy and followed Pauline into the house. She led the way to her own little bedroom. It was the most comfortable in the house and that was the one she wanted Jim Clanton to have.

Chapter VI

Billie Asks a Question

Roubideau rounded up next day his beef stock and sold two hundred head to the drover. During the second day the riders were busy putting the road brand on the cattle just bought.

"Don't bust yore suspenders on this job, boys," Webb told his men. "I'd just as lief lie up here for a few days while Uncle Sam is roundin' up his pets camped out there. Old man Roubideau says we're welcome to stick around. The feed's good. Our cattle are some gaunted with the drive. It won't hurt a mite to let 'em stay right here a spell."

But on the third day came news that induced the Missourian to change his mind. Jean, who had been out as a scout, returned with the information that a company of cavalry had come down from the fort and that the Apaches had hastily decamped for parts unknown.

"I reckon we'll throw into the trail again tomorrow, Joe," the drover told Yankie. "No use wastin' time here if we don't have to stay.

We'll mosey along toward the river. Kinder take it easy an' drift the herd down slow so as to let the cattle put on flesh. Billie an' the kid can join us soon as they're fit to travel."

The decision was announced on the porch of the Roubideau house. Its owner and his daughter were present. So was Dad Wrayburn. The Texan old-timer snorted as he rolled a cigarette.

"Hm! Soft thing those two boys have got sittin' around an' bein' petted by Miss Polly here. I've a notion to go an' bust my laig too. Will you nurse me real tender, ma'am, if I get stove up pullin' off a grand-stand play like they done?"

"The hospital is full. We haven't got room for more invalids, Mr. Wrayburn," laughed the girl.

"Well, you let me know when there's a vacancy, Miss Polly. My sister gave me a book to read onct. It was 'most twenty years ago. The name of it was 'Ivanhoe.' I told her I would save it to read when I broke my laig. Looks like I never will git that book read."

By daybreak the outfit was on the move. Yankie trailed the cattle out to the plain and started them forward leisurely. Webb had allowed himself plenty of time for the drive. The date set for delivery at the fort was still distant and he wanted the beeves to be in first-class condition for inspection. To reach the Pecos he was allowing three weeks, a programme that would let him bed the herd down early and would permit of drifting it slowly to graze for an hour or two a day.

The weeks that followed were red-letter ones in the life of Jim Clanton. They gave him his first glimpse of a family life which had for its basis not only affection, but trust and understanding. He had never before seen a household that really enjoyed little jokes shared in common, whose members were full of kind consideration the one for the other. The Roubideaus had more than a touch of the French temperament. They took life gayly and whimsically, and though they poked all kinds of fun at each other there was never any sting to their wit.

Pauline was a famous little nurse. It was not long before she was offering herself as a crutch to help young Clanton limp to the sunny porch. Two or three days later Billie joined his fellow invalid. From where they sat the two young men could hear the girl as she went about her work singing. Often she came out with a plate of hot, new-baked cookies for them and a pitcher of milk. Or she would dance out without any excuse except that of her own frank interest in the youth she shared with her patients.

One of the Roubideau jokes was that Polly was the mother of the family and her father and Jean two mischievous little boys she had to scold and pet alternately. Temporarily she took the two cowpunchers into her circle and browbeat them shamefully with an impudent little twinkle in her eyes. Whatever the state of Billie's mind may have been before, there can be no doubt that now he was fathoms deep in love. With hungry eyes he took in her laughter and raillery, her boyish high spirits, the sweet tenderness of the girl for her father. He loved her wholly — the charm of her comradeship, of her swift, generous impulses, of that touch of coquetry she could not entirely subdue.

Pierre had been a chasseur in the Franco-Prussian War. His daughter was very proud of it, but one of her games was to mock him fondly by swaggering back and forth while she sang:

"Allons, enfants de la patrie,
Le jour de gloire est arrivé."

When she came to the chorus, nothing would do but all of them must join. She taught the words and tune to Prince and Jimmie so that they could fall into line behind the old soldier and his son:

"Aux armes, citoyens! formez vos bataillons!
Marchons! Marchons!
Qu'un sang impur abreuve nos sillons."

It always began in pretended derision, but as she swept her little company down the porch all the gallant, imperishable soul of France spoke in her ringing voice and the flash of her brown eyes. Surely her patriotism was no less sound because the blood of Alsace and that of Tennessee were fused in her ardent veins.

The wounds of the young men healed rapidly, and both of them foresaw that the day of their departure could no longer be postponed. Neither of them was yet in condition to walk very far, but on horseback they were fit to travel carefully.

"We got all the time there is. No need of pushin' on the reins, but I reckon the old man isn't payin' us fifty dollars a month to hold down the Roubideau porch," said Prince regretfully.

"No, we gotta light a shuck," admitted Jim, with no noticeable alacrity. He was in no hurry to leave himself, even if he did not happen to be in love.

Billie put his fortune to the touch while he was out with Polly rounding up some calves. They were riding knee to knee in the dust of the drag through a small arroyo.

The cowpuncher swallowed once or twice in a dry throat and blurted out, "I got something to tell you before I go, Polly."

The girl flashed a look at him. She recognized the symptoms. Her gaze went back to the wave-like motion of the backs of the moving yearlings.

"Don't, Billie," she said gently.

Before he spoke again he thought over her advice. He knew he had his answer. But he had to go through with it now.

"I reckoned it would be that way. I'm nothin' but a rough vaquero. Whyfor should you like me?"

"Oh, but I do!" she cried impulsively. "I like you a great deal. You're one of the best men I know — brave and good and modest. It isn't that, Billie."

"Is there — some one else? Or oughtn't I to ask that?"

"No, there's nobody else. I'm awfully glad you like me. The girl that gets you will be lucky. But I don't care about men that way. I want to stay with dad and Jean."

"Mebbe some day you may feel different about it."

"Mebbe I will," she agreed. "Anyhow, I want you to stay friends with me. You will, won't you?"

"Sure. I'll be there just as long as you want me for a friend," he said simply.

She gave him her little gauntleted hand. They were close to a bend in the draw. Soon they would be within sight of the house.

"I'd say 'Yes' if I could, Billie. I'd rather it would be you than anybody else. You won't feel bad, will you?"

"Oh, that's all right." He smiled, and there was something about the pluck of the eyes in the lean, tanned face that touched her. "I'm goin' to keep right on carin' for my little pal even if I can't get what I want."

She had not yet fully emerged from her childhood. There was in her a strong desire to comfort him somehow, to show by a mark of special favor how high she held him in her esteem.

"Would you — would you like to kiss me?" she asked simply.

He felt a clamor of the blood and subdued it before he answered. It was in accord with the charm she held for him that her frank generosity enhanced his respect for her. If she gave a royal gift it was out of the truth of her heart.

Without need of words she read acceptance in his eyes and leaned toward him in the saddle. Their lips met.

"You're the first — except dad and

Jean," she told him.

The feeling in his primitive heart he could not have analyzed. He did not know that his soul was moved to some such consecration as that of a young knight taking his vow of service, though he was aware that all the good in him leaped to instant response in her presence, that by some strange spiritual alchemy he had passed through a refining process.

"I'm comin' back to see you some day. Mebbe you'll feel different then," he said.

"I might," she admitted.

They rounded the bend. Clanton, on horseback, caught sight of them. He waved his hat and cantered forward.

"Say, Billie, how much bacon do you reckon we need to take with us?"

In front of the house Pauline slipped from her horse and left them discussing the commissary.

Chapter VII

On the Trail

The convalescents rode away into a desert green with spring. The fragrant chaparral thickets were bursting into flower. Spanish bayonets studded the plains. Everywhere about them was the promise of a new life not yet burnt by hot summer suns to a crisp.

During the day they ran into a swamp country and crossed a bayou where cypress knees and blue gums showed fantastic in the eerie gloom of the stagnant water. From this they emerged to a more wooded region and made an early camp on the edge of a grove of ash trees bordering a small stream where pecans grew thick.

Shortly after daybreak they were jogging on at a walk-trot, the road gait of the Southwest, into the treeless country of the prairie. They nooned at an arroyo seco, and after they had eaten took a siesta during the heat of the day. Night brought with it a thunderstorm and they took refuge in a Mexican hut built of palisades and roofed with grass sod. A widow lived alone in the jacal, but she made them welcome to the best she had. The young men slept in a corner of the hut on a dry cowskin spread upon the mud floor, their saddles for pillows and their blankets rolled about them.

While she was cooking their breakfast, Prince noticed the tears rolling down her cheeks. She was a comely young woman and he asked her gallantly in the bronco Spanish of the border if there was anything he could do to relieve her distress.

She shook her head mournfully. "No, señor," she answered in her native tongue. "Only time can do that. I mourn my husband. He was a drunken ne'er-do-well, but he was my man. So I mourn a fitting period. He died in that corner of the room where you slept."

"Indeed! When?" asked Billie politely.

"Ten days ago. Of smallpox."

The young men never ate that breakfast. They fled into the sunlight and put many hurried miles between them and their amazed hostess. At the first stream they stripped, bathed, washed their clothes, dipped the saddles, and lay nude in the warm sand until their wearing apparel was dry.

For many days they joked each other about that headlong flight, but underneath their gayety was a dread which persisted.

"I'm like Doña Isabel with her grief. Only

time can heal me of that scare she threw into Billie Prince," the owner of that name confessed.

"Me too," assented Clanton, helping himself to pinole. "I'll bet I lost a year's growth, and me small at that."

Prince had been in the employ of Webb for three years. During the long hours when they rode side by side he told his companion much about the Flying V Y outfit and its owner.

"He's a straight-up man, Homer Webb is. His word is good all over Texas. He'll sure do to take along," said Billie by way of recommendation.

"And Joe Yankie — does he stack up A 1 too?" asked the boy dryly.

"I never liked Joe. It ain't only that he'll run a sandy on you if he can or that he's always ridin' any one that will stand to be picked on. Joe's sure a bully. But then he's game enough, too, for that matter. I've seen him fight like a pack of catamounts. Outside of that I've got a hunch that he's crooked as a dog's hind leg. Mebbe I'm wrong. I'm tellin' you how he strikes me. If I was Homer Webb, right now when trouble is comin' up with the Snaith-McRobert outfit, I'd feel some dubious about Joe. He's a sulky, revengeful brute, an' the old man has pulled him up with a tight rein more 'n once."

"What do you mean — trouble with the Snaith-McRobert outfit?"

"That's a long story. The bad feelin' started soon after the war when Snaith an' the old man were brandin' mavericks. It kind of smouldered along for a while, then broke out again when both of them began to bid on Government beef contracts. There's been some shootin' back an' forth an' there's liable to be a whole lot more. The Lazy S M — that's the Snaith-McRobert brand — claims the whole Pecos country by priority. The old man ain't recognizin' any such fool title. He's got more'n thirty thousand head of cattle there an' he'll fight for the grass if he has to. O' course there's plenty of room for everybody if it wasn't for the beef contracts an' the general bad feelin'."

"Don't you reckon it will be settled peaceably? They'll get together an' talk it over like reasonable folks."

Billie shook his head. "The Lazy S M are bringin' in a lot of bad men from Texas an' the Strip. Some of our boys ain't exactly gun-shy either. One of these days there's sure goin' to be sudden trouble."

"I'm no gunman," protested Clanton indignantly. "I hired out to the old man to punch cows. Whyfor should I take any chances with the Snaith-McRobert outfit when I ain't got a thing in the world against them?"

"No, you're no gunman," grinned his friend in amiable derision. "Jimmie-Go-Get-'Em is a quiet little Sunday-go-to-meetin' kid. It was kinder by accident that he bumped off four Apaches an' a halfbreed the other day."

"Now don't you blame me for that, Billie. You was hell-bent on goin' into the Roubideau place an' I trailed along. When you got yore pill in the laig you made me ride up the gulch alone. I claim I wasn't to blame for them Mescaleros. I wasn't either."

Prince had made his prophecy about the coming trouble lightly. He could not guess that the most terrible feud in the history of the West was to spring out of the quarrel between Snaith and Webb, a border war so grim and deadly that within three years more than a hundred lusty men were to fall in battle and from assassination. It would have amazed him to know that the bullet which laid low the renegade in Shoot-a-Buck Cañon had set the spark to the evil passions which resulted in what came to be called the Washington County War. Least of all could he tell that the girl-faced boy riding beside him was to become the best-known character of all the desperate ones engaged in the trouble.

Chapter VIII

The Fight

Half a dozen cowboys cantered up the main street of Los Portales in a cloud of dust. One of them, older than the rest, let out the wild yell he had known in the days when he rode with Quantrell's guerrillas on the infamous raids of that bandit. A second flung into the blue sky three rapid revolver shots. Plainly they were advertising the fact that they had come to paint the town red and did not care who knew it.

The riders pulled up abruptly in front of Tolleson's Gaming Palace & Saloon, swung from their horses, and trailed with jingling spurs into that oasis of refreshment. Each of them carried in his hand a rope. The other end of the rawhide was tied to the horn of a saddle.

A heavy-set, bow-legged man led the procession to the bar. He straddled forward with a swagger. The bartender was busy dusting his stock. Before the man had a chance to turn, the butt of a revolver hammered the counter.

90

"Get busy here! Set 'em up, Mike. And jump!" snarled the heavy man.

The barkeeper took one look at him and filed no demurrer. "Bad man" was writ on every line of the sullen, dissipated face of the bully. It was a safe bet that he was used to having his own way, or failing that was ready to fight at the drop of the hat.

Swiftly the drinks were prepared.

"Here's how!"

"How!"

Every glass was tilted and emptied.

It was high noon by the sun and Tolleson's was practically deserted. No devotees sat round the faro, roulette, and keno tables. The dealers were asleep in bed after their labors. So too were the dance girls. The poker rooms upstairs held only the stale odor of tobacco and whiskey. Except for a sleepy Negro roustabout attendant and two young fellows at a table well back from the bar, the cowboys had the big hall all to themselves.

The bar was near the front of the barnlike room and to the right. To the left, along the wall, were small tables. Farther back were those used for gaming. In the rear one corner of the floor held a rostrum with seats for musicians. The center of the hall was kept clear for dancing. Three steps led to a door halfway back on the left-hand side of the building.

They communicated with an outer stairway by means of which one could reach the poker rooms.

The older of the two young men at the table nodded toward the roisterers and murmured information. "Some of the Snaith-McRobert crowd."

His companion was seated with his back to the bar. He had not turned his head to look at those lined up in front of the mirrors for drinks, but a curious change had come over him. The relaxed body had grown rigid. No longer was he lounging against the back of his chair. From his eyes the laughter had been wiped out, as a wet sponge obliterates writing on a slate. All his forces were gathered as if for instant action. He was tense as a coiled spring. His friend noticed that the boy was listening intently, every faculty concentrated at attention.

A man leaning against the other end of the bar was speaking. He had a shock of long red hair and a squint to his eyes.

"Sure you're right. A bunch of Webb's gunmen got Ranse — caught him out alone and riddled him. When Webb drove through here two days ago with a herd, his killers bragged of it. Ask Harsha up at the Buffalo Corral if youse don't believe me. Sure as hell's hot we got to go on the war-path. Here, you

Mike! Set 'em up again."

The boy at the table had drawn back his lips so that the canine teeth stood out like tusks. There was something wolfish about the face, from which all the color had been driven. It expressed something so deadly, so menacing, that the young man across from him felt a shock almost of fear.

"We'd better get out of here," he said, glancing toward the group near the front door.

The other young man did not answer, but he made no move to leave. He was still taking in every syllable of what the drinkers were saying.

The ex-guerrilla was talking. "Tha's sure sayin' something, Hugh. There ain't room in New Mexico for Webb's outfit an' ours too."

"Better go slow, boys," advised another. He was a thick-set man in the late thirties, tight-lipped and heavy-jawed. His eyes were set so close together that it gave him a sinister expression. "Talkin' don't get us anywhere. If we're goin' to sit in a game with Homer Webb an' his punchers we got to play our hand close."

"Buck Sanders, segundo of the Lazy S M ranches," explained again the young man at the table in a low voice. "Say, kid, let's beat it while the goin' is good."

The big bow-legged man answered the foreman. "You're right, Buck. So's Hugh. So's the old rebel. I'm jus' servin' notice that no bunch of shorthorn punchers can kill a brother of mine an' get away with it. Un'erstand? I'll meet up with them some day an' I'll sure fog 'em to a fare-you-well." He interlarded his speech with oaths and foul language."

"I'll bet you do, Dave," chipped in the man next him, who had had a run-in with the Texas Rangers and was on the outskirts of civilization because the Lone Star State did not suit his health. "I would certainly hate to be one of them when yore old six-gun begins to pop. It sure will be Glory-hallelujah for some one."

Dave Roush ordered another drink on the strength of the Texan's admiration. "Mind, I don't say Ranse wasn't a good man. Mebbe I'm a leetle mite better 'n him with a hogleg. Mebbe — "

"Ranse was good with a revolver all right, but sho! you make him look like a plugged nickel when you go to makin' smoke, Dave," interrupted the toady.

"Well, mebbe I do. Say I do. I ain't yet met up with a man can beat me when I'm right. But at that Ranse was a mighty good man.

They bushwhacked him, I'll bet a stack of blues. I aim to git busy soon as I find out who done it."

The red-headed man raised his voice a trifle. "Say, you kid — there at the table — come here an' hold these ropes! See you don't let the hawsses at the other end of 'em git away!"

Slowly the boy turned, pushing his chair round so that he half-faced the group before the bar. He neither rose nor answered.

"Cayn't you-all hear?" demanded the man with the shock of unkempt, red hair.

"I hear, but I'm not comin' right away. When I do, you'll wish I hadn't."

If a bomb had exploded at his feet Hugh Roush could not have been more surprised. He was a big, rough man, muscular and sinewy, and he had been the victor of many a rough-and-tumble fight. On account of his reputation for quarrelsomeness men chose their words carefully when they spoke to him. That this little fellow with the smooth, girlish face and the small, almost womanish hands and feet should defy him was hard to believe.

"Come a'runnin', kid, or I'll whale the life out of you!" he roared.

"You didn't get me right," answered the boy in a low, clear voice. "I'm not comin' till I get ready, Hugh Roush."

The wolf snap of the boy's jaw, the cold glitter in his eyes, might have warned Roush and perhaps did. He wondered too, how this stranger knew his name so well.

"Where are you from?" he demanded.

"From anywhere but here."

"Meanin' that you're here to stay?"

"Meanin' that I'm here to stay."

"Even if I tell you to git out of the country?"

"You won't be alive to tell me unless you talk right sudden."

They watched each other, the man and the boy. Neither as yet made any motion to draw his gun, the younger one because he was not ready, Roush because he did not want to show any premature alarm before the men taking in the scene. Nor could he yet convince himself, in spite of the challenge that rang in the words of the boy, of serious danger from so unlikely a source.

Dave Roush had been watching the boy closely. A likeness to some one whom he could not place stirred faintly his memory.

"Who are you? What's yore name?" he snapped out.

The boy had risen from the chair. His hand rested on his hip as if casually. But Dave had observed the sureness of his motions and he accepted nothing as of chance. The experience of Roush was that a gunman lives longer if he is cautious. His fingers closed on the butt of the revolver at his side.

"My name is James Clanton."

Roush let fall a surprised oath. "It's 'Lindy Clanton you look like! You're her brother — the kid, Jimmie."

"You've guessed it, Devil Dave."

The eyes of the two crossed like rapiers.

"Howcome you here? Whad you want?" asked Roush thickly.

Already he had made up his mind to kill, but he wanted to choose his own moment. The instinct of the killer is always to take his enemy at advantage. Clanton, with that sixth sense which served the fighter, read his purpose as if he had printed it on a sign.

"You know why I'm here — to stomp the life out of you an' yore brother for what you done to my sister. I've listened to yore brags about what you would do when you met up with them that killed Ranse Roush. Fine! Now let's see you make good. I'm the man that ran him down an' put an end to him. Go through, you four-flushin' coward! Come a-shootin' whenever you're ready."

The young Southerner had a definite motive in his jeering. He wanted to drive his enemies to attack him before they could come at him from two sides.

"You — you killed Ranse?"

"You heard me say it once." The eyes of the boy flashed for a moment to the red-headed man. "Whyfor are you dodgin' back of the bar, Hugh Roush? Ain't odds of two to one good enough for you — an' that one only a kid — without you runnin' to cover like the coyote you are? Looks like you'll soon be whinin' for me not to shoot, just like Ranse did."

If any one had cared to notice, the colored roustabout might have been seen at that moment vanishing out of the back door to a zone of safety. He showed no evidence whatever of being sleepy.

The silence that followed the words of the boy was broken by Quantrell's old grayback. Dave Roush was a bad man — a killer. He had three notches on his gun. Perhaps he had killed others before coming West. At any rate, he was no fair match for this undersized boy.

"He's a kid, Dave. You don't want to gun a kid. You, Clanton — whatever you call yourself — light a shuck pronto — git out!"

It is the habit of the killer to look for easy game. Out of the corner of his eye the man who had betrayed 'Lindy Clanton saw that Hugh was edging back of the bar and dragging out his gun. This boy could be killed safely now, since they were two to one, both of them experts with the revolver. To let him escape would be to live in constant danger for the future.

"He's askin' for it, Reb. He's goin' to get it."

Dave Roush pulled his gun, but before he could use it two shots rang out almost simultaneously. The man at the corner of the bar had the advantage. His revolver was in the clear before that of Clanton, but Jim fired from the hip without apparent aim. The bullet was flung from the barrel an imperceptible second before that of Roush. The gunman, hit in the wrist of the right hand, gave a grunt and took shelter back of the bar.

The bystanders scurried for safety while explosion followed explosion. Young Clanton, lightfooted as a cat, side-stepped and danced about as he fired. The first shot of the red-headed man had hit him and the shock of it interfered with his accuracy. Hugh had disappeared, but above the smoke the youngster still saw the cruel face of Devil Dave leering triumphantly at him behind the pumping gun.

The boy kept moving, so that his body did not offer a static target. He concentrated his attention on Dave, throwing shot after shot at him. That he would kill his enemy Clanton never had a doubt. It was firmly fixed in his mind that he had been sent as the appointed executioner of the man.

It was no surprise to Jim when the face of his sister's betrayer lurched forward into the smoke. He heard Roush fall heavily to the floor and saw the weapon hurled out of reach. The fellow lay limp and still.

Clanton did not waste a second look at the fallen man. He knew that the other Roush, crouched behind the bar, had been firing at him through the woodwork. Now a bullet struck the wall back of his head. The red-headed man had fired looking through a knot-hole.

The boy's weapon covered a spot three inches above this. He fired instantly. A splinter flew from a second hole just above the first. Three long, noiseless strides brought Clanton to the end of the bar. The red-headed man lay dead on the floor. The bullet had struck him just above and between the eyes.

"I reckon that ends the job."

It was Jim's voice that said the words, though he hardly recognized it. Overcome by a sudden nausea, he leaned against the bar for support. He felt sick through and through.

Chapter IX

Billie Stands Pat

Clanton came back out of the haze to find his friend's arm around his waist, the sound of his strong, cheerful voice in his ears.

"Steady, old fellow, steady. Where did they hit you, Jim?"

"In the shoulder. I'm sick."

Billie supported him to a chair and called to the bartender, who was cautiously rising from a prone position behind the bar. "Bring a glass of water, Mike."

The wounded man drank the water, and presently the sickness passed. He saw a little crowd gather. Some of them carried out the body of Hugh Roush. They returned for that of his brother.

"Dave ain't dead yet. He's still breathing," one of the men said.

"Not dead!" exclaimed Clanton. "Did you say he wasn't dead?"

"Now, don't you worry about that," cautioned Prince. "Looks to me like you sure got him. Anyhow, it ain't your fault. You were that quiet and game and cool. I never saw the beat."

The admiration of his partner did not comfort Jim. He was suspiciously near a breakdown. "Why didn't I take another crack at him when I had the chance?" he whimpered. "I been waitin' all these years, an' now — "

"I tell you he hasn't a chance in a thousand, Jim. You did the job thorough. He's got his."

Prince had been intending to say more, but he changed his mind. Half a dozen men were coming toward them from the front door. Buck Sanders was one of them, Quantrell's trooper another. Their manner looked like business.

Sanders was the spokesman. "You boys ride for the Flying V Y, don't you?" he asked curtly.

"We do," answered Billie, and his voice was just as cold. It had in it the snap of a whiplash.

"You came in here to pick trouble with us. Your parner — Clanton, whatever his name is — gave it out straight that he was goin' to kill Roush."

"He didn't mention you, did he?"

"The Roush bothers were in our party. We ride for the Lazy S M. We don't make distinctions."

"Don't you? Listen," advised Prince. In

102

five sentences he sketched the cause of the trouble between Jim Clanton and the Roush brothers. "My bunkie didn't kill any of the Roush clan because they worked for Snaith and McRobert. He shot them for the reason I've just given you. That's his business. It was a private feud of his own. You heard what was said before the shootin' began," he concluded.

"Tha's what you say. You'll tell us, too, that he got Ranse Roush in a fair fight. But you've got to show us proof," Sanders said with a sneer.

"I expect just now you'll have to take my word and his. I'll tell you this. Ranse Roush was a renegade. He was ridin' with a bunch of bronco bucks. They attacked the Roubideau place an' we rode — Jim an' I did — to help Pierre an' his family. We drove the 'Paches off, but they picked up Miss Pauline while she was out ridin' alone. We took after 'em. I got wounded an' Jim here went up a gulch lickety-split to catch the red devils. He got four 'Paches an' one hell-hound of a renegade. Is there a white man here that blames him for it?"

When all is said, the prince of deadly weapons at close range is the human eye. Billie was standing beside his friend, one hand resting lightly on his shoulder. The cowpuncher was as lithe and clean of build as a mastiff, but it was the steady candor of his honest eye that spoke most potently.

"Naturally you tell a good story," retorted the foreman with dry incredulity. "It's up to you to come through with an explanation of why Webb's men have just gunned three of our friends. Your story doesn't make any hit with me. I don't believe a word of it."

"You can take it or let it alone. It goes as I've told it," Prince cut back shortly.

Another man spoke up. He was a tinhorn gambler of Los Portales and for reasons of his own foregathered with the Snaith-McRobert faction. "Look here, young fellow. You may or may not be in this thing deep. I'm willin' to give you the benefit of the doubt if my friends are. I'd hate to see you bumped off when you didn't do any of the killin'. All we want is justice. This is a square town. When bad men go too far we plant 'em on Boot Hill. Understand? Now you slide out of the back door, slap a saddle on your bronc, an' hit the high spots out of here."

"And Clanton?" asked Billie.

"We'll attend to Clanton's case."

A faint smile touched the sardonic face of Prince. "What did you ever see me do to give you the notion that I was yellow, Bancock?"

"This ain't your affair. You step aside an' let justice — "

"If those that holler for justice loudest had it done to them there would be a lot of squealin' outside of hogpens."

"You won't take that offer, then?"

"Not this year of our Lord, thank you."

"You've had your chance. If you turn it down you're liable to go out of here feet first."

Not a muscle twitched in the lean, brown face of the young cowpuncher. "Cut loose whenever you're ready."

"Hold yore hawsses, friend," advised the ex-guerrilla, not unkindly. "There's no occasion whatever for you to run on the rope. We are six to two, countin' the kid, who's got about all he can carry for one day. We're here askin' questions, an' it's reasonable for you to answer 'em."

"I have answered 'em. I'll answer all you want to ask. But I'd think you would feel cheap to come kickin' about that fight. My friend fought fair. You know best whether your friends did. He took 'em at odds of two to one, an' at that one of your gunmen hunted cover. What's troublin' you, anyhow? Didn't you have all the breaks? Do you want an open an' shut cinch?"

"You're quite a lawyer," replied Dumont, the man who found the climate of Texas unhealthy. "I reckon it would take a good one to talk himself out of the hole you're in."

Billie looked at the man and Dumont decided that he did not have a speaking part in the scene. He was willing to remain one of the mob. In point of fact, after what he had seen in the last few minutes, he was not at all anxious to force the issue to actual battle. A good strong bluff would suit him a great deal better. Even odds of six to two were not good enough considering the demonstration he had witnessed.

"What is it you want? Another showdown?" asked Clanton unexpectedly.

Quantrell's man laughed. "I never did see such a fire-eater."

He turned to his companions. "I told you how it would be. We can't prove a thing against the kid except that he was lookin' for a fight an' got it. He played the hand that was dealt him an' he played it good. I reckon we'll have to let him go this time, boys."

"We'll make a mistake if we do," differed Sanders.

"You'll make one if you don't," said Prince pointedly.

He stood poised, every nerve and muscle set to a hair-trigger for swift action. Of those facing him not one of the six but knew they would have to pay the price before they could exact vengeance for the death of the Roush brothers.

"What's the use of beefing?" grumbled a one-armed puncher in the rear. "They shot up three of our friends. What more do you want?"

"Don't be in a hurry, Albeen," advised Billie. "It's easy to start something. We all know you burn powder quick. You're a sure-enough bad man. But I've got a hunch it's goin' to be your funeral as well as mine if once the band begins to play."

"That so?" replied Albeen with heavy sarcasm. "You talk like you was holdin' a royal flush, my friend."

"I'm holdin' a six-full an' Clanton has another. We're sittin' in strong."

Dumont proposed a compromise. "Why not just arrest 'em an' hold 'em at Bluewater till we find whether their story is true?"

"Bring a warrant along before you try that," Billie countered. "Think we were born yesterday? No Lazy S M sheriff, judge, an' jury for me, if you please."

The old guerrilla nodded. "That's reasonable, too. We haven't got a leg to stand on, boys. This young fellow's story may be true an' it may not. All we know is what we've seen. Clanton here took a mighty slim chance of comin' through alive when he tackled Dave an' Hugh Roush. I wouldn't have give a chew

107

of tobacco against a week's pay for it. He fought fair, didn't he? Now he's come through I'll be doggoned if I want to jump on him again."

"You're too soft for this country, Reb," sneered Albeen. "Better go back to Arkansas or wherever you come from."

"When I get ready. You don't mean right away, Albeen, do you?" demanded the old-timer sharply.

"Well, don't hang around all day," said Prince, his eye full on that of the foreman. "Make up your minds whether you want to jump one man an' a wounded boy. If you don't mean business I'd like to have a doctor look at my friend's shoulder."

Sanders's eyes fell at last before the quiet steadiness of that gaze. With an oath he turned on his heel and strode from the gambling-hall. His party straggled morosely after him. The old raider lingered for a last word.

"Take a fool's advice, Prince. There's a gun-barrel road leads out of town for the north. Hit it pronto. Stay with it till you come up with Webb's herd. You won't see his dust any too soon."

"I guess you're right, Reb," agreed Prince.

"You know I'm right. Just now you've got the boys bluffed, but it isn't going to last. They'll get busy lappin' up drinks. Quite a crowd of town toughs will join 'em. By night they'll be all primed up for a lynching. I'd spoil their party if I was you by bein' distant absentees."

"Soon as I can get Jim's shoulder fixed up we'll be joggin' along if he's able to travel," promised Billie.

"Good enough. And I'd see he was able if it was me."

Chapter X

Bud Proctor Lends a Hand

After the doctor had dressed the wounded shoulder he ordered Clanton to go to bed at once and stay there. "What he needs is rest, proper food, and sleep. See he gets them."

"I'll try," said Billie dryly. "Sometimes a fellow can't sleep when he's got a lead pill in him, doctor. Could you give me something to help him forget the pain an' the fever?"

The doctor made up some powders. "One every two hours till he gets to sleep. I'll come and see him in the morning. You're at the Proctor House, aren't you?"

"Yes."

"Is Roush goin' to live?" asked Jim.

The professional man looked at the boy speculatively. He wondered whether the young fellow was suffering qualms of conscience. Since he did not believe in the indiscriminate shooting in vogue on the frontier, he was willing this youngster should worry a bit.

"Not one chance for him in a hundred," he replied brusquely.

"That's good. I'd hate to have to do it all over again. Have you got the makin's with you, Billie?" Clanton asked evenly.

"I've got a plain and simple word for such killings," the doctor said, flushing. "I find it in my Bible."

"That's where my dad found it too, doctor."

With which cryptic utterance Clanton led the way out of the office to the hotel.

Jimmie lay down dressed on the bed of their joint room while his friend went down to the porch to announce to sundry loafers, from whom the news would spread over town shortly, that Clanton had gone to sleep and was on no account to be disturbed till morning.

Later in the afternoon Billie might have been seen fixing a stirrup leather for Bud Proctor, the fourteen-year-old heir of the hotel proprietor. He and the youngster appeared

110